The Urbana Free Library

To renew materials call
217-367-4057

THE GOD BOX

ALSO BY ALEX SANCHEZ

Rainbow Boys
Rainbow High
Rainbow Road
So Hard to Say
Getting It

THE
GOD
BOX

ALEX SANCHEZ

SIMON & SCHUSTER BOOKS FOR YOUNG READERS
NEW YORK LONDON TORONTO SYDNEY

SIMON & SCHUSTER BOOKS FOR YOUNG READERS

An imprint of Simon & Schuster Children's Publishing Division

1230 Avenue of the Americas, New York, New York 10020

This book is a work of fiction. Any references to historical events, real people, or real locales are used fictitiously. Other names, characters, places, and incidents are products of the author's imagination, and any resemblance to actual events or locales or persons, living or dead, is entirely coincidental.

Scripture quotations are from the *King James Version of the Bible*; the *Revised Standard Version of the Bible*, copyright 1946, 1952, 1959, 1973; and the *New Revised Standard Version Bible*, copyright 1989, by the Division of Christian Education of the National Council of the Churches of Christ in the United States of America. Used by permission. All rights reserved.

Book design by Jeremy Wortsman

The text for this book is set in Hoefler Text.

Glossary of Spanish Words and Phrases appears on page 249.

Manufactured in the United States of America

10 9 8 7 6 5 4 3 2 1

Library of Congress Cataloging-in-Publication Data

Sanchez, Alex.

The God box / Alex Sanchez.—1st ed.

p. cm.

Summary: When openly gay Manuel transfers to Paul's high school, Paul, a born-again Christian, begins to question his own sexuality.

ISBN-13: 978-1-4169-0899-9 (hardcover : alk. paper)

ISBN-10: 1-4169-0899-4 (hardcover : alk. paper)

[1. Homosexuality—Fiction. 2. High schools—Fiction. 3. Schools—Fiction. 4. Friendship—Fiction. 5. Christian life—Fiction.] I. Title.

PZ7.S19475God 2007

[Fic]—dc22   2006033121

FIRST
EDITION

*To those who believe in a loving God
and those who struggle to love themselves*

ACKNOWLEDGMENTS

With gratitude to my editor, David Gale; my agent, Miriam Altshuler; associate editor Alexandra Cooper; and all those who contributed to the creation of this book with their encouragement and feedback, including Tommie Adams, David Bissette, Theerasak Boonprajam, Bob Bozek, Bill Brockschmidt, Zach Brokenrope, Justin Cannon, David Chen, Robert Harris and Michael Davies, Bill Hitz, Charles Keener, Jingjo Kongmun, Erica Lazaro, Jayeson Owen, Guillermo Porras, John Porter, John "J.Q." Quiñones, and Pattawish Thitithanapak. Thank you all.

"There is a principle which is a bar against all information, which is proof against all arguments and which cannot fail to keep a man in everlasting ignorance—that principle is contempt prior to investigation."

HERBERT SPENCER

THE GOD BOX

1

" SEX AND RELIGION DON'T MIX,"

MY GRANDMA ONCE TOLD ME. "THE CHURCH SHOULD STAY OUT OF PEOPLE'S PANTS."

That random memory flashed through my mind the first morning of senior year, as I tugged my red rubber WHAT WOULD JESUS DO? wristband—*snap!*—against my wrist. I hoped the sting would help me forget the sex dream that had woken me. But it didn't.

I climbed from bed, hurried through my Bible reading and prayers, then raced through my shower, all the while trying to stop thinking about the dream.

When I arrived at homeroom, my girlfriend, Angie, had already snagged us a couple of seats together. She'd been my best friend since kindergarten, when my family moved from Mexico to Texas. Now I surprised her with the latest CD of one of our favorite Christian rock bands.

"No way!" Her bright brown eyes gazed up at me like I was the only one in her world. "You're so awesome. Thanks!"

While she scanned the CD's song list, I glanced up. A lanky boy I'd never seen before stepped through the doorway. Tiny hoops pierced both ears and his left eyebrow—surprising for our conservative little west Texas town, where even a single earring could get a guy accused of "going gay." His black wavy hair and cedar skin hinted he was most likely Mexican, and his cinnamon-colored eyes almost pulled me toward him. Who was he?

The boy sauntered toward an empty seat where Jude Maldonado—a ratty guy who came to school mostly to make life hell for everybody—had his dirt-smeared cowboy boots kicked up.

"'Sup?" the new guy asked Jude, friendly-like. "Mind if I sit here?"

"You blind?" Jude sneered. "The seat's taken."

All of homeroom turned to watch as New Boy calmly raised his hands.

"Whoa, easy! Keep your chair."

"Here's a seat," Angie, always the rescuer, called over.

"Thanks." The boy walked over with a broad smile. "My name's Manuel."

"I'm Angie. This is Paul."

"Paul?" Manuel locked onto my eyes, as if peering inside me, with a look that was part mischief and part something else. "Not Pablo?"

"Paul," I said firmly. Although my birth certificate actually did say Pablo, I didn't want to be constantly reminded I was from Mexico. I wanted to be American; I didn't want to be different.

During the remainder of homeroom I tried not to stare at Manuel. What was the strange pull I felt toward him, almost like some force stronger than my own? Did he know me from some-where? And what was up with those earrings?

Throughout morning classes my thoughts kept returning to him. Nervously, I tugged at my WWJD wristband—a habit I had picked up from a friend who used to bite his fingernails like crazy. In order to quit, he started snapping a rubber band against his wrist whenever he caught himself. The pain of the snap, although merely a sting, had helped him stop. In my case, I hoped the trick would stop my mind from thinking things I didn't want to think.

When the lunch bell rang, I eagerly headed to the cafeteria. My lunch group consisted of Angie and two other girls, Dakota and Elizabeth, who were as opposite as hot and cold. Dakota was gangly and tall, with curls of fiery red hair flaring all over the place; she was editor of the school newspaper, Honor Society president, and flexibly progressive. In contrast, Elizabeth was Barbie-doll petite and impeccably blonde, a cheerleader, student council vice president, and adamantly conservative.

Both were feisty and fiercely opinionated. The big difference between them was that Dakota was warm and never harsh. Elizabeth acted warm, but she could be cold as an icicle. The two of them, Angie, and I had been friends since middle school. We were all smart, ranking in the top ten percent of our class, and we all belonged to our Christ on Campus Bible Club.

For as long as I can remember, my closest friends have always been girls. I'm not sure why. I just found early on that generally girls were more open to telling you what was on their minds and listening to what was on yours. You could talk to them about emotional and spiritual stuff, like why somebody wasn't getting along with someone else, or how a certain song made you want to dance or cry, or how you felt God was calling you to do something.

I had guy friends too, but they tended to be more guarded about venturing into discussions much beyond sports, cars, games, or sex. My Christian guy friends were a bit more open to at least talking about God-related stuff, but even at Bible Club the girls did most of the talking. The few guys who attended mostly lobbed scripture verses as though pitching softballs.

In any case, I didn't mind being the only male at our lunch table. It made me feel special. The girls turned to me for advice.

Like today: Elizabeth had fought with her boyfriend, Cliff, because she'd seen him talking with his ex. Angie thought Elizabeth was being too severe. Dakota suggested Elizabeth get more info rather than give him the silent treatment. Elizabeth frowned at their opinions, then asked what I thought.

"Well . . ." I gave a diplomatic shrug. "You really think you should crucify the guy just for talking with somebody?"

Elizabeth frowned at that, too, while Angie glanced across the cafeteria. "Hey, there's Manuel."

She waved and I turned to see the new guy holding his tray, scanning the room for a place to sit.

"Ooh, he's cute. Is he single?" Dakota pushed the red curls back from her face as Manuel jostled toward us.

"Hey, can I sit with you guys? I was hoping to see you."

As Manuel set his tray down, Angie introduced him to the others.

"Hi!" Dakota flashed a smile. "Where you from?"

As Manuel ate his spaghetti, he told us that he'd moved from Dallas (the nearest big city to us), his parents were originally from Mexico, his mom had gotten a job as a math professor at the little college in our town, and his dad worked as a sales manager for some company.

I only half listened to what he said, paying more attention to his voice. It was soft and smooth, not gravelly like mine. I'd never liked my voice. And every time he looked at me, it was like *kapow!* Something happened inside me that I couldn't explain.

Then Elizabeth asked, "Are you a Christian?"

"Some days more than others." Manuel gave a relaxed grin. "But I try to be."

Elizabeth's brow knitted in confusion, and I was puzzled too. Either you were a Christian, meaning you accepted Jesus Christ as your Lord and savior, or you didn't and you weren't.

Angie and Dakota moved on to other new-friend questions: Manuel's favorite color? Purple. Favorite season? Spring. Favorite ice cream? Chocolate Chip Cookie Dough.

He asked us the same sort of stuff and then said, "Hey, does your school have a GSA?"

"A what?" Angie's nose crinkled with curiosity.

"A gay-straight alliance," Dakota interjected.

At the mention of the word "gay," I recalled the dream that had woken me that morning, and my face flamed.

"My cousin told me," Dakota continued, "that they started a GSA at her school in Houston. She said it caused a huge ruckus. Some churches even tried to stop it."

"Ugh!" Elizabeth paled in horror. "They'd never allow a group like *that* here."

"They barely even let us have dances," Angie complained.

"So . . ." Dakota, intrepid journalist and always to the point, leaned toward Manuel. "Are *you* gay?"

I expected him to laugh or get angry, but he calmly twirled his spaghetti noodles. "Yep."

Elizabeth's jaw dropped. Angie's eyes grew wide. And my heart skipped a beat. He couldn't possibly mean it. Could he?

"Don't worry." Manuel glanced around at us, half grinning and half serious. "It's not contagious."

Dakota pealed with laughter, while the rest of us sat stunned. How could he joke like that? Didn't he realize the consequences of what he was saying? Students would shun and ridicule him— or worse. He *had* to be kidding.

"Are you serious?" Angie asked, and Manuel nodded.

Elizabeth braced herself on the table. "You mean you're a practicing homosexual?"

Manuel studied her a moment, as if debating whether to take her question seriously. "Well, actually, I think I've got the hang of it by now."

Elizabeth frowned, and Angie commented, "I don't think any of us have ever met anybody gay before."

Manuel gazed toward me. Quickly I averted my eyes. Why was he looking at *me*?

"But you *can't* be homosexual *and* Christian," Elizabeth sputtered. "That's impossible!"

"Well . . ." Manuel gave a casual shrug, although his voice sounded a little defensive. "What about John Three-Sixteen? Or did I overlook the fine print?"

In our little corner of the Bible Belt, it wasn't unusual for someone to cite the famous verse: *For God so loved the world that he gave his only Son, that whoever believes in him should not perish but have eternal life.* But I'd never heard anybody quote it to include someone gay. I'd been taught that gay or lesbian people had turned away from God.

As I glanced up at the girls, a million questions swirled in my mind. If Manuel truly was gay (which I still couldn't believe he'd actually admit), then why was he quoting Scripture? Had he ever actually read the Bible? Didn't he understand he was going to hell?

My friends and I stared across the table at one another, as if each expected one of the others to defuse the bomb of confusion that had landed in our midst. And inside myself, doubts and worries I'd fought off for years bombarded me.

Without anyone noticing, I slipped my hands beneath the lunch table and snapped my wristband against my wrist.

2

MY EARLIEST MEMORY

OF BECOMING A CHRISTIAN TAKES PLACE AT THE LITTLE
CHURCH MY MA JOINED WHEN MY FAMILY MOVED TO TEXAS.
One wall of my Sunday school classroom displayed a bright
life-size mural of Jesus draped in pristine robes. Handsome, white-
skinned, and blue-eyed, he sat surrounded by beaming children
from different nations. One boy wore a turban, another a serape. A
girl wore a kimono. Each child leaned forward as if listening raptly,
while Jesus pointed toward the billowy clouds above him. Though
the painting now sounds sort of contrived, when I was a boy it
impressed me vividly.

I sat in the front row, staring at the mural, while hearing the
passionate stories of Moses, David, St. Paul, and Jesus. I wanted to
be like them: brave, pure, and good. I wanted to feel God's strength
and love.

For my First Communion present, my ma gave me a leather-
bound Holy Bible. The rich, clean smell of glue and fresh ink seeped
into my lungs as I turned the crisp tissue-paper pages with their
shining gold edges. I carefully ran my small hands across the words
Jesus spoke (printed in red) and the multicolored maps of the Holy

Land. So began my love for the book that would guide my life.

All through grade school I carried my Bible everywhere, memorizing whole chunks of Scripture, striving to show God how much I loved him. I'm not exactly sure why winning God's approval was so important to me, but it was.

Then, in middle school, my faith received a huge test: puberty. My health classes had prepared me for the biological consequences. My voice started to change and my first pubic fuzz appeared. But no one had forewarned me that the most noteworthy consequence for boys might pop up inside my pants at moments that totally mystified me. (Like at little league, when a teammate scratched his tightly uniformed thigh, or at Vacation Bible School, each time my suntanned youth minister leaned close and I smelled his musky cologne.) At home in my room I pondered my unwanted physical reactions and began to detect a worrisome pattern: They were all directed toward guys.

A sickening feeling gripped my stomach. Around that same time I had begun to hear in church that homosexuality was a sin and that "Sodomites" were destined to hell. I didn't want to sin, and I definitely didn't want to be condemned to hell. So why was I having these feelings?

At school one boy who the other guys said was "queer" got beaten up nearly every day. I watched and recalled the story of the Good Samaritan. I wanted to help him. But what if people began to think I was gay too? Instead I turned away.

I began to be on guard—even when asleep. Although my health texts had advised me to expect sex dreams, mine weren't about the opposite sex like those books said. In my dreams I was being hugged and kissed *by boys*.

I woke up in a sweat, confused and terrified. After fumbling for the light, I scrambled to my knees beside the bed.

"Why am I feeling this way?" I asked God. "You know I don't want to. Why is this happening to me?"

I listened in silence, waiting for an answer. But none came.

Too ashamed to talk to anyone about it, I went back to my health books, desperate for hope. To my relief, I discovered two tiny sentences buried in a footnote:

> During puberty some girls and boys may feel sexual curiosity toward others of the same sex. Such feelings are a temporary phase that will soon pass.

I drank from that promise like from some spring in a desert of doubt. And just as I'd tried to bury the fact that I was Mexican, I stuffed the possibility I might be gay into a box deep inside my heart.

To escape thinking about it, I involved myself big-time in sports, competing in swimming, track, and especially cross-country, going on long runs and praying with each step. I spoke openly to everyone about being a Christian. And to Angie I professed my love.

She and I had been pretty inseparable ever since my family had arrived from Mexico. At the time I didn't speak a word of English. The boys in class cracked up and made fun of me, but the girl beside me with the sleek black ponytail told them, "Shush!" and gently corrected my pronunciation.

I repeated the words she taught me over and over, determined to get them exactly right, till she'd finally tell me, "Take it easy! You're too hard on yourself." The guys teased me that I'd catch girl cooties, but I ignored them. Like Angie's name suggested, she was kind of an angel for me. By second grade I had progressed to the advanced reading group, stopped speaking Spanish altogether, and started going by Paul instead of Pablo.

Angie and I sat side by side at lunch, hung out at each other's homes after school, talked for hours on the phone, and IMed way past bedtime. In middle school, at a birthday party truth-or-dare game, Angie and I kissed for the first time. It was just a peck, really. But it made us officially boyfriend and girlfriend.

After that we walked hand in hand at the mall, went to dances together, and gave each other gifts and heart-shaped cards. By high school, we were voted Cutest Couple, even though we never majorly made out—much less did anything approaching sex.

I never spoke to her about the confused feelings that troubled me, maybe because I feared talking about it would make it more real. I wasn't ready for that. And besides, how could I explain what was happening when I didn't understand it myself? Instead I prayed for God to change me and hoped that Angie wouldn't end up hurt. What if she did find out my secret thoughts?

On the outside, I was a model of all-American heterosexual Christian boyhood. (Being tall for my age no doubt helped.) But on the inside, I felt like a fraud, smaller than a bug.

3

SNAP!

I POPPED MY WWJD BAND AGAINST MY WRIST AS THE END-OF-LUNCH BELL CLANGED THAT FIRST DAY OF SENIOR YEAR. Elizabeth stood hurriedly, almost knocking over her chair. "Well . . ." She gave Manuel a tight-lipped smile. "It's certainly been interesting meeting you."

Dakota steadied Elizabeth's chair and told Manuel, "I'd love to interview you for the school paper sometime."

Angie gathered her tray and offered, "Let me know if you need help finding your way around."

I merely mumbled, "See you," and got up to leave.

"Hey, Pablo!" Manuel reached out, handing me a slip of paper. "Here's my screen name and phone number."

I gritted my teeth, trying to be polite. "I told you, my name's not Pablo. It's Paul."

"Okay, sorry, Paul." He gave me a big full-on smile. "You want to hang out after school?"

"Can't. I've got choir practice." I grabbed my tray to leave, glancing at the screen name, *GetReal_BeReal2312*.

"Hey." Manuel stopped me again. "Can I have yours?"

I grappled for an excuse. Couldn't he take a hint? Reluctantly, I jotted down *Jesus_Rules_316* along with my cell number.

"Cool." Manuel beamed. "Thanks."

All during afternoon classes, I stared out the window at the school's parched September lawn, too angry at myself to focus on my class work. Why had I given some admitted homosexual my screen name and cell number? Was I stupid? No, I was *beyond* stupid. How could I undo what I had done? Simply not answer if he contacted me? For now, there was only one thing I could do: pray.

I'd never understood the debate over prayer in schools. Whenever I wanted to pray, it didn't matter where I was—in a classroom, at a school football game, or in the crowded cafeteria—I simply did it. I didn't need any constitutional amendment for permission. I knew Jesus was with me at all times and everywhere. I merely needed to speak his name in my heart.

As I did now: *Jesus, I'm really scared. I know I shouldn't have given Manuel my screen name and phone number. Please forgive me. And could you maybe have him lose it? Or at least not call me? I ask you this with all my heart. In your name. Amen.*

After school I met Angie in the seniors' parking lot to go to church choir practice. When she saw me, her brow creased with concern. "What's the matter?"

"Nothing." I forced a smile, but she didn't buy it.

"Hey, it's me." She pouted and tossed me her car keys. "I can tell when something is bothering you."

Cagily, I slid into the seat next to her. How could I explain how angry I was at myself for giving Manuel my info and how scared I was he'd call? As I started the car engine, I fumbled for something to tell her. "Um, I don't know. I guess maybe I'm nervous about the coming weekend."

That wasn't a total lie. Several times a year our church's youth choir performed at the main Sunday worship. I loved singing and connecting to God that way, but as every performance approached, I'd feel a little jittery.

"You always stress . . ." Angie reached across the seat and squeezed my shoulder. "But every time you do fine. Relax."

The touch of her hand soothed like a balm. Even though it sometimes annoyed me how she could keep so cool when I felt ready to lose it, her steadfast calm was also one of the things I loved most about her.

Choir rehearsal that afternoon was uneventful, with no calamities or screw-ups. Singing always lifted my heart and put me at peace. After practice, Angie invited me over to her house to eat and study together, as she often did.

She lived about six blocks from me, in a ranch-style house with a St. Francis birdbath in the front yard to welcome any passing creature. Angie was a little crazy when it came to animals, trying to save them from themselves, from each other, and from humans. One time, it was a squirrel jolted by an electric line; another time, a frog trapped in a swimming pool. At least once a month I helped her take some critter to the vet to have it mended or healed. Every tree in her yard had a carefully placed birdhouse, and each morning and evening she fed a gathering of strays.

"Be careful," I'd tease her, "or you'll grow to be some kooky old cat lady who smells like tuna."

In truth I admired her a lot—her strength and kindness. At times her heart seemed bigger than all of Texas.

Tonight, after I helped her dish out the dog and cat food, replenish the water bowls, and fill the bird feeders, we had dinner with her mom and dad: veggie burgers, tomatoes, corn chips, and zucchini. (Naturally, Angie was a vegetarian, refusing to eat "anything that has a face.")

After we had finished eating and loaded the dishwasher, we went to Angie's room and listened to the CD I'd given her in homeroom, each of us saying which songs we liked best. As we listened, Angie sat at her computer, a cat perched on her lap, and researched a passage from the Gospel of John for our Christ on Campus meeting the following day. Each group member rotated leading our Bible studies, and tomorrow was Angie's turn.

Meanwhile, I lay on the carpet and worked on my homework for AP English: a report on Jane Austen's *Pride and Prejudice*, which I'd had to read over the summer. I was writing about the lead characters and how Miss Bennet's stubborn prejudice contrasted with Mr. Darcy's obnoxious pride.

Suddenly Angie announced, "We should invite Manuel."

At the mention of his name, my stomach gave a lurch. Ever since choir practice I'd managed to put him out of my mind. Now he suddenly barged in again, and all of my anxiety along with him.

"To Bible Club tomorrow," Angie clarified. "Let's invite him."

I glanced up at her. "You serious?"

"Sure. Why not?"

"Why *not*?" I sat up on the carpet. "Because, *duh*! He says he's gay!"

"So?" Angie continued scrolling through the web page she was studying. "He said he's a Christian."

I let my pen drop. "And I suppose if he were a serial killer who claimed to be Christian you'd want to invite him too?"

Angie pursed her lips a moment, thinking. "Yeah. Maybe. Didn't Jesus reach out to *everyone*—especially people whom others wanted nothing to do with?"

I folded my arms across my chest. "I don't recall Jesus ever reaching out to anyone gay."

"Well," Angie retorted, "I don't recall Jesus reaching out

to any American teenage boys either—or people in a thousand other categories."

I frowned, annoyed—and stumped—by her logic.

"Besides," Angie continued, "not every single soul Jesus reached out to is listed in the Gospels. And how do we know that some of the people who are mentioned weren't gay?" She reached down and nudged my shoulder. "Hey, come on. The poor guy is new. He doesn't have any friends. Remember Matthew Twenty-five? 'I was a stranger and you welcomed me . . . As you did it to one of the least of these my brethren, you did it to me.'"

Among our group we often quoted Scripture. But Angie had a particular knack for citing verses that made you feel like a hard-hearted creep if you argued against them.

"He's going to get his butt kicked," I grumbled, "when the word gets out he's gay."

"All the more reason"—Angie returned her attention to the computer screen—"he needs us as friends."

While she continued preparing her Bible study, I tugged nervously at my wristband. I knew that when Angie made up her mind about something, there was no stopping her.

Inside my head I tried to picture Manuel at our Bible Club. How could we discuss Holy Scripture with someone avowedly homosexual in our midst? How would Elizabeth and the others react? And where would all this lead? The words of Second Corinthians rang in my brain: *Be ye not unequally yoked together with unbelievers.* Except that Manuel claimed he *was* a believer.

I tried to go back to my homework paper but couldn't concentrate. "I've got to go." I gathered my stuff off the carpet and stood up.

Angie gazed over from the computer, giving me a curious look. "You okay?"

"Yeah." I felt too mixed-up to reveal what was really going on. "Call you later, okay?"

Walking home, I tried to sort out my feelings, most of all my annoyance at Angie. Manuel wasn't some injured baby possum fallen from a tree. Why was she so interested in him?

When I got home, my pa was in the kitchen on the phone with his girlfriend and drinking a glass of buttermilk. At forty-one, he had begun to show his age. When Ma had died five years earlier from cancer, his mustache had started to gray and little lines had started forming at the corners of his eyes.

A year ago he had met Raquel, and she began patiently courting him. Even before Ma's death Pa had been kind of an introvert. He worked in landscaping and had always seemed more at ease with plants than with people. Raquel seemed good for him. I liked her.

After Pa hung up, we talked for a few minutes, and then I headed to my room. I tossed my backpack onto the bed and checked my computer. An IM from *VetGirl-888* (Angie) awaited me: *Guess what? Did you ever notice that John is the only Gospel with the story of the woman at the well? Or the woman taken in adultery? That story isn't even in any of the earliest versions of John.*

Angie was always coming up with little known factoids like that.

Really? I asked, glad to take my thoughts off Manuel.

Cool, huh? Angie replied. *Doesn't it make you wonder how many other Gospel stories failed to make the cut?*

I wondered if she was going to harp again on whether some Bible characters were secretly gay.

Suddenly, another message popped up, and little blisters of sweat exploded on my forehead. The IM was from *GetReal_BeReal2312:*

Sup amigo? Enjoyed meeting u and ur chick friends. C ya tomorrows.

I stared at the message, my stomach churning. Why on earth had I given him my screen name? Should I respond now? He hadn't asked for a response. Better not. Nevertheless, I added him to my buddy list.

I tried working on my *Pride and Prejudice* paper some more, in and around messaging Angie. But I didn't tell her about Manuel's IM. I guess I didn't want to get into it again with her.

Around midnight I readied for bed and got on my knees to pray, as I did every night. I started by giving thanks for my pa, Angie, and all the blessings in my life. Then, as usual, I reviewed my day. Since God obviously hadn't made Manuel lose my screen name, I wasn't sure what to pray about that.

"Again, forgive me, Lord, for giving Manuel my info . . ."

But then Angie's words crossed my mind—about reaching out to Manuel—and made me feel all tangled up inside. Unable to sort it out, I simply added him to my prayer list of people.

I climbed into bed, hoping that would be the end of it. But his face wouldn't leave me, as I pictured him in the cafeteria, reaching out to me with his big full-on smile.

4

MY SECOND MORNING OF SENIOR YEAR,

I HIT SNOOZE ON MY ALARM ABOUT A MILLION TIMES. BY NOW WORD ABOUT THE NEW GUY AT SCHOOL BEING GAY HAD SURELY SPREAD LIKE WILDFIRE. AND WHAT WOULD HAPPEN IF HE DID COME TO BIBLE CLUB?

NOT WANTING TO THINK ABOUT IT, I PULLED THE COVERS OVER MY HEAD AND PLUNGED BACK TO SLEEP.

"*Mijo*, you're going to be late," Pa said, shaking my foot.

All my life he'd woken me up like that, as though I were some tree he'd planted and he wanted to make sure it had taken root. It was kind of annoying, mostly because after that I could never fall back to sleep.

Reluctantly, I got up and slogged through my shower, double-tasking with prayers. As I approached school, my stomach burbled with anxiety at the prospect of seeing Manuel. I imagined pandemonium, with people hurling insults at him and throwing things. Yet amazingly, when I arrived at homeroom, Manuel and Angie sat chatting and smiling, as normal as could be. And none of the other students were giving them weird or scornful looks.

Why weren't people freaking out? Hadn't the news spread

about Manuel's announcement? Or was it no big deal after all? Maybe students in our small town were simply too shocked to believe a classmate would openly admit to being gay.

As I stepped warily between the desks, Manuel grinned at me, and a ray of sun shone across his wavy hair.

My morning classes blurred past without incident. I handed in my halfhearted *Pride and Prejudice* report, and my class discussed how pride and prejudice stand in the way of relationships. I didn't pay much attention. I was too preoccupied, worrying if Manuel would sit with us again at lunch.

When I got to the cafeteria, my three "chick friends" (as Manuel had called them) were already at our table. I set my tray down just as Elizabeth asked Angie, "That new guy isn't going to sit with us from now on, is he?"

"I don't know." Angie calmly sipped her carton of apple juice.

"Because if he is"—Elizabeth stabbed her fork into a batter-fried shrimp—"I can't sit with y'all anymore."

"But he's so cute!" Dakota grinned. For a Christian, she could look surprisingly devilish. "Why don't you want him to sit with us?"

"You know why." Elizabeth glowered at her. "Because he's living in sin."

I sat down and quietly dug into my lasagna, anxious to see where the conversation would go.

Angie stared across the table at Elizabeth and quoted Romans: "'All have sinned and fall short of the glory of God.'"

"Yes, I do know that, thank you. But he's unrepentant."

"So, do you want to tell him not to sit here?" Dakota asked.

Elizabeth wiped her hands with a napkin. "I'm not the one who invited him in the first place."

From across the lunchroom, I noticed Manuel approaching our table and murmured to our group, "Here he comes."

"Hey." Manuel smiled. "Is it okay if I sit with you guys again?"

Elizabeth darted a look of disapproval at us. A batter crumb was sticking to her pale pink lipstick.

Angie turned away from her and told Manuel, "Of course."

"Have a seat." Dakota pulled a chair out for him.

Elizabeth opened her mouth, about to say something, just as her boyfriend, Cliff, strode over, on his way to his usual table with his football teammates.

"Hey," he said to our group. "How's it going?"

Cliff was a large straw-haired boy with a hard jaw and muscle-packed body. A linebacker on the varsity team, his massive shoulders gave him the appearance of being about to burst from his clothes at any moment, like the Incredible Hulk.

Elizabeth gave him a frosty glance, apparently still angry at him for talking to his ex. But Cliff seemed indifferent.

"We'll be meeting for Bible Club in room 132." His gruff, husky tenor added to the impression of contempt. "Let everyone know." His steely blue eyes shifted to Manuel, focusing on his eyebrow ring.

"Cliff?" Dakota said. "Meet Manuel."

"'Sup?" Manuel nodded to him and Cliff replied, "You coming to Bible study this afternoon?"

Elizabeth's jaw clenched at the suggestion. Mine did too.

"Yeah, come!" Angie cut in. "I was going to invite you."

"Thanks." Manuel smiled at the offer. "I'd like to, but I've got a dentist appointment after school."

Elizabeth's face relaxed, mirroring my own relief.

"But hey," Manuel said, "can I take a rain check?"

"Of course." Cliff's eyes flashed restlessly around the room. "Anytime."

Elizabeth stood abruptly and said to Cliff, "Can I talk with you?"

"Yeah, sure." Cliff looked a little taken aback by her sudden change toward him. "See y'all later."

Elizabeth whisked her tray off the table, leading Cliff away. After a few steps she said something to him, and he paused a moment, glancing over his shoulder at us with a hard gaze. Had Elizabeth told him about Manuel?

While Angie, Dakota, and I silently watched them continue across the cafeteria, Manuel sliced into his roast beef.

"The food's pretty decent here," he commented, oblivious to the lunch table melodrama that had just played out.

5

BIBLE CLUB MET

ON A FAIRLY LOOSE SCHEDULE, SINCE ALL OF US WERE
HEAVILY INVOLVED IN AFTER-SCHOOL ACTIVITIES. OUR
CLUB ADVISOR, VICE PRINCIPAL RUSSELL, LEFT US PRETTY
MUCH ALONE, PROBABLY FIGURING WE WERE GOOD
CHRISTIAN KIDS UNLIKELY TO GET INTO ANY TROUBLE.

I was walking down the hall toward room 132 when Elizabeth and
Cliff came from the opposite direction, murmuring in low voices.

"Hey!" Cliff's eyes latched onto me. "Why didn't you warn me
that guy was gay?"

"*Warn* you?"

"Yeah!" Cliff leaned into me. "Why were you sitting with him
at lunch?"

Even though Cliff was only slightly taller than me, his muscles
made him seem twice as large. Nevertheless, his hostile tone annoyed
me. "I didn't sit with him. He sat with us."

"Same thing," Cliff sneered. "Watch out you don't get
a reputation."

His comment irritated me, mostly because I knew it was true.
But what was I supposed to do about it?

Inside the classroom, Angie and Dakota had already begun moving chairs into a circle, assisted by a half dozen other students. It was

a warm afternoon, and the AC had already been shut off, so I opened the windows, hoping the fresh air would help calm me down.

I had always loved our school club Bible studies. I cherished the fellowship of the Spirit and valued hearing the perspectives of my friends.

As everybody got settled, Angie, as the day's leader, asked Elizabeth to start us in prayer.

"Heavenly Father," Elizabeth began, "we ask your Holy Spirit to cleanse our hearts and open our minds to receive your Holy Word. We ask you this in Jesus' name. Amen."

"Amen," everyone echoed.

For our discussion, Angie had selected John 4, the story of the woman at the well. It had always been one of my favorites. I loved the image of Jesus as "living water," able to quench any thirst for all eternity.

Each of us had brought his or her own Bible. I'd brought the one my ma had given me for First Communion. Over the years its leather cover had grown worn, the pages had gotten dog-eared, and countless verses had been underlined, marking my spiritual growth.

Angie began reading the chapter aloud, telling how Jesus traveled to Galilee and "'had to pass through Samar'ia.'"

"As I researched that passage," Angie interjected, "I read a commentary that said this wasn't literally true."

Cliff glanced up from his Bible, shooting a look at Angie. As a fundamentalist minister's son, he believed passionately in the inerrancy of the Bible. Anytime anyone questioned the literalness of a passage, Cliff debated it vehemently.

"In fact," Angie continued, "most Jewish people in Jesus' time traveled from Judea to Galilee through the Jordan Rift Valley in order to avoid passing through Samaria. They believed Samaritan people were ritually unclean and that contact with them would render a Jewish person unclean too. So Jews went out of their way. The phrase 'He had to pass' was probably a traditional way of saying the events that transpired were no accident but happened as part of God's will."

Cliff leaned back in his seat, apparently satisfied that Angie's explanation hadn't discredited Holy Scripture.

Angie continued reading to us from the chapter. Jesus met a woman at Jacob's well: "'Jesus said to her, "Give me a drink." For his disciples had gone away into the city to buy food. The Samaritan woman said to him, "How is it that you, a Jew, ask a drink of me, a woman of Samar'ia?" For Jews have no dealings with Samaritans.'"

"Okay." Angie paused again and her voice became animated. "I thought this was really interesting. When Jesus asked the Samaritan woman for a drink, he violated a number of ancient customs. First, that Jesus even started a conversation with a Samaritan demonstrated a rejection of Jewish mores of that time. Second, that Jesus would talk with a woman *as an equal* went against a culture of male superiority. Restrictions against speaking with women were so strict that a rabbi (or teacher, such as Jesus) wasn't even allowed to speak with his own wife, daughter, or sister in public. And third, that Jesus started a conversation with a woman he knew (as we'll read later) to have a bad moral reputation was even more shocking and significant. So, for Jesus to travel through Samaria and speak with and share a drinking vessel with a Samaritan woman he knew to have a bad rep put his own reputation at risk."

As Angie spoke, I recalled Cliff's caution before our meeting about risking *my* rep through association with Manuel.

"What this passage says to me," Angie continued, "is how no one was—or *is*—beyond the love of Jesus, regardless of their tribe, gender, or sexuality."

At the word "sexuality" our entire group looked up at Angie.

In the three-plus years I'd gone to Bible Club, no one had *ever* talked about anything remotely related to sex. Why was she bringing it up now?

The silence in the room weighed so heavy I could practically hear my own heart beat.

Elizabeth finally asked, "What exactly do you mean by sexuality?"

"Well," Angie replied, "In verse eighteen, Jesus reveals to the woman his supernatural knowledge that 'you have had five husbands, and he whom you now have is not your husband.' Clearly, this woman's love life wasn't 'one man, one woman, till death do us part.' Jesus knew this, and yet he reached out to her. He didn't judge her. He didn't condemn her. He didn't try to change her. Nor did he get into a scriptural debate. Instead he asked her to share a cup of water with him."

Angie paused and scanned our group for reactions. I followed her gaze.

Cliff bent forward, muscles taut, as if about to tackle, but waiting. Meanwhile Elizabeth sat with her arms folded and her jaw set. Though obviously disturbed by Angie's interpretation, both Cliff and Elizabeth seemed unsure how to challenge it.

Others in our little circle kept their eyes trained on their Bibles. Either they agreed with Angie or they were too uncertain to speak up.

As for me, I wasn't exactly sure what I thought. This was turning out like no Bible discussion we'd had before, and the silence was making me nervous.

"I can see your point," I ventured, "about Jesus being accepting and nonjudgmental, but didn't he also want the woman to believe in him and change her ways?"

Heads nodded eagerly in agreement. But before Angie could answer, Dakota tossed a grenade that sent the discussion in a different direction. "So, by sexuality, would you include gay and lesbian people?"

Everyone snapped to attention again. Sweat built on my forehead. It was the first time anybody had ever brought up the topic of gays in Bible Club.

Angie gave a confident nod to Dakota. "I think that's consistent with the passage."

"Wait a sec!" Cliff burst out. "To claim Jesus reached out to people is way different from saying he approved of them. The Bible clearly states that homosexuality is an abomination."

I tensed in my seat. Thank God Manuel wasn't here. I wished I weren't either.

"God created Adam and Eve," Elizabeth added, "not Adam and Steve."

Without missing a beat Dakota asked, "Then who created Steve?"

Elizabeth smirked at the question. "If people hear the Word of God and keep sinning, they're not believers."

"They're wolves in sheep's clothing," Cliff agreed.

"And are you without sin?" Angie calmly asked.

"First Corinthians Five-Eleven," Cliff shot back. "Don't 'associate with any one who bears the name of brother if he is guilty of immorality'—"

"But what about Romans Two-One?" Aaron Esposito, a heavyset boy, interjected. "'. . . By the standard by which you judge another you condemn yourself, since you, the judge, do the very same things.'"

Here we go, I thought. *Proof-text volleyball.* We'd gotten into debates like this before, where each side spiked and volleyed Scripture quotes. Sometimes it seemed that if you looked hard enough, you could find a Bible verse to justify anything.

"If you accept gays," Elizabeth sputtered, "you're saying that what they do is okay. And if you say gay is okay, what's to stop *everybody* from becoming gay?"

Dakota rolled her eyes. "Would *you* become gay?"

"No!" Elizabeth scrunched her nose in disgust. "But I don't want my children to be gay."

Dakota widened her eyes in mock surprise. "I never knew you had kids." She abruptly turned to me. "Did you know she had kids?"

I kept my mouth shut, growing warmer as the girls grew louder— and felt like a phony for not revealing my own inner turmoil.

"Ha, ha," Elizabeth sneered at Dakota. "This isn't a joke, you know."

"Okay," Dakota said in pretend seriousness. "So, you're worried about your *imaginary* children."

Elizabeth shook with rage. "I'm thinking about the children I plan to have and all the other children in the world who shouldn't be told that something is okay when it's clearly a sin!"

The two girls leaned toward each other. Were they about to come to blows? Eager to defuse the tension, I raised my hands into a *T* formation. "Can we get back to the passage?"

Dakota and Elizabeth became quiet. Everybody else—even Cliff—exhaled a sigh of relief. Angie returned to reading aloud about Jesus being the living water, something which it seemed like we all could use a big dose of. My throat felt dry as dust.

No one said much else after we finished reading the passage. I think we were all too stunned by how angry the discussion had gotten. We closed the meeting in prayer and put the chairs back in order. And I slinked out the door, feeling like I had dodged a bullet.

6

ARRIVING HOME FROM BIBLE STUDY,

I TOSSED MY BACKPACK TO THE FLOOR AND COLLAPSED INTO BED. WHAT SHOULD HAVE BEEN MY DREAM SENIOR YEAR WAS TURNING INTO A NIGHTMARE.

Cliff's and Elizabeth's comments hadn't totally surprised me. Their attitudes about gay people were the same as those I'd heard at church and Sunday school—and just as unsettling, if not worse.

I wished I could have spoken up and explained that a person might not necessarily *want* to have gay feelings and that it might not be so easy to get rid of them. But no way could I say that. People might suspect I'd had thoughts about kissing and doing lusty things with guys.

As I lay in bed, I cupped my hands behind my head and stared up at the ceiling. A crack had been inching its way across the plaster for years, like some slowly growing tree branch. I'd once asked Pa about it, a little worried the roof might crash in on me, but he'd told me not to worry. "It's just from the foundation settling."

Inside my jeans pocket, my cell phone rang. It was Angie. "Why'd you take off so fast after Bible study?"

Me, sitting up: "Because it was crazy!"

Angie: "Yeah. I never expected that big a rise."

Me: "Was Dakota *trying* to antagonize them?"

Angie: "You think?"

I couldn't tell if she was sarcastic or serious. A moment later, my call-waiting clicked. It was Elizabeth calling to ask why I hadn't sided with her at the Bible study.

I asked if I could call her back, then Dakota clicked in, asking, "Did Elizabeth call you?"

My gut clenched uneasily. The multiple calls got pretty insane for a while as I tried to juggle all three girls; then I finally managed to get off the phone. It wasn't the first time I'd gotten caught in the middle of their squabbles. Pa had once referred to the group as my harem. *As if!* I wondered how Abraham, Isaac, and my other Old Testament heroes had managed multiple wives. Wasn't one plenty?

I took a deep breath, hoping to rally myself to get up and out of bed. But instead, I crashed asleep. Next thing I knew, Pa was shaking my foot and peering at me with concern.

"Something wrong, *mijo?*"

"Um, no," I lied, recalling Bible study.

"You sure?" Pa insisted. "You didn't look so good this morning, either."

"I'm okay—just tired from school." I rubbed my eyes. "I'll go start dinner." He and I took turns making dinner, and tonight was my turn.

"Never mind," Pa told me. "Let's go get pizza."

I didn't argue.

Pa and I had always gotten along well. When my ma died, he'd taken her death pretty hard, and started to drink every night, from the time he got home until he was drunk. He hadn't been a mean drunk, but he would get depressed, telling me over and over, "*Te quiero, mijo.* You know I love you."

The way he kept repeating it had frightened me. What if something happened to him, too? I felt like I had to be strong for him—and for me. That's when I started making dinner for us, mostly easy stuff like macaroni and cheese or tuna fish sandwiches. When he fell asleep on the couch, I covered him with a blanket. In the morning I made coffee and woke him so he'd get to work on time.

Although I realized something was very wrong with Pa, I felt too afraid to tell anyone. What if they tried to take me away from him? I had just lost one parent; the thought of losing another terrified me. But Angie came over to my house too often to keep it from her. When she found out what was happening, she swatted my arm. "Why didn't you tell me?"

"Please, don't tell anyone," I begged. "Promise?" But she wouldn't.

The evening after that, the doorbell rang, and I peeked out the window to see Angie with a big man in a crisp blue suit. I kept quiet, pretending no one was home. But when the bell rang again, my pa woke from the couch and told me, "Answer it, *mijo*."

When I opened the door, Angie gave me a hard look and introduced her evangelical minister, Pastor José. From his tan, jowly face gleamed a confident smile. As he shook my hand, his eyes roved around the living room, completing their arc on my pa and the beer bottles beside him.

Pa had never been a big fan of religion. Ma had had to practically drag him to church. And when she died, he stopped going altogether, instead muttering under his breath at God. But tonight Pa listened respectfully to Angie's minister and left his beer aside.

"I understand the hurt you feel," Pastor told Pa. "You must've loved your wife very much, but drinking isn't going to bring her back. You know that. You need to think about your son. That's what your wife would've wanted, isn't it?"

My pa gazed toward the floor, his face red from the alcohol—and shame.

After talking a while, Pastor José asked Pa if he could pray with him, and Pa nodded. Angie took my hand while I looked on, and the minister prayed:

"Lord and Father, source of all our strength, we ask you to fill this man with your courage and help him to overcome the pain in his heart . . ."

While Pastor José spoke, his voice genuine and heartfelt, I prayed too, hoping with all my heart that God would answer.

"We ask you this in Jesus' name," the pastor concluded. "Amen."

And although it was barely a whisper, my pa responded, "Amen."

The following Sunday morning, Angie and her mom came to fix Pa and me scrambled eggs and pancakes. For the first time since Ma's funeral, Pa put on a tie. And after breakfast we all headed to Pastor José's church.

Through the I Am The Way Church, Pa began to attend Alcoholics Anonymous. With the help of AA he stopped drinking and got back to normal. Actually, better than normal: He started to help me with homework, attended parent-teacher conferences, and read the Bible almost daily. The church gave him a new lease on life, and one Sunday he stuck a bumper sticker on his truck that read: *The Bible says it. I believe it. That settles it!*

Five years had passed since then, and each year we spoke less and less about my ma. I never mentioned how painfully I missed her, not wanting to risk making him drink again. Instead, our conversations stuck to safe subjects: my school, choir practice, sports, his work, when Abuelita (his ma, my grandma) would come visit us again from Mexico . . .

Tonight during dinner we talked about college. Although Pa had slowly built his gardening business to include a plant nursery, five staff, and three trucks, he had never gone to college. He'd always made it clear he expected me to go. I'd be the first in my family.

I worried how Pa would get along without me. He and I had become pretty emotionally dependent on each other. Maybe I also worried a little bit how *I* would get along without *him*.

He must have sensed my nervousness, because between pizza bites he told me, "I'm proud of you, *mijo*. You'll do fine."

After dinner he dropped me off at home and went to one of his regular AA meetings. As I was stepping up our front walkway, my cell phone rang with a number I didn't recognize.

"Hey, it's Manuel. How'd your Bible study go this afternoon?"

I had managed to put our heated Bible discussion out of my mind during dinner. Now the memory flooded back. Did I really want to go into it with Manuel?

"Um, it went okay."

"Yeah? What passage did you read?"

"John Four." I turned the key to the front door. "The woman at the well."

"Oh, yeah," Manuel said. "I love that: Jesus, the living water."

It surprised me that he knew the passage. I still didn't get how he could accept being gay and consider himself a Christian. Did he pray? Did he really know Jesus?

"Let me know when you guys meet again," Manuel continued, "so I can go."

"Uh-huh," I mumbled, while thinking, *No way*.

He chatted a few more minutes about school and stuff, as if he were my buddy. I didn't want to be his buddy. I wanted him to go away and leave me alone. After saying good-bye I chucked my phone onto the bed and groaned in frustration. "Why me?"

Later, I said my prayers, reviewing the day—listing the bad

things I'd done and the good things I'd left *undone*. But once again I had a hard time deciding what I should and shouldn't have done. Should I have sided with Elizabeth at lunch? Or had I done right by keeping silent? During Bible Club, should I have joined Angie and Dakota in speaking up for gay people? Or should I have joined Elizabeth and Cliff in speaking out against them? Was I resisting evil by at least trying to keep my distance from Manuel? Or was I turning my back on him?

"Please help me, Jesus," I whispered, my thoughts and feelings all twisted up again. "Forgive me, and help me do better tomorrow."

As I tried to get to sleep, I kept thinking about Jesus and the woman at the well—and about Manuel at our lunch table. I snapped my wristband against my wrist, trying to stop thinking about him. And in my heart I asked Jesus, *What would you do?*

7

THE FOLLOWING MORNING

WHEN I ARRIVED AT HOMEROOM, MANUEL AND ANGIE
WERE ALREADY THERE, CHATTING QUIETLY.

I said hi and sat down beside them. Suddenly I got the feeling
people were staring over at us. But when I looked around, people
glanced away. Was I getting paranoid?

The bell rang, followed by announcements blasting from
the loudspeaker. When the end-of-homeroom bell rang, people
clamored out of the room. And in the last row, Jude Maldonado
announced to one of his buddies: "If I saw two guys walk down the
street holding hands, I'd take a baseball bat and kill them."

An angry flush crept up the back of my neck. That moment
made me want to pound Jude, even though I'd never been in a fight
in my life. Impulsively, I turned to face him.

"Yeah?" Jude glared back at me. "What are you looking at?"

I stared at him a moment, sizing him up. Then I turned away,
annoyed at myself. His stupid comments didn't merit attention.
But at the same time he'd fueled my suspicions: Had people begun
to talk about Manuel?

While I sat in morning classes, an even tougher question

weighed on my mind: If I associated with Manuel, would people start talking about *me*?

When lunchtime arrived, I stood in the food line, gazing across the cafeteria at my lunch table. Angie and Dakota were talking with Manuel, but Elizabeth was conspicuously absent. That didn't totally surprise me. She was probably still riled at Dakota for making fun of her in Bible study.

"What can I get you today?" The cafeteria lady smiled at me.

Glancing down at the aluminum trays, I settled on the fried chicken; then I trudged toward my table.

"Hi." Angie pulled a chair out for me.

As I set my tray down, I noticed Elizabeth sitting across the room with Cliff, several of his football teammates, and some of their girlfriends. Manuel followed my gaze and asked, "How come Elizabeth isn't sitting with us?"

I glanced away, letting Angie and Dakota respond. "I think she wants to keep closer tabs on Cliff," Angie told Manuel.

"She's jealous of his ex," Dakota added.

Manuel's eyebrows arched up, as if he sensed there was more. Angie and Dakota exchanged a look.

"Well, actually . . ." Dakota pushed a loose strand of red curl behind her ear. "She also thinks we shouldn't associate with somebody . . . gay."

"Ah." Manuel nodded. Then he glanced over at me, as if once again implying I might be gay. But this time I refused to look away. Let him think what he wanted.

"Look . . ." Manuel set his fork down from his lasagna. "I don't want to break up your group. I'll go sit somewhere else."

"No," Angie protested. "You don't have to do that."

"Yeah, please don't!" Dakota agreed. "Elizabeth will get over it."

I stayed silent, biting into a chicken wing. Even though I felt bad for Manuel, the prospect of not having to be seen with him offered some relief.

"No, better I go," Manuel said, grabbing his tray. He pasted on a smile, but it seemed like the saddest smile in the world. "Thanks for letting me sit with you guys."

Angie called after him. "Manuel!"

He ignored her calls and wandered across the cafeteria. I watched him, curious who he'd sit with, but I wasn't able to see where he ended up. When I glanced back at Angie and Dakota, both were glowering at me.

"What?" I asked innocently.

"You *know* what." Dakota's gray eyes were smoldering.

"Why didn't you say anything?" Angie elaborated.

"Because he's right." I tossed down my chicken wing. "He *is* breaking up our group."

"No, he's not!" Dakota argued. "Elizabeth's the one breaking it up."

Angie clenched her jaw, not saying another word. I knew that meant she was angry. But what could I say? I focused on my chicken till the bell rang.

After school, when I met Angie in the seniors' lot to go to choir practice, she didn't toss me her car keys. Instead, she drove.

Halfway to church she said, "Can I ask you something?"

From experience I knew that that question signaled the start of an argument. I sat up in my seat, bracing myself. "Yeah."

"Why don't you like him?"

Obviously, she meant Manuel. I took a breath and chose my words carefully. "It's not that I don't like him. I just don't want to hang out with him. And I don't think you should either."

Angie stopped the car for a red light and gave me a sideways glance. "Are you jealous of him?"

"Jealous?" The question confused me. "He's gay! Why would I be jealous?"

"I don't know." She turned the car into the church parking lot.

I slid down in my seat, irritated by the conversation. "He's bad news."

"Well," Angie said, "if you don't want to hang out with him, that's up to you. But I don't care if he is gay. I like him."

"Fine." I gave a shrug, not wanting to argue anymore.

After choir practice she didn't invite me over for dinner. When I asked if she wanted to come over to my house, she merely said, "I can't tonight. Thanks."

Once I arrived home, I tried my best to put any more thoughts of Manuel out of my mind. I made my pa and me meat loaf and corn for dinner. Later that evening I was doing homework at my computer when an IM from *GetReal_BeReal2312* appeared:

Sup? I hope I didn't screw up u guys' friendship with Elizabeth.

I stared at the message, debating whether to respond. I didn't want to encourage him. Finally, I typed, *That's okay.*

Manuel replied at once: *If u don't want to talk to me at school, just tell me.*

His words made me feel like a creep. Could he tell I didn't want to be seen with him? Our town and school were too small to truly avoid someone. Besides, even when I disliked somebody, I always tried my best to get along.

My leg jiggled nervously as I told Manuel, *Don't worry about it.*

I hoped that might end our conversation, but unfortunately, he seemed to take it as an invitation to friendship: *Wanna hang out this weekend?*

My hands fumbled across the keyboard. *I'm kind of busy with a concert at church.*

I waited, hoping he'd take the hint.

OK, he replied. *Good luck with it. Knock 'em alive!*

I let out a sigh. Later, when I said my prayers and reviewed the day's events, one question Angie had asked kept reverberating in my brain: Was I jealous of Manuel?

I still didn't understand why she'd asked that—and I had no idea what to pray in response.

8

EVEN THOUGH I HAD TOLD MANUEL

IT WAS OKAY TO TALK TO ME AT SCHOOL, I STILL FELT NERVOUS ABOUT IT. WHEN I GOT TO HOMEROOM THE FOLLOWING MORNING, I HUNG OUT AT MY LOCKER AND CHATTED WITH FRIENDS, WAITING FOR THE BELL TO RING BEFORE GOING IN TO SIT BESIDE HIM.

My fears weren't groundless. As the week progressed, the stares and whispers about him multiplied:

"Did you hear that new guy is *gay*? He said so himself."

"Oh, my God! You serious? That's so *gross*!"

On Friday afternoon when the final bell rang, I bolted out the door, welcoming the weekend.

Saturday morning, I slept till nearly noon. Then I spent most of the afternoon doing homework and chores: laundry, vacuuming, washing Pa's truck . . .

Around six, Raquel came over for dinner with Pa. After gabbing with her a while, I drove over to Angie's. Saturday was our regular date night. We almost always did the same thing: go out for dinner and a movie, usually by ourselves, though sometimes with friends. There wasn't much else to do.

Tonight I took her a little stuffed panda I'd picked up at the store, even though she'd gotten over her anger at me about Manuel. At her house I helped with the evening feeding of adopted cats and dogs. Then for our own dinner we agreed on the little Chinese restaurant, one of the few options for eating out in our town.

On our drive Angie was in a sweet, happy mood. She smiled at me, played with the panda, and rubbed my hand between hers. Over dinner we talked about our upcoming SATs and about universities for next year. We had discussed going to college together, and Angie wanted to apply to Texas A&M's veterinary school. Her life's dream was to be a vet. Mine was to be a minister.

We made it through our veggie pot stickers, Ma-Po tofu, and stir-fried eggplant without any mention of Manuel. When we broke open our fortune cookies, Angie's said: *If you think the sea is blue and I think it's green, why try to convince you?*

"That's true!" Angie laughed, her ponytail bouncing back. I loved her laugh—self-assured and joyful.

My fortune said: *For sunlight to shine through a window, the blinds must be raised.*

To me, both messages seemed kind of, like, *duh.*

After dinner we headed to a movie at our town's one dinky little mall—or, as we called it, the (s)mall. The film was a romantic comedy that followed the standard Hollywood formula: boy meets girl, loses girl, and wins girl back. Along the way, boy and girl get into a heavy make-out session and usually land in bed.

In contrast, Angie and I had been a couple for nearly five years but had never gone beyond making out, much less landed in bed. After all, we were Christians. At least that's how I rationalized it. I didn't admit that my passion for her all took place above my waist. I'd never thought about sex with her. Instead, I tried to be the perfect boyfriend, imitating the romantic gestures I'd watched Pa show my ma: I held doors for Angie, gave her chocolates on Valentine's Day, slipped my jacket onto her shoulders if she felt cold . . .

I loved her—of that I had no doubt. Aside from my family, she was the most important person in the world to me. She was funny, fun, kind, smart, and always there for me. I loved the time we spent together, whether talking, studying, praying, or just hanging out. Even when we argued, I never stopped loving her. But as much as I wanted to, I felt none of the lusty in-love-ness I watched on screen, even when we kissed or slow-danced.

One lunchtime during sophomore year Dakota had stirred up a discussion about what constituted premarital sex. "To me," she argued, "that only means you can't have intercourse."

"No way!" Elizabeth protested. "Sex includes *any* kind of sex."

"What do you guys think?" Dakota asked Angie and me.

"Well," Angie replied, "I think it's a personal decision between two people and God."

Then the three girls shifted their gaze to me.

"Um . . ." I poked my fork into my mashed potatoes. "I think, um, a couple should wait on *anything* sexual till marriage."

And secretly, I prayed that when the time came God would make me *want* to have sex with a woman.

In tonight's silly comedy, the girl mistook the boy, a lab janitor, for a rocket scientist. Hoping to score an easy lay, he went along with the mistaken identity. But then he found himself falling in love and feared that if she found out who he really was, he'd lose her.

Although it was a lame story, I laughed—probably from nerves. What if Angie found out *my* secret? Would she still love me? I didn't want to hurt her. But I didn't want to lose her either. She wasn't just my *girl*friend; she was my *best* friend.

Angie stroked my hand in the darkness of the theater, glancing at me every time the couple kissed—and when they landed in bed. Her longing was obvious.

I squeezed her hand but kept my eyes glued to the screen, praying, *Please, God, make me feel toward Angie like the guy in the movie feels toward his girl . . . like every other normal boy in the world feels, except me.*

At the climax of the film, the girl discovered the truth about the boy, and they had a blowout of anger. He apologized. And she decided she loved him anyway, for who he was inside, not what he was outside. Happy ending, blah, blah, blah . . . The moral eluded me. My life was no silly Hollywood movie.

As I drove Angie back to her house, the moon was up, and little thin clouds were whipping across it, going south. Angie leaned close to me, light-voiced, her hair fragrant.

I parked the car and laid my arm across her shoulder. Angie rested her head on my chest and hummed a little bit of some hymn.

Eventually, we kissed. I didn't mind kissing her; I just wished that I felt more. After several minutes I pulled away and reached for the door handle, expecting Angie to climb out too, so I could walk her up the front steps—always the ideal gentleman. Except tonight she remained in the car seat beside me, studying my face.

I let go of the door handle. "What's the matter?"

She gave her head a little shake. "You're always the first to pull away."

"Huh?"

"When we kiss," Angie explained, "you always pull away first."

A faint band of sweat beaded on my forehead. Was she suspecting something?

"Um, sorry." I put my arm around her again and resumed kissing.

"Okay!" Angie pulled away, giggling. "You're so funny sometimes."

I laughed too, from anxiety. Then I walked her to the front door. On the steps we kissed again, and once more I waited for her to pull away first.

She gazed into my eyes and told me, "I love you."

"I love you too," I echoed, meaning it.

After one last peck she said, "Good night," and stepped inside. But as always she waited till I'd started the car before shutting off the porch light.

And I drove home, thinking about the silly movie.

9

SUNDAY MORNING I WOKE UP

**THINKING ABOUT OUR YOUTH CHOIR PERFORMANCE—
FEELING MORE EXCITED AND NERVOUS THAN EVER.**
In our town, the church that you went to defined what group
you belonged to—kind of like whom you sat with at lunch. It
seemed like we had a church on almost every corner. When
meeting someone for the first time, folks would ask, "Where do
you worship?"

The I Am The Way Church was one of our area's largest con-
gregations, holding English and Spanish services for more than
two thousand members in a building bigger than our high school.

Five years ago, when I first went with my pa and Angie, I had
never been to a charismatic church before. At the solemn little cha-
pel Pa and I had attended with Ma, people knelt in silent prayer,
listening to the musty organ while waiting for service to start.

Here, even before the service began, churchgoers stood and
prayed out loud, some at full voice, raising their hands in the air.
And when Pastor José strode in, a full-throttle band and jubilant
choir accompanied his arrival, while people swayed their bodies,
clapped to the music, and practically danced in the aisles.

That Sunday, Pastor José had preached about how Jesus softened our hardened hearts, quoting from Matthew: "'Come to me, all who labor and are heavy laden, and I will give you rest. Take my yoke upon you, and learn from me; for I am gentle and lowly in heart, and you will find rest for your souls.'" People started speaking in tongues, received the laying on of hands, and fell backward ("slain in the Spirit," Angie later explained), while I shifted in my seat, a little nervous.

When I gazed at Pa for reassurance, I was surprised to see a river of tears streaming down his face for the first time in the weeks since Ma had died. And when Pastor José invited all who wanted to be made new in Christ Jesus to come forward, my pa responded.

I craned my neck to watch, not wanting to let him out of my sight. When he returned from the altar, he stood straight and smiled peacefully, his eyes no longer dimmed by Ma's death but glowing with light. It was uncanny. Had Jesus truly made him new?

That afternoon I asked Pa, "What do people pray for when they kneel at the altar?"

His dark brown eyes gazed at me softly. "They ask Jesus to come live in their hearts."

At my ma's church, the pastor and Sunday school teachers had mostly spoken about Jesus as living in the past, ascending into heaven, and sitting at the right hand of the Father until the day he'd come again in glory.

But as I recalled the Sunday school mural of Jesus, my entire body surged with excitement. Could Jesus come to live in my heart now, *today*?

The following Sunday, when Pastor José announced the altar call, I edged forward in my seat, eager but unsure.

"Go ahead, *mijo*," Pa whispered. "Don't be afraid."

I stepped tentatively toward the altar, while the congregation joined the choir in singing:

Just as I am, without one plea,
But that thy blood was shed for me,
And that thou bidst me come to thee,
O Lamb of God, I come, I come.

Knees trembling, I knelt beside the others and uttered this simple but heartfelt prayer: "Dear Jesus, I believe you lived and died for us. Please forgive all my sins and come live in my heart. I love you. Amen."

I returned to my seat, tears pouring down my face, out of control. Pa wrapped his arms around me so tightly I could feel his heart beat. And I felt God's love surround me. At that moment, being a Christian seemed so simple.

I quickly grew to love this church. The music made me want to sing. The swaying and dancing gave me the feeling of worshipping with my whole body, not just my thoughts. I was able to spend more time with Angie. But most of all I loved that church for bringing Jesus into my heart. I'd seen how he had changed my pa, and I believed he could change me.

Now, as I polished my shoes and dressed in my best church clothes for our choir concert, I asked Jesus, *Please help me calm down and use my voice to share your Spirit.*

Then I asked Pa to drive us to church, so I could rehearse in my mind for one last time the hymns we'd sing.

10

DESPITE MY WORRIES,

OUR YOUTH CHOIR PERFORMANCE CAME OFF GREAT. IT
FELT ALMOST ELECTRIC, LIKE GOD WAS IN OUR MIDST,
RADIATING THROUGH OUR VOICES. AS I LOOKED AT ANGIE
AND OUT OVER THE CONGREGATION, I COULD FEEL HIS
LOVE AND ENERGY IN OUR HEARTS.

"I think that was your best performance ever." Pa clapped me
on the back after the service. He said that every time. I knew he
was proud of me largely because he dreaded standing up in front
of groups.

"Thanks." I smiled.

Like she did every Sunday, Pa's girlfriend invited us for lunch
after church. Today she made *arroz con pollo*, chicken and rice. I
loved her cooking, and by dessert time I was stuffed. After we
cleared the table, Pa stayed to spend the afternoon at Raquel's, and
I drove home.

I was in my bedroom, changing out of my church clothes, when
my cell rang. I glanced at the screen: It was Manuel. Reluctantly, I
answered. "Yeah?"

"Hey, *amigo*!" Manuel said cheerily. "I made a coconut

custard flan that's got your name all over it. You want to come hang out?"

"Um . . ." Unsure what to respond, I plopped down on my bed and peeled off my dress shoes. "Thanks, but, um, I've got a load of stuff to do."

"No problem. I'll bring it over. You'll love it. Guaranteed!"

"Look . . ." I emptied my pockets and tugged my slacks off, debating the idea of a known gay guy coming over. "I appreciate it, but I just had a big lunch."

"Then you can save it for later. Come on, man. You've got to help me. Otherwise I'll pig out till I blimp out."

I unbuttoned my shirt, annoyed by his insistence. "I wish I could, but I've really got a ton of chores and stuff to do."

"*Amigo*, please?" Manuel paused, and his voice became soft. "I miss my friends back home. I hardly know anyone here. Can't I just come over for a little while? I'll help you with stuff."

I thought for a moment, recalling Angie quoting Matthew: *I was a stranger and you welcomed me . . . As you did it to one of the least of these my brethren, you did it to me.*

"All right." I gave an irritated sigh. "Come on over." After giving him directions I hung up and finished changing into a T-shirt, shorts, and flip-flops. Then I picked up the Sunday newspaper my pa had left scattered in the living room and tried to think up an excuse to politely get rid of Manuel. I was cleaning out the coffee-maker from the morning when the doorbell rang.

"'Sup?" Manuel greeted me at the door, flan in hand. "Wait till you taste this baby. I brought extra for your mom and dad. Are they home?"

"Nope." I didn't mention that my ma had died. I didn't usually talk about that till I knew someone better. I didn't want people feeling sorry for me.

"Do you have any brothers and sisters?" Manuel asked, as he followed me to the kitchen.

"No, just me." I stored the flan in the fridge. It looked good, but I was still full from lunch.

"Lucky you," Manuel continued. "I've got a bossy older brother and a pain-in-the-butt kid sister. How was your church concert?"

"Great." I told him about our choir performance, and since I still hadn't figured out how to get rid of him, I poured us a couple of Cokes. "Where do you go to church?"

"Right now . . ." Manuel sipped his Coke. "We're trying out different churches, looking for a welcoming congregation."

I wasn't sure what he meant by that. Wasn't every Christian congregation supposed to be welcoming? Nonetheless, I didn't suggest he try my church. That was the last thing I needed.

"So, what can I help you with?" he asked.

"Huh?"

"You said you had chores to do."

I hadn't expected him to take that seriously. "Don't worry about it," I told him.

He gave me a sidelong glance, as if grasping what had happened.

To change the subject I suggested, "You want to play a video game?"

Even though I had a fairly boring room, Manuel walked around it slowly, checking out every poster (mostly Christian singers and bands) and each of my school and team awards, like he was really interested. None of my guy friends ever did that. They normally went straight to my games.

"What's so interesting?" I asked.

"Just looking." Manuel shrugged. "You can tell a lot about a person from their room."

He glanced across my desk at the little maple-wood "God Box"

Pa had given me. Carved atop the lid was the Serenity Prayer:

> *God, grant me the serenity*
> *To accept the things I cannot change,*
> *Courage to change the things I can,*
> *And wisdom to know the difference.*

Pa had explained that you were supposed to write down a specific prayer and fold it into the box, giving your problem up to the Lord. Over time there had been exams I'd prayed to pass, cross-country races I'd asked to win, Abuelita's gallstone operation I'd prayed for her to get through, my pa's sliced tendon I'd begged for him to heal from . . . When Angie told me her dad might take a job in another town, I'd prayed for her not to move. All of these and other problems, decisions, and fears I'd put into that box. Whenever it got too crammed, I took out the old scraps of paper and read back over them.

Almost everything I'd prayed and stressed over had somehow gotten resolved. Tests had been passed (or failed, but the world hadn't ended), Abuelita had survived her gallstone operation, Pa's tendon had healed, and Angie's dad had gotten a promotion, so she hadn't had to move. But there remained one thing I'd prayed about in a million different ways, giving it up to the Lord over and again. Yet no matter how many times I entered it into the God Box, the thing still hadn't gone away—the issue I felt terrified Manuel would open the box and see.

To my relief, he only ran his finger along the carved lid and said, "I love that prayer."

Then he picked up the gold-framed photo of me when I was six years old, together with my ma at the community pool where she'd taught me to swim.

"Is that your mom?" Manuel said. "She's pretty."

"Thanks." I stared at the photo, even though I knew it so well that I could see it with my eyes closed. "She died when I was twelve."

"Oh, I didn't know." He put his hand on my shoulder. "I'm sorry, man."

"It's okay." I felt the gentle weight of his hand and could sense he only meant to be friendly, nothing lustful by it. Nevertheless, I wasn't sure how I felt about a gay guy touching me. When he finally removed his hand, I felt relieved.

Then he picked up the photo of Angie and me in our formals at junior prom. "You and she seem pretty close."

"Yeah," I replied. "We've been going together since seventh grade."

"You mean *dating*?" Manuel's voice rose in surprise.

"Yeah. Dating." Irritated, I yanked the photo away and set it back on the desk. "You got a problem with that?"

"No, I just thought . . ." He peered directly into my eyes like on that first morning. This time I knew what he was thinking.

"I'm not gay," I said defiantly.

"Okay." He shrugged.

"I don't want you to think I'm gay," I insisted. "'Cause I'm not."

"Yeah, I got that." He stared at me and I felt a little foolish. "Mind if I sit down?" he asked.

I nodded, and he deposited himself onto the carpet. Running his palm across the weave, he announced, "I miss my boyfriend."

The comment startled me. I'd never imagined he might have a *boyfriend*.

"We've been together a year." Manuel pulled out his wallet. "Here's a photo of us at *our* junior prom."

In the snapshot he stood beside a boy with curly blond hair and brilliant blue eyes. Both of them wore tuxes and bright wide grins. I could hardly believe it. "You went to prom together?"

"Yep." Manuel nodded proudly. "We were the first same-sex couple at our school."

"And no one did anything?" I tried to imagine two guys trying that in our town. They'd probably get bashed in the head with a baseball bat, like Jude Maldonado had threatened.

"Nope. It was fun." Manuel sighed wistfully and wrapped his arms around his knees. "I miss him so much."

Manuel's longing seemed to fill the room. I had never heard anyone describe somebody gay like this: as a real person capable of loving and missing someone. I knew how much I'd miss Angie if she and I were separated, except . . .

That feeling of being a fraud returned. Even though I knew Manuel and his boyfriend were sinning by being gay, I couldn't help wondering: Weren't they being more honest than I was with Angie?

I handed him back the snapshot and turned to my video games. "What do you want to play?"

We spent the next couple of hours playing games and listening to CDs. I lost track of time till Manuel said, "I'd better go and let you do your stuff. Thanks for letting me come over."

Now I kind of didn't want him to go. I'd actually had a fun time with him. As I peered out the blinds, watching him walk away down the sidewalk, I felt that odd, uneasy tug again.

When Pa got home, I pulled the coconut flan from the fridge. We each had a slice and split the third piece. I've always had a weakness for coconut.

"It's almost as good as your ma's was." Pa smiled. "Who made it?"

I shrugged. "A friend."

Later that evening, when Angie phoned, I debated whether to tell her about Manuel and decided she was bound to find out anyway. "Um . . . Manuel came by."

"You asked him over?" Angie laughed. "I thought you said he was bad news."

"He *invited himself* over. What was I supposed to tell him?"

"Uh-huh," she said. "Well, good. He needs some friends."

"But why *me*?" I asked.

"Because you're a good guy," she replied.

When I undressed for bed that night, my thoughts remained on Manuel. But not Manuel hunched over the video game controller; Manuel laying his hand on my shoulder . . . and telling me about his boyfriend.

What would it feel like to have a boyfriend? I wondered. *What would it feel like to dance with a boy?*

Almost immediately, a wave of guilt washed over me. Once again, I wrote down my same prayer: *Dear Lord, please take away these feelings. You know which ones. In Jesus' name I ask you. Thank you. Amen.*

I folded it up and placed it in my God Box, hoping this time the Lord would answer.

11

AT SCHOOL THE FOLLOWING WEEK,

IT SEEMED AS IF AT EVERY TURN I HEARD THE WORD
"GAY." THAT IN ITSELF WASN'T NEW OR UNUSUAL. PEOPLE
HAD ALWAYS USED "GAY" AND THE LIKE AS PUT-DOWNS:
"THAT'S SO GAY." "YOU'RE SUCH A FAG." "THOSE STRING
BEANS ARE SO QUEER."

Teachers ignored the remarks, silently turning away. I did too. At times I even said stuff like that myself, not giving it much thought. But since Manuel's arrival, every time I heard it, I flinched. *Why did he have to come to our school?*

One morning in homeroom, before the bell, Jude Maldonado sneered at Manuel, "Hey, is it true you're a fag?"

The room became quiet as everyone waited for the response.

Manuel slowly turned. "Why?" he asked Jude. "Are *you?* If you are, I'm not interested."

Students giggled, but it sounded a little nervous. I felt too tense to laugh.

Jude glared back at Manuel and clenched his fists. Clearly, he didn't like being made fun of. In a voice that gave me chills, he warned, "You'd better watch your back, man."

"Lookit!" Manuel emitted an exaggerated sigh. "Would you stop trying to flirt? I told you I'm not interested."

Again, laughter, though even less than before. As we left homeroom, I whispered to Manuel, "One day, you're going to get your butt kicked serious."

"Won't be the first time. Besides, I didn't start it. I'm just being myself. You want me to hide my light under a bushel?"

"No, but do you have to shine it in people's faces?"

Although a smile pressed onto his lips, he looked me in the eye for a long moment, a little sad. "That's just how I am, *amigo*. Can't help it. Sometimes I say dumb things."

I watched him stride away and shook my head in frustration—at him for the antagonism he was provoking . . . and at myself for caring.

Later that week, I was studying with Angie one evening when I noticed a stack of library books on her desk.

Angie read more than anybody else I knew, about all sorts of stuff: autobiographies of world leaders, stories about girls and horses or boys and their dogs, romance novels with sappy cover illustrations, explanations of quantum physics and string theory . . .

No doubt she had been influenced by our school librarian, Mrs. Ramirez, who constantly nagged us: "Read! Free your minds!" Once, Mrs. R. had lectured me: "When I was in school, my library barely had as many books as you see there." She pointed at a single stack of shelves across the room. "You don't realize how lucky you are. You have so much you can read—about almost *anything*."

In fact I liked to read. But with school, church, and sports, who had the time to check out everything Mrs. R. recommended?

Now, as I glanced at the books on Angie's desk, I shifted

uneasily. One was about teenage sexuality. The other two were novels about gay and lesbian teens.

"You want to borrow one?" Angie asked, noticing me.

"No." I swallowed the guilty lump in my throat. "What are you reading them for?"

"Just curious." She returned her gaze to her computer, and I looked over at the novels again. What stories did they tell? Did they turn out happy or depressing?

Angie darted another glance at me. I hunched over my math book, trying to force my mind back to my homework.

It seemed as though everywhere I went, my unwanted thoughts followed me—even in my own home. Manuel had begun to call or come over often, either to do homework or just to hang out, often bringing treats. He loved to make desserts.

When my pa met him, they seemed to get along okay. "You're a good cook," Pa told him. But afterward Pa asked me, "Why does he have an earring in his eyebrow?"

"Um, I don't know." I shoved my hands into my pockets. "He's from Dallas."

Pa pondered that explanation, then shook his head. "It looks *maricón*"—the Spanish word for "queer."

I cringed. What would Pa say if I told him, "Well, Manuel *is* a *maricón*"?

Pa didn't say anything else about him, but he still looked at Manuel a little curious-like whenever he came over.

I wondered how my ma would have reacted to Manuel. Would she have liked him? I still thought about her a lot—every day, during prayers and in between. I tried to remember the happy times we'd shared, but it was hard not to also recall her long suffering in and out of hospitals.

During the two years of her illness I had prayed for her

nearly every waking hour, faithfully asking God to heal her in Jesus' name. Over and over I read the Bible passages where Jesus healed the sick, lame, and blind. But Ma never got better, only worse. The day after my twelfth birthday, with Pa and me by her bedside, she died in the hospital.

I couldn't understand why God hadn't healed my ma. Hadn't Jesus said, *Whatever you ask in my name, I will do it?*

The adults in my life tried to console me. My pa steadied my shoulder, not saying much, in his usual reserved way.

My Sunday school teacher told me, "The Lord has a reason for everything. Now he has a new angel in heaven."

And Abuelita explained, "Sometimes, when God doesn't answer our prayers, it doesn't mean he didn't hear us; it just means he has a different plan for us."

I knew that those grown-ups were trying to reassure me, but their words only stirred doubts. What if the Lord decided he wanted my pa in heaven too? Where would that leave me? And if God didn't answer our prayers, what was the point? If he was going to do whatever he wanted anyway, how could I trust him?

For a twelve-year-old boy, the image of an unresponsive and unpredictable God capable of wreaking such pain wasn't much comfort. There had to be some other explanation. Maybe I just hadn't prayed hard enough. Or maybe God had ignored my prayers because of those other thoughts I'd had.

Once again I tried to put my feelings away and prayed even harder, recalling the verse in Matthew: *Be perfect, as your heavenly Father is perfect . . ."*

Maybe that way nothing else bad would happen.

12

SOMETIMES WHEN MANUEL PHONED

TO HANG OUT, I TOLD HIM, "I'M BUSY." LOTS OF TIMES
I HONESTLY *WAS* BUSY WITH CHOIR, HONOR SOCIETY,
OR HANGING OUT WITH ANGIE. AT OTHER TIMES I JUST
DIDN'T WANT TO DEAL WITH HIM.

HE MESSED WITH MY MIND TOO MUCH.

One moment I wanted to shake him and say, "Stop being gay! It's wrong." But the next minute I was mesmerized by stories about him and his boyfriend, Bryan. Like how they'd kissed the first time at a movie theater and ended up making out so much that neither could remember how the film ended. Or how they'd slow-danced together at junior prom and their principal nearly had a coronary.

As Manuel talked, I caught myself staring at him—at his playful eyes and thick wavy hair. His hair had a good smell that I couldn't quite place—sort of a mix of mint and sage. When I went to the supermarket, I uncapped shampoos, testing to find out what brand he used. When I finally discovered it, I told myself that I was buying it because of the good smell. But from then on, each time I showered I thought of Manuel.

And yet even though I thought about him in secret, I still resisted being his friend. He was opening up something inside me that I didn't want opened up.

During the day I avoided him as much as possible. And after school I never let myself be the one to phone him. But I couldn't deny that I was looking forward to his calls and visits.

One evening when he didn't phone or show up, I found myself checking my cell every few minutes, hoping for a text message. Of course, *I* could have phoned *him*, but I didn't.

When dinnertime came, Pa said, "You made a lot of food tonight."

"I know," I mumbled. "I thought Manuel might come over."

But he never showed up. After Pa and I had cleared the supper dishes, I tested my phone's dial tone to make sure it was working. Manuel never called that night. I went to bed angry at him—and myself.

The next morning I awoke with fresh resolve to ignore him and stop liking him so much. I arrived at homeroom expecting to find him and Angie joking and talking as usual. But instead, he was staring silently out the window. It was the first time I'd seen him sulk.

"What's up with him?" I whispered to Angie.

Manuel overheard and muttered, "Bryan dumped me."

I recalled the photo of the two of them in their tuxes, so happy-looking. Why had they broken up?

"He says it's too hard," Manuel mumbled, "to do the LDR thing."

I gave Angie a questioning glance, and she explained: "Long-distance relationship."

"I told him that I'd visit him at Thanksgiving," Manuel continued, "but he says that's too long to wait. The jerk!" Even though Manuel's tone was angry, his eyes glistened with tears.

I felt sad for him—and disappointed with myself for not having phoned him the night before. What kind of selfish friend was I, not having even considered that something might have happened?

That evening when Manuel didn't call, I stared at my phone. Then, for the first time, *I* phoned *him*.

13

OVER THE NEXT SEVERAL AFTERNOONS

I LISTENED — SOMETIMES PATIENTLY, AT OTHER TIMES UNEASILY — WHILE MANUEL LAY ON MY BEDROOM CARPET, STARING UP AT THE CEILING, AND RECOUNTED THE STORY OF HIM AND HIS (NOW EX-) BOYFRIEND.

"The first time I saw Bryan was at his locker. My heart went tumble, literally. I tripped over somebody's books in the hallway like a total klutz. His eyes were this amazing aqua blue color, like oceans in some cruise ship commercial . . . and his smile was bright as the moon. Any time I went near him, I got all goofy and tongue-tied. I thought my heart would explode. But I kept wondering, *What if he isn't gay?*"

Manuel paused, gazing toward me. Was he wondering the same thing about me? Even though I had told him I wasn't, it felt like he was seeing inside me again.

"So?" I gestured to him to get on with the story. "What did you do?"

"So . . ." Manuel continued, "we started hanging out, till I couldn't stand not knowing anymore. One afternoon he and I were walking home, and I asked, 'Are *you* . . . ?' I was too nervous to actually say the word 'gay' to him, but he knew what I meant. 'Yep.' He broke into a smile. 'Are *you?*'"

Manuel stared at me as if now asking *me* the same question. When I didn't answer, he proceeded with his story. "I couldn't stop thinking about him. I was crazy insane certain that I had met my life partner. He was my first real love." Manuel exhaled a weary sigh. "I guess that's why it hurts so much."

Manuel wiped his cheek, and I squirmed in my chair. It was the first time since grade school a guy had cried in front of me. A part of me wanted to reach out and hold him. He looked so vulnerable. But what if I got swept into something I couldn't handle?

Instead, I tugged nervously at my wristband, wondering how it would feel if Angie and I broke up. Would she feel as hurt as Manuel? Would I? Was I in love with Angie the same way Manuel had been with Bryan? The same way my other friends were crazy in love with their crushes? Could I ever be in love with *anyone* that way?

My thoughts spun in circles. Once again Manuel was confusing me.

"Want to play a video game?" I asked. "To help take your mind off him?" Without waiting for Manuel's response, I got up and jammed a cartridge into the game box.

During the next couple of weeks, Manuel slowly got over his breakup with Bryan. One afternoon he invited me over to his house.

Before that, I hadn't felt comfortable going over. I'm not sure why. Maybe it had to do with meeting him on his own turf. Or maybe I was nervous that his family might be as unconventional as he was. But as I got to know them, they turned out to be as normal as any of my other friends' families.

His dad was dark-skinned, curly-haired, and outgoing. Whenever he was home, he seemed to be on business calls, sometimes in English, other times in Spanish, but he always stopped to ask how I was. His mom, the college teacher, was usually either grading papers at a cluttered desk in the living room or preparing dinner in the kitchen. His older brother studied chemistry at UT Austin but came home every other weekend. His twelve-year-old sister often had a friend over, and they would whisper and giggle together in her room.

Manuel's bedroom was unexpectedly commonplace—as messy as most of my guy friends' rooms, strewn with clothes and video game cartridges. A Bible and glossy magazines lay heaped on the nightstand. Posters lined the walls. I noticed that they were all of openly gay stars: Elton John, k.d. lang, George Michael, Melissa Etheridge . . .

During that first visit, I sat down in his desk chair and scanned a bulletin board jumbled with photos and notes. In the middle was a quote from someone named Lynn Lavner:

The Bible contains six admonishments to homosexuals and 362 admonishments to heterosexuals. That doesn't mean that God doesn't love heterosexuals. It's just that they need more supervision.

Staring at the quote, I whispered, "Does your family know? I mean, about you?"

"I think so." A sheepish grin wandered across Manuel's face. "When I was in eighth grade, my dad caught me making out—with a boy."

I sat up, trying to picture the scene. "What happened?"

"What could he say?" Manuel shrugged. "He squeezed my shoulder, all fatherly-like, and said, 'You know, *mijo*, boys don't normally kiss other boys.' Maybe he thought that would stop me. But it actually helped me to figure things out. The next night at dinner I announced, 'I guess I'm gay.'"

Manuel's matter-of-factness put me at the edge of my seat. What would *my* pa say to something like that? "Then what happened?"

Manuel's grin grew wider. "I think Dad had already told my mom, because she said, 'If you are, that's okay.' Then Dad said something like, 'We'll always love you, no matter what.' My brother only said, 'Yeah, I figured you were.' And my sister was like, 'Really? That's cool.' It was all disappointingly undramatic."

I didn't get that. "Did you want it to be dramatic?"

"I guess not." Manuel thought for a moment. "Well, maybe a *little* dramatic."

His honesty could be disarming. Yet there was an aspect of his being gay that I still couldn't accept. One afternoon, between computer games, I asked, "But don't you realize it's a sin?"

Manuel gave me a questioning look. "You mean being gay?"

I nodded and folded my arms, bracing for an argument. "You understand you're going to hell, don't you?"

"No," Manuel said, his voice confident. "That doesn't make sense. Ever since I first started going to church nursery school, I was taught that God loves me just as I am, just as my mom and dad love me, no matter what. So . . . why on earth would a good and loving God create ten percent of people with a sex drive oriented toward the same gender, and at the same time condemn them to hell for it?"

He raised his eyebrows, waiting for my answer. I stared back, uncertain. I'd always been told that gay people were godless. Obviously, Manuel wasn't.

When I failed to respond, he filled in: "The logic of condemning people for how they were born is just . . . just . . . backward. It's like when they used to blame lepers or mentally ill people, claiming that God was punishing them. Why should I believe that I'm sick or sinful or going to hell for something I didn't choose and can't change? I don't buy that."

It took me a moment to collect my thoughts. "It's not proven that people are born gay."

"Well," Manuel argued, "it's not proven that people are born *straight*, either, but no one challenges them about it."

"But homosexuality is unnatural," I protested.

"Is it?" Manuel argued. "Do you know that homosexual courtship, mating, and parenting are scientifically documented in more than four hundred fifty animal species?"

"Is that really true?" I asked—even though I could recall times when I'd seen male dogs, or horses, or cattle mount each other.

"Look it up on the Web," Manuel replied. "What's unnatural is homophobia. *Homo sapiens* is the only species in all of nature that responds with hate to homosexuality."

His comment made me think back to a psychology class where we'd studied how both hate and love were learned behaviors. And I remembered thinking how important it was that Jesus had come to teach us how to love.

"But what about AIDS?" I asked Manuel. "You don't think AIDS is God's punishment for gay people?"

"First of all," Manuel answered, "I don't believe in a sadistic God who thinks up ways to punish us. Is that what you believe in?"

"No. But I think he tries to tell us when we're doing something wrong."

"Through cruelty?" Manuel shook his head. "I think that's the wrong image of God, the one that Jesus came to correct. I believe suffering is just a sucky part of life—*everybody's* life. As Jesus said in Matthew: God *'makes his sun rise on the evil and on the good, and sends rain upon the just and the unjust.'*"

Once again Manuel's citing of Scripture confounded me.

"And as for AIDS," he continued, "it's hurt a lot more straight than gay people, including millions of children. And do you realize lesbians have the lowest HIV rate of *any* group? If AIDS is a punishment from God, then he must *love* lesbians!" Manuel grinned for a moment before turning serious again. "To link gay people and AIDS is simply . . ."—he paused as if measuring his words—". . . ignorant."

I folded my arms more tightly across my chest. Manuel was taking every church view I'd heard against homosexuality and blowing it away—blowing *me* away.

I stared at him a long time, too annoyed to say anything, till at last I grumbled, "I'm going home."

And yet, as I wandered through the evening twilight toward my house, I found my annoyance turning into prayer. "Could Manuel possibly be right?" I whispered to Jesus.

When I got home, Pa was asleep on the couch, one shoe on and the other fallen off, snoring like he does. I stood there for a while, quietly watching him sleep and thinking about what Manuel had said about coming out to his family.

Then I went to make dinner.

14

THE NEXT DAY I FOUND MYSELF

AT MANUEL'S HOUSE ONCE AGAIN, ARGUING IN THE KITCHEN WHILE HELPING HIM MAKE BROWNIES. THE SMELL OF CHOCOLATE FILLED THE AIR AS I CHALLENGED HIM: "OKAY, THEN, WHAT ABOUT 'LOVE THE SINNER BUT HATE THE SIN'?"

"What about it?" Manuel calmly sliced the brownies. "I mean, think about that. Isn't it like saying, 'I love left-handed people but hate that they're left-handed.' Is that really love? Or is that saying, 'I'm willing to love you as I'd like you to be, not as you are'? Either God's love is unconditional or it's not."

Once again Manuel had stumped me.

"Besides . . ." He handed me a steaming hot brownie. "Did Jesus ever say, 'hate the sin'? Or was his message, love the sinner and forgive sins, for who of you is without sin?"

"Yeah," I replied, "but he also said, 'Go, and sin no more.' You think we should just let people do whatever they want and stand by doing nothing?"

"No." Manuel led me to his bedroom. "If somebody is obviously hurting someone, of course you should stop them.

But if I choose to love another guy, who am I hurting?"

"When you sin," I recited automatically, and dropped down onto his carpet, "you hurt God, others, and yourself."

Manuel shook his head and sat down beside me. "How is love between two people a sin? Love isn't about gender; it's about two souls uniting. But okay, let's just suppose it is a sin. Then isn't that between God and the people involved? Who are you to judge? Isn't that the whole point in John's story of the woman taken in adultery? Time and again, Jesus' message was, 'How can you say, "Let me take the speck out of your eye," when there is the log in your own?'"

I blew on my brownie to cool it and wondered, *Why am I trying to argue with a sinner who obviously has no desire to repent?* And yet I found it hard to pull away.

"You know the most amazing thing about Jesus?" Manuel exclaimed. "It's not that he performed miracles. It's that he was who he was, no matter what. He raged at religious leaders, questioned prophets, and challenged teachers to stop being dishonest hypocrites, knowing he'd get slammed for it. Jesus hung out with outcasts and sinners because they weren't pretending to be anything other than who they were. He had the courage to be himself, every time he encountered anyone—whether it was a leper or a temple leader, a fisherman or a rich young ruler. He was true to who he was—always and everywhere—and that's what he calls *us* to do. To follow Jesus means that *we've* got to be real."

This gospel according to Manuel was unlike any I'd ever heard. Pastor José and my Christian friends often spoke about Jesus being real to us, but I'd never heard them talk about Jesus calling *us* to be real. But then again, Manuel was nothing like any other Christian I had ever met.

"Don't you see?" Manuel's voice filled with passion. "Jesus

didn't only *command* us to love God, one another, and ourselves. He *showed* us how: by being himself, by being real, whether he was accepting the cheers of the palm-waving crowd or later hanging on the cross, questioning God and forgiving those who jeered him. His message stayed the same: Be true to who you are, knowing the cost. How else can you worship the Creator of all being, the great 'I am,' except by being the person that God created you to be? Have the guts to be real!"

I listened quietly, feeling a little shell-shocked.

"Are *you* real?" Manuel asked, peering at me with his soul-searching look. "Who are you, really?"

I stared at him, no longer knowing. Who was I? Who did God create me to be? Was I truly a born-again Christian straight boy being tempted by the sin of homosexuality? Or was I trying to be somebody I wasn't because I couldn't accept who I really was?

Manuel gazed at me patiently, waiting for my response, as my head began to throb.

"I need to go," I said quietly. Then I stood up with my brownie and gathered my things.

When I got home, I decided to go for a long, long run, hoping the exercise would clear my mind.

15

NO MATTER HOW MUCH MANUEL

CONFUSED ME WITH HIS RADICAL IDEAS, I FOUND MYSELF
UNABLE TO STAY AWAY. ONE DAY I KICKED HIM OUT OF MY
ROOM, TELLING HIM, "YOU NEED TO GO NOW."

"Okay." He grinned. "Try not to miss me too much."

Yeah, right, I thought, snapping the band against my wrist. And
yet the next evening I was calling him to ask, "You want to come
hang out?"

I wasn't sure who was crazier, him or me. During prayers one
night I'd ask forgiveness for hanging out with Manuel, but the next
day I'd thank Jesus for bringing him into my life. I couldn't stop
thinking about Manuel, and every time I stormed away from him,
swearing never to return, five minutes later I wanted to come running back.

On top of everything, Manuel had the annoying habit of sometimes referring to God as "she."

"I wish you'd stop that," I told him over pretzels at my house.
"The Bible says God created man in *his* image, not *her* image."

"But," Manuel argued, "doesn't St. Paul say in Galatians that in
Christ 'there is neither male nor female'? Why should we portray

God as some old bearded guy, or even a man at all? Since we don't have a pronoun for a Supreme Being so infinite that it's called the 'I am,' why not give equal time to calling God 'she'?"

I didn't know what to answer. Was Manuel nuts or a genius? He made my brain feel like a pretzel, all twisted up inside.

"You want to know what I *really* think?" Manuel continued.

"No," I lied, knowing he'd tell me anyway.

Which he did: "I think *we've* created God in *our* image, instead of the other way around. It's like we've built this little box and tried to cram the infinity of God into it, too afraid that if we let him out, she might challenge us too much. Then we'd have to crucify and kill him." Manuel scratched his forehead beneath his bangs as if recalling something. "Hey, wait a minute. That story sounds familiar. I think I read about that actually happening once, about two thousand years ago."

I shook my head, both irritated and intrigued. Even when we argued, it felt as though Manuel was reaching parts of my mind and heart that had never been touched before.

The afternoons I didn't spend with him, I continued to spend with Angie, going to choir practice together, hanging out, or taking some wounded creature to the vet. Sometimes she asked casually about my time with Manuel, like she'd ask about time I spent with any other guy friend.

"Manuel's a nut," I'd tell her, and leave it at that, feeling too mixed-up to discuss it further.

"Well . . ." She gave a little smile and laughed. "I'm glad you're over your bias against him."

On Saturday nights she and I continued going to dinner and the movies, and afterward parked outside her house. In the car I'd lay my arm across her shoulder and feel her warmth. A different boy might have tried to feel something else, too. I felt proud that I didn't, and yet it also continued to worry me.

One afternoon with Angie something happened which I doubt I'll ever forget: She and I were eating PBJ sandwiches and watching a movie in her family room, when something slammed into the plate-glass window. *Bam!* Loud, like a softball. "What was *that*?" Angie and I looked at each other.

Suddenly her eyes widened in fear. "Oh, my God!" She bolted to the window, slid it open, and quickly knelt on the outside landing.

I leaned over her shoulder and saw a tiny bird—a sparrow or something—motionless, tumbled over. "Is it still alive?"

Angie scooped it into her palm, gently folding its wings, and pressed its tiny breast to her ear. Then she did something I never imagined possible: She cupped her lips over its teeny beak, breathed and paused, breathed and paused . . .

I stared in wonder. Could she actually bring the little creature back to life?

Its chest began moving. It shook its head, blinked its eyes open, and gazed at Angie.

She set it down on the ground. It hopped a few steps, turned to look back up at her, and then fluttered away.

"Thank you, Jesus," Angie said, as the sparrow circled and flew to a birdhouse. Then she took my hand, and we returned to watching the DVD—or tried to. I felt too in awe of what she had done. My heart swelled with love for her, more than ever.

When I got home that night, I prayed again: "Please, God. Please make me feel the only thing missing in my love for Angie." But when I climbed into bed and closed my eyes, it was Manuel's face I saw leaning over me, and his wavy hair.

16

DURING LUNCHTIME AT SCHOOL

I CONTINUED TO SIT WITH ANGIE AND DAKOTA, BUT ELIZABETH NEVER REJOINED OUR GROUP. WHEN I SAID HI TO HER IN THE HALL, SHE ARRANGED HER MOUTH CAREFULLY INTO A SMILE, BUT HER "HI" SEEMED FORCED AND COLD.
I wanted to talk to her about coming back to our group, but what if she confronted me about where I stood on homosexuality and Manuel? I decided, *Better just leave it.*

In the cafeteria Manuel now sat with a hodgepodge group he'd brought together one at a time—the kids that most people in school avoided. First, there was Rufus Santana, a starry-eyed stoner who reeked of marijuana and always wore a goofy grin. He was nice enough, but severely spacey.

Across from him sat Gerald Grissom, a quirky, self-proclaimed atheist Goth boy who'd worn a black trench coat every day during freshman year till he got nicknamed Columbine, provoking Mr. Arbuthnot (our principal) to institute a "no coats during school hours" policy. But even without the coat Gerald still seemed weird.

Next to him sat Maggie McGhee, whose name was scrawled on boys' restroom stalls for supposedly "putting out." Gossip was she'd already had one abortion, marking her with the equivalent of a scarlet letter—at least during school hours.

Beside her sat Janice Salazar, who had definitely gotten pregnant but opted to have the baby. And yet, in spite of her decision, people now avoided her, too, as if pregnancy might be contagious. Actually, I didn't hang out with her either.

And last was Stephen Marten, the boy from middle school whom other boys had beaten up and called "queer"—while I turned away.

I never would have expected a group of such different personalities to sit together, but I guess it made sense: They were all outsiders, just like Manuel.

Some afternoons he would invite me to hang out with him and one of them, but I always made up some excuse. He must have gotten the message, because eventually he stopped asking. Nevertheless, he still wanted to hang out with *my* friends. At his house one evening he asked, "When is your group having its next Bible study?"

"Um . . ." I knew our Bible Club was scheduled for that Wednesday, but I also recalled what a disaster our last meeting had been. So I looked away and lied: "Um, I'm not sure when it is." Afterward, I prayed for God's forgiveness.

My fib did no good anyway. Angie or Dakota must have told Manuel about the meeting, because when I arrived at Bible Club, he was already there with them. My stomach slid down to my shoes.

Across the circle of chairs sat Elizabeth and Cliff, darting glances at Manuel while murmuring in low voices with two other girls.

Angie motioned to an empty seat she'd saved for me.

Cliff had volunteered to lead that day's discussion, about the Sermon on the Mount, another of my Scripture favorites. He asked Elizabeth to start us off in prayer, but when she had finished, he unexpectedly announced, "Instead of the Sermon on the Mount, I think we should discuss Genesis Nineteen."

I blinked at him in surprise. We had never changed the scheduled passage at the last minute. People hastily flipped through their Bibles to recall what Genesis 19 was about. But I already knew. It told the story of Sodom and Gomorrah.

Angie looked worriedly at Manuel and objected, "We didn't prepare for that."

"Okay, let's take a vote," Cliff replied, as if he had anticipated the objection. "Majority rules. All those opposed to changing today's reading, raise their hands."

Angie, Dakota, Aaron Esposito, and I lifted our hands. I'd assumed Manuel would too, but he didn't.

"You can vote too," I whispered to him.

"Thanks. I will." But he still didn't raise his hand.

"Those in favor of changing the reading?" Cliff asked, raising his arm alongside Elizabeth and the two other girls. That made it a tie, four against four, except . . . Manuel also raised his hand.

Everyone in the circle stared at him. Even Cliff eyed him suspiciously.

"It's one of my favorites." Manuel smiled. Was he being sarcastic?

"All right then." Cliff cleared his throat. "Genesis Nineteen." He began reading aloud, "'The two angels came to Sodom in the evening—'"

"Excuse me," Manuel interrupted. "But the story really starts in chapter eighteen."

Cliff peered at him warily, as if suspecting a trap. "We voted to read chapter *nineteen*."

"All right." Manuel shrugged. "But the story starts in chapter eighteen."

Cliff resumed reading about how Lot, a nephew of Abraham,

rose to meet the two male angels at the city gate and invited them to spend the night at his house: They said, "No; we will spend the night in the street." But he urged them strongly; so they turned aside to him and entered his house; and he made them a feast, and baked unleavened bread, and they ate.'"

I tugged nervously at my wristband, knowing we were about to get to the bad part.

"'But before they lay down, the men of the city, the men of Sodom, both young and old, all the people to the last man, surrounded the house; and they called to Lot, "Where are the men who came to you tonight? Bring them out to us, that we may know them."'"

From Sunday school I knew that to "know" someone was often the Biblical way of saying to have sex. But in this passage it confused me. Did it mean that every single male in the city—"both young and old . . . to the last man"—was homosexual? That seemed kind of unlikely. But if they weren't, then why would they all have mobbed the house demanding to "know" the visiting strangers?

My palms started to sweat as Cliff pressed on with his reading: "'Lot went out of the door to the men, shut the door after him, and said, "I beg you, my brothers, do not act so wickedly. Behold, I have two daughters who have not known man; let me bring them out to you, and do to them as you please; only do nothing to these men, for they have come under the shelter of my roof."'"

"Can we stop a moment?" Dakota cut in. "If Lot, Abraham's nephew, is supposed to be a righteous, good, God-loving guy, how can he offer his two virgin daughters to be raped?"

"I agree," Angie spoke up. "What kind of dad is that? Isn't he just as bad as the rest of the Sodomites?"

Cliff thought for a moment and replied, "No. He knew the men outside were gay, so they wouldn't want his daughters."

"Wait a minute." Dakota shook her head. "Lot offered his daughters knowing they'd be refused? Then why'd he offer them? That doesn't make any sense."

I sat up in my seat, agreeing with the girls, but Cliff ignored their arguments and resumed reading aloud. In the following verses, the men of Sodom indeed refused Lot's offer of his daughters, telling him, "'Now we will deal worse with you than with them.' Then they pressed hard against the man Lot, and drew near to break the door. But the men put forth their hands and brought Lot into the house to them, and shut the door. And they struck with blindness the men who were at the door of the house, both small and great, so that they wearied themselves groping for the door."

As Cliff continued reading out loud, I turned the page, leaving a sweaty thumbprint.

"'Then the men said to Lot, "Have you any one else here? Sons-in-law, sons, daughters, or any one you have in the city, bring them out of the place; for we are about to destroy this place, because the outcry against its people has become great before the LORD, and the LORD has sent us to destroy it." So Lot went out and said to his sons-in-law, who were to marry his daughters, "Up, get out of this place; for the LORD is about to destroy the city." But he seemed to his sons-in-law to be jesting.'"

"Whoa, whoa, whoa!" Dakota interrupted again. "Lot went out to the mob to get his *sons-in-law*, who were to marry his *daughters*? So, were his sons-in-law also gay?"

Cliff scowled at her, thinking again. "Yeah. Apparently. That's why they get destroyed with the rest."

"What *I* don't get," Angie cut in, "is where were the women of the city during all this? Or were they supposedly also gay?"

"I'd like to say something," Manuel spoke up. "Maybe the story isn't really about homosexuality, but about rape. If the angels had been female, and the men of Sodom said they wanted to 'know' them against their will, would people claim that the story shows *heterosexuality* is a sin?"

Everyone in our circle turned to him, faces blank. It was the first time I'd ever heard anybody approach the story that way.

"The story is about homosexuality," Cliff insisted. "The angels weren't female. You're trying to change the story."

"No, I'm not." Manuel replied. "I'm trying to look at it without a homophobe bias. The men of Sodom wanted to rape the strangers. The fact that the angels were men isn't the point. The point is that the people of the city wanted to hurt visiting strangers. The story isn't antigay; it's antiviolence."

Cliff shook his head, unpersuaded. "The Bible says homosexuality is a sin." He quickly thumbed through his Bible to a page he'd marked. "Leviticus Eighteen-Twenty-two: 'You shall not lie with a male as with a woman; it is an abomination.'"

I slinked down in my seat, cowering at the verse.

But Manuel shrugged, unfazed. "So, are lesbians okay?"

"You're mocking God's Word," Cliff said, his fists curling.

"No, I'm just trying to understand," Manuel retorted. "In Leviticus Eleven, the Bible indicates that eating any seafood other than fish is an abomination. So does anyone who eats shrimp commit a lesser abomination than homosexuality?"

"That's ridiculous," Elizabeth said, glaring at Manuel.

"The Bible," Cliff insisted, "is the inerrant Word of God."

Manuel cocked his head. "And does that make *you* inerrant to interpret it?"

"God, I hope not," Dakota groaned, pushing back her red curls.

"I don't interpret the Bible," Cliff replied proudly. "I just believe it. I believe everything in this book." He pointed his Bible at Manuel. "Do *you* believe everything in this book?"

In response, Manuel glanced around the group and back to Cliff. "Do you even know what 'abomination' means in the Old Testament? It meant unclean and impure. Leviticus describes an ancient code of cleanliness and ritual purity. It forbade sex between men because Jewish people of that time thought it was unclean, similar to talking to a Samaritan or eating shrimp or pork—not because those things were evil or wrong in themselves. St. Paul clarified in Romans Fourteen-Fourteen, 'I know and am persuaded in the Lord Jesus that nothing is unclean in itself; but it is unclean for anyone who thinks it unclean.' Can't you understand that?"

"I understand," Cliff replied icily, reading again from his Bible, "Leviticus Twenty-Thirteen: 'If a man lies with a male as with a woman, both of them have committed an abomination; they shall be put to death, their blood is upon them.'"

"Well, I'm gay." Manuel edged forward in his seat. "Do you think *I* should be put to death?"

I sat listening, sure that Cliff would back down. I never expected the words that came out of his mouth: "That's what the Bible says. It's our job to obey."

The room fell silent as the rest of us sat startled. Even Elizabeth looked shocked.

I sat up in disbelief. "You don't mean that."

"And who should put me to death?" Manuel challenged Cliff. "You?"

Cliff hesitated. Was he considering the possibility?

Aaron Esposito spoke up. "The Bible also says, 'Thou shalt not kill.'"

Cliff glared at him. "Obviously, it makes exceptions."

"For gay people?" Manuel asked.

Cliff nodded. "That's what it says."

Angie called out, "Guys, stop it. This is crazy."

"Can I ask you something else?" Manuel said to Cliff. "Do you have a weekend job?"

"Yeah," Cliff replied cautiously.

"Including Sundays?"

"Sometimes."

"Well, doesn't Exodus Thirty-five-Two proclaim that for working on the Sabbath *you* also should be put to death?"

"That's different," Elizabeth interjected. "In Mark, Jesus proclaims, 'The Sabbath was made for man, not man for the Sabbath.'"

Manuel turned to her. "You mean Jesus corrected the inerrant word of God?"

"Jesus was the Word made flesh," Cliff replied, sounding almost enlightened.

"Exactly!" Manuel nearly leaped out of his seat. "Don't you get what that means? He showed us how to question, think, and not make an idol of the Bible. Time and again, he challenged those who followed the Law—including Leviticus—to look into their hearts. Is it such a stretch to think that if Jesus had said anything at all about homosexuality, it might've been that it's not the gender of your partner that matters, but what's in your heart?"

"Listen!" Cliff ordered Manuel. "If you don't believe in the Bible, then maybe you should just leave."

Manuel gazed at the rest of us. "So, is this like a cult where you can't disagree?"

"Of course you can disagree," Angie encouraged him.

"Then I disagree." Manuel frowned at Cliff. "How can you proclaim the Bible inerrant and claim to take it literally, but pick and choose to believe one part and not the other?" He glanced around our group. "I love the Bible. But I believe it's meant to soften our hearts, not harden them."

With that, he stood and grabbed his backpack.

"Manuel!" Angie called, but he was already out the door. She got up, glowering at Cliff, and followed after Manuel, still calling him. Dakota strode behind her, but not before telling Cliff, "You're a Neanderthal, you know that?"

I wanted to follow too, and yet I remained seated, still too rattled from the debate.

"Let's get back to the story," Cliff told us, but Aaron spoke up: "I think we should stop for today."

"Yeah," the rest of us agreed.

One of the girls closed our meeting with a prayer. Then we replaced our chairs in order, and I headed home, exhausted.

17

A NORTHER STARTED TO BLOW IN

AS I DROVE HOME FROM BIBLE STUDY, STILL FEELING A
LITTLE UNNERVED BY CLIFF AND MANUEL'S SHOWDOWN
OVER THE SODOM STORY.

When I got to my room, I went to my desk and gathered every
Bible translation, concordance, dictionary, and commentary I
owned. I also pulled up my favorite Bible website, determined to
figure out for myself what the story of Sodom was really about.

"Jesus, please guide me," I prayed. "I'm trying hard to understand, but I need your help." Then I opened my Bible to Genesis
18, the chapter immediately preceding the angels' trip to Sodom, as
Manuel had suggested.

The passage began with Abraham sitting at the door of his tent
in the heat of the day. *He lifted up his eyes and looked, and behold, three
men stood in front of him. When he saw them, he ran from the tent door to
meet them, and bowed himself to the earth, and said, "My lord, if I have found
favor in your sight, do not pass by your servant. Let a little water be brought,
and wash your feet, and rest yourselves under the tree, while I fetch a morsel of
bread, that you may refresh yourselves, and after that you may pass on . . ."*

Apparently, one of the three men was the Lord and the other

two were angels. After a meal, the visitors turned their attention to Sodom, to which they were traveling, and the Lord confided in Abraham his plans for the city: *"Because the outcry against Sodom and Gomor'rah is great and their sin is very grave, I will go down to see whether they have done altogether according to the outcry which has come to me; and if not, I will know."*

As I read the passage, I wondered, *why wasn't the "very grave" sin identified?* It seemed odd that the Lord didn't know what was going on in the world and had to check on reports. Wasn't the Creator all-knowing? I kept reading.

The two angels turned and headed toward Sodom, but Abraham still stood before the Lord, concerned about his nephew, Lot, and his family, who lived in Sodom. Abraham drew near to God and began to bargain, reminding him of his divine and righteous nature: *"Wilt thou indeed destroy the righteous with the wicked? Suppose there are fifty righteous within the city; wilt thou then destroy the place and not spare it for the fifty righteous who are in it? Far be it from thee to do such a thing, to slay the righteous with the wicked, so that the righteous fare as the wicked! Far be that from thee! Shall not the Judge of all the earth do right?"*

The Lord, apparently persuaded by Abraham, agreed, *"If I find at Sodom fifty righteous in the city, I will spare the whole place for their sake."*

Abraham continued to bargain God down, to forty-five, forty, thirty, twenty, and finally ten. Then the Lord went his way, Abraham returned to his home, and I turned the tissue-thin page to the next chapter, 19.

As I reread our Bible study passage, the whole Sodom story seemed even more twisted than before. Once more I wondered, could *all* the males in the city, young and old, have been gay? One of my commentaries suggested that the original language could be interpreted as meaning that both the men *and* women of Sodom wanted to "know" the angels. But that only furthered Manuel's argument that the story wasn't about homosexuality, but about rape.

I also recalled Dakota's point: How could Lot have offered up his daughters? What kind of dad would do that? How could God consider him righteous and spare him?

Then there were the verses where the angels tell Lot's family, *"Flee for your life; do not look back or stop anywhere in the valley; flee to the hills, lest you be consumed . . ." But Lot's wife behind him looked back, and she became a pillar of salt.*

God turned Lot's wife to salt simply because she looked back? Wasn't that a bit harsh?

Then the story got even more confusing. Lot and his two daughters went to live in caves, and the daughters conspired: *"Our father is old, and there is not a man on earth to come in to us after the manner of all the earth. Come, let us make our father drink wine, and we will lie with him, that we may preserve offspring through our father."*

Wait a minute. Were these the same two daughters that God supposedly spared for being righteous? Yet they got their very own dad drunk and had sex with him without even his knowledge or consent. Wasn't that considered rape?

Through their incest the daughters bore two sons, who became the fathers of the Moabites and Ammonites. And that was the full story of Sodom, so often held up as a condemnation of homosexuality.

I leaned back in my desk chair, staring at my cherished Bible. How could anyone take a story about mob violence, attempted gang rape, a God who doesn't know what's going on, sin that isn't specified, a woman being nuked to salt, and daughter-father incest, and use that story to condemn homosexuality?

And yet, hadn't I been taught for years to read the story that way?

I recalled Manuel's photo of his boyfriend and him at prom, wearing tuxes and smiles. How was that anything like the story of Sodom?

In Sunday school on various occasions my teachers had explained that we needed to view certain practices accepted in the Bible, such as polygamy and slavery, in their historical-cultural context. But then didn't *everything* in the Bible need to be viewed in context, including attitudes toward homosexuality?

To be sure that I wasn't making a mistake, I decided to search my concordance for every other Biblical reference to Sodom I could find.

In Isaiah 1 and 3, the prophet implied that Sodom was destroyed for a bunch of evildoings and a failure to *do good; seek justice, correct oppression* . . . But there was no reference even hinting at homosexuality.

The book of Jeremiah compared the prophets of Jerusalem to the Sodomites: *I have seen a horrible thing: they commit adultery and walk in lies; they strengthen the hands of evildoers, so that no one turns from his wickedness; all of them have become like Sodom to me, and its inhabitants like Gomor'rah.* Again, no link to homosexuality.

Ezekiel stated, *Behold, this was the guilt of your sister Sodom: she and her daughters had pride, surfeit of food, and prosperous ease, but did not aid the poor and needy. They were haughty, and did abominable things before me; therefore I removed them, when I saw it.* Once again, no mention of homosexuality.

In Zephaniah, I found this passage: *Moab shall become like Sodom, and the Ammonites like Gomor'rah, a land possessed by nettles and salt pits, and a waste for ever . . . This shall be their lot in return for their pride, because they scoffed and boasted against the people of the LORD of hosts.* But weren't the Moabites and Ammonites the descendents of Lot and his daughters, who had been spared for supposedly being righteous?

In Judges 19, a story almost identical to Genesis 19 occurs, about a city named Gibeah, in which a Levite and his concubine are given hospitality by an old man. The men of Gibeah gather, demanding, *"Bring out the man who came into your house, that we may know him."* Instead, the old man hands over the concubine, who is raped so savagely that she dies. That grisly story reminded me of Manuel's question: If the angels in the Sodom story had been female (like the concubine), would *heterosexuality* be condemned? Not likely. Was that why I never heard anyone cite the Gibeah story?

Finally, even in Matthew 10, when Jesus himself sent out his disciples to do God's work, he alluded to Sodom, not in terms of homosexuality, but in terms of inhospitality: *"If any one will not receive you or listen to your words, shake off the dust from your feet as you leave that house or town. Truly, I say to you, it shall be more tolerable on the day of judgment for the land of Sodom and Gomor'rah than for that town."*

No reference to sex, but a clear warning against failing to welcome God's messengers.

If homosexuality truly was the sin of Sodom, then why did no other book in the Bible mention anything about homosexuality or even homosexual rape in relation to the Sodom story? Instead, each additional reference created a clearer image of the Sodomites as prideful, unjust, unwelcoming, and inhospitable to strangers, to the point of violence.

So, was the story of Sodom really about God's wrath over homosexuality?

I closed my Bible, exhausted and yet also unexpectedly calmed. Verses of Scripture that had frightened me for years suddenly seemed far less intimidating. After all, I'd never threatened or abused strangers—or anyone. Even if I didn't like somebody, I tried to be nice. And I had definitely never ever even *imagined* raping someone.

After today's Bible study, even the ominous injunctions of Leviticus no longer seemed quite so menacing. Nevertheless, when my cell phone rang, I jumped.

It was Angie: "Dakota and I decided we need to start a GSA."

"Huh?" I gripped the phone, recalling what the initials stood for: gay-straight alliance.

"After today's Bible study," Angie explained, "we think we need to do something before somebody gets killed. So we're going to start a GSA. We want you to help us."

I sat up in my desk chair. My calm of a moment earlier evaporated as my confusion returned. "You serious?"

"Yep. Dakota's looking up stuff about GSAs on the Web right now. We'll talk about it at lunch tomorrow, okay?"

By the time I said prayers that night, my head was once again a jumble of thoughts: about Bible study, Cliff's belief that gay people should be killed, Manuel opening my eyes to reading Bible passages in a way I'd never read them before, and my best friends' plan to start a GSA.

18

BY LUNCHTIME THE NEXT DAY

ANGIE HAD STOPPED BY THE MAIN OFFICE AND PICKED
UP THE APPLICATION FORM REQUIRED TO ORGANIZE A
SCHOOL CLUB. SHE AND DAKOTA WERE TALKING
EXCITEDLY ABOUT IT WHEN I GOT TO OUR TABLE.

"You really think Mr. Arbuthnot will allow a GSA?" I asked,
secretly hoping our principal wouldn't.

"He has to." Dakota shoved her curls behind her ear and
explained: "According to the websites I researched, the Supreme
Court ruled that GSAs are covered under the . . . wait, I wrote
it down . . ." She opened her reporter's notebook to a page of
scribbles. "Here it is: the federal Equal Access Act, created to allow
school Bible clubs like ours. The act states that all public schools
receiving federal funding must allow *any* school club to be organized, so long as the group is student-initiated."

"I asked Manuel," Angie interjected, "to explain to us how
they formed a GSA at his old school." She glanced across the cafeteria. "Here he comes."

For the first time since Elizabeth ditched our group, Manuel
once again joined our table. I gazed around the lunchroom to see if

anyone was watching. Even though I hung out with him after school, that was different; no one saw us. Now I ducked down in my seat.

Angie noticed and gave me a puzzled look. "Are you okay?"

"Fine," I muttered, and tried to listen to Manuel.

"At my old school," he explained, "most of our GSA members were actually straight. Ironically, the gay and lesbian kids were too closeted and afraid to come to meetings—at least at first. But once they saw the support of straight students, they started coming out."

Angie leaned across the table to show us our school's application form. It required at least four students to officially organize a school club. One by one Angie, Dakota, and Manuel each signed their names to the form. I watched, sweat trickling down my back. Did I really want to put my name down?

Manuel handed me the pen.

I stared at the dotted line. "Um, I want to think about it."

Angie and Dakota peered across their lunch trays at me.

"Why?" Manuel asked, a grin tugging at his lips. "You afraid people might think you're gay?"

"No!" I said it louder than I intended, wishing Manuel had never come to our school.

"Then what do you need to think about?" Angie asked softly.

I folded my arms and slumped farther down in my chair. "I just want to think about it, that's all."

"Well . . ." Dakota shrugged. "If you don't want to do it, we can find someone else."

"Go ahead," I shot back. I didn't like being pressured. "I said I want to think about it. Okay?"

The three of them were quiet, exchanging looks. Angie, ever the peacemaker, said, "Well, in the meantime we'll need to find a sponsor. Every group has to have one."

I thought about all the teachers who ignored the "that's so gay" remarks and silently turned their backs. Maybe I didn't need to be so worried about the GSA. After all, would any teacher actually be willing to sponsor the club? I doubted it.

19

AS THE WEEK PROGRESSED,

IN MY MIND I DEBATED WHETHER OR NOT TO SIGN THE
GSA APPLICATION. AND IN MY HEART I ASKED JESUS,
*PLEASE HELP ME. EVERYTHING SEEMS SO CONFUSED. I'VE ALWAYS
TRIED TO DO WHAT YOU WANTED. WHAT SHOULD I DO NOW?*
Meanwhile, Angie and Dakota began asking teachers to sponsor
the club. During lunchtime the girls reported what had happened,
and I listened intently, too anxious to eat much.

Angie had first approached six-foot-three Ms. Lanier, the
unmarried girls' gym teacher, who—rumor claimed—was a lesbian.

"No way!" she had told Angie. "You want me to lose my job?"

Next, Dakota had asked Mr. Oglethorpe, our ancient history
and world civ teacher. He was one of the nicest teachers at school,
but a little deaf and verging on senile.

"When I told him it was a gay-straight alliance"—Dakota
rolled her eyes in exasperation—"he thought I meant some
sort of glee club. When I tried to explain the purpose was to
combat homophobia, he said he couldn't support any organization that advocated violence. At that point I gave up."

Angie proceeded to describe her encounter with Mrs. Lee, a

math teacher: "She peered over her little half-moon glasses at me and whispered, 'It's that new boy, isn't it? The one with the eyebrow ring? I knew he was trouble from the moment I saw him.'"

Dakota told us how Mr. Wendt, the English teacher, had told her, "I'd like to help you. Really, I would. But I have to choose my battles wisely, and frankly, I doubt this one stands a chance in Hades. I'm still getting grief for teaching *Slaughterhouse-Five* last year."

I recalled how a group of parents had tried to get him fired for teaching a book that they said promoted sex and filthy language.

Out of all the teachers Angie and Dakota had asked, not a single one would sponsor the GSA.

"So now what do we do?" Dakota gazed, droopy-faced, across the table at Angie and me.

"We keep asking," Angie insisted. "Till somebody says yes."

"But what if no one will do it?" I asked.

Dakota gave me a disappointed frown. "That's not what you're hoping, is it?"

"Um, no," I said, though I wasn't sure I meant it. My feelings about everything, including Angie, the Bible, what to believe, and especially about Manuel, were shifting every minute.

Each time I saw him, I was aware of feelings growing inside me, unlike any I'd ever experienced. Even though he exasperated me at times, I couldn't stop thinking about him. And the more I tried to control my thoughts, the more they seemed to buck me.

Adding to my confusion, it seemed like the antigay stuff at school was getting worse. One morning in homeroom, I noticed that Jude Maldonado had written on his desktop, "Manuel Cordero is a fag." Crude stuff like that began to appear on desks in every class I had with Jude: "Manuel likes dick," "E-mail Cordero for butt sex."

One day in the hallway, between classes, Cliff pulled me aside.

"We need to talk." His steel gray eyes drilled into me. "People are asking me why you hang out with that queer."

I cringed, recalling Cliff's death-to-gays remark. "So?"

"So . . ." Cliff narrowed his eyes at me. "What am I supposed to tell them?"

"I don't care." Of course I really *did* care. But what could I do?

That afternoon I was walking down the hall, when a group of guys passed me and coughed the word, "Faggot!" I pretended like I didn't hear them, but inside I churned with emotion: wanting to smack them, or hide, or scream, or cry . . .

In the evening, alone in my room, I asked Jesus to guide me. "I'm so confused. Everything seems all wrong. Why is this happening?"

Another day, Elizabeth cornered me at my locker. "I'm really concerned about you, Paul. I want you to know I'm praying for you." That came as no surprise. Every once in a while she'd gaze across the cafeteria, glaring at Dakota, and text me: *I'm praying 4 u in Jesus' name.*

The following day at lunch I told Angie and Dakota, "I've decided to sign the GSA application."

The girls exchanged a look, and Angie said, "Thanks, but, um . . . we already got someone else."

"Really?" My skin prickled with curiosity. "Who?"

"Stephen Marten," Dakota replied.

I glanced across the lunchroom toward Manuel's table. The boy who since middle school had gotten called "queer" was now smiling and laughing.

"So, um, is he really gay?" I said.

Angie shrugged. "I didn't ask."

"It's a gay-*straight* alliance," Dakota reminded me. "As a ground rule, we don't ask people's sexual orientation."

"Even so . . ." I picked at my chicken salad. "People will assume anyone who goes is gay. I'm already getting flack just for hanging out with Manuel."

"You are?" Angie's eyes grew huge with worry. "What kind of flack?"

I pushed my tray aside, too frustrated to eat. "Like guys calling me names and saying stuff."

Dakota squared her shoulders as if ready to defend me. "Has anyone tried to hurt you physically?"

"No." Her concern made me feel better.

Angie sighed. "I think it's harder for guys than girls."

"At least with girls," Dakota agreed, "you don't have to worry as much about violence."

"How can we help?" Angie reached over and laid her hand on mine.

I shook my head in dismay. Even though I appreciated their offer, I knew I was on my own. Guys would view any sort of help from girls as only further reason to accuse me of being gay. "There's nothing you can do," I said.

Later that week I was walking toward my car when a school bus passed and someone yelled out the window, "Homo!"

I whirled around to see who'd said it, but they had ducked back inside the roaring bus. I kicked the sidewalk and resumed walking, feeling like Armageddon was approaching.

20

WHEN THE LAST BELL RANG

BEFORE THANKSGIVING BREAK, I BOLTED OUT THE
DOOR. BESIDES BEING EAGER TO GET AWAY FROM ALL THE
SCHOOL STRESS, I'D BEEN LOOKING FORWARD TO
ABUELITA COMING TO VISIT US FROM MEXICO. I LOVED
HER A LOT, AS MUCH AS I LOVED MY PA. AFTER SCHOOL,
I DROVE THE HOUR TO ABILENE TO PICK HER UP AT THE
AIRPORT.

As Abuelita shuffled through the gate, I ran up, stooping over her
tiny frame and into her outstretched arms. She pressed her bony
face against my cheek, and I breathed in her delicate rose perfume.
Then she grabbed my shoulders, staring at me through the chunky
glasses that magnified her charcoal-black eyes, making them huge
and bright.

"Let me look at you, *mi amor*. Every time I see you, you're even
more tall and handsome than ever." She always said stuff like that,
making me blush and smile.

On the drive home she asked me about Pa and his girlfriend,
and about school and Angie. "And what about *you*?" She clutched
my hand tightly. "Are you happy, Pablito?"

Abuelita was the only person in the world I let call me that—the kid form of Pablo. I nodded earnestly in response. Sitting beside her, I was the happiest I'd been in weeks.

When we arrived home, I carried her suitcase into the guest bedroom, but she only took a moment to get settled before heading to the kitchen. Abuelita took that room over whenever she visited, warming it with her presence and filling our house with sounds and smells that carried me back to when I was a little kid in Mexico: the sizzle of sautéed peppers, the steaming hiss of a pressure cooker full of beans, the bubbling boil of posole stew, the sweet smell of masa, and the *slap, slap, slap, slap* of Abuelita's hands patting tortillas . . . Even though Pa and I got along okay batching it, having Abuelita home made everything better.

At mealtimes she set an extra place, to remind us of those who didn't have enough to eat—and of the Lord's presence among us. To Abuelita, God was a member of the family—someone to talk to and reckon with.

Oftentimes I'd come home and hear her in the middle of a conversation. I had to look around to check: Was anyone human actually there? Or was she talking to Jesus again? Her chats with God weren't like most prayers—at least not like mine. She could get into real arguments, nearly shouting at the Lord.

As a boy I'd wondered what to make of Abuelita, but Ma had reassured me: "Don't worry, *mijo*. That's just how she is."

Over the years I had gotten used to the quirkiness. I admired her faith, and I think she paved the way for my own relationship with Jesus.

On Thanksgiving morning, I woke up early to help Abuelita make her best-turkey-on-earth recipe, *mole poblano de guajolote*, with the magical ingredient, melted chocolate. She knew how much I loved chocolate. My mouth watered the entire time we were making it.

Pa invited Raquel and some of their friends. And later in the day, after we'd finished our feast, Angie came over, bringing a pumpkin custard pie. The three of us sat in the kitchen, and Abuelita told us funny stories about growing up in her Mexican farm town: having to run away from snakes in the outhouse; how mischievous girls at her convent school secretly tacked their nun's habit to a chair to find out if she was bald, so that when the sister stood up, her headdress pulled off; and the cooking disaster when Abuelita became a restaurant chef and used too many chili peppers. I loved her stories and laughed so much that my ribs hurt.

After Angie left, I was helping Abuelita unload the dishwasher when she abruptly asked, "Are you in love with her?"

I almost dropped the cup I was storing. *Why is she asking that? What should I answer? Am I in love with Angie? I want to be.*

Abuelita adjusted her clunky glasses and peered at me with her enormous eyes. "If you're not," she said sternly, "don't mislead her, *mi amor*. Be honest with her—and yourself."

I swallowed what felt like a pumpkin-sized knot in my throat and looked away. Why was she telling me this?

But she gently took my chin and turned my face back to her. "Have you ever been in love?"

I hesitated, recalling Manuel's description of being head over heels about Bryan, and comparing it with Angie and me.

"Um, I don't know."

"If you don't know," Abuelita said sternly, "then you haven't. When you're in love, you'll know."

I quietly put away the last of the dishes, aching to confess to her all the turmoil bottled up inside me: my unwanted attraction toward guys, my fear of going to hell because of it, how much I *wanted* to be in love with Angie, and how confused I felt about the new boy at school named Manuel. I wanted to tell Abuelita all of it.

But I couldn't. It was too much to sort out. Instead, I changed my clothes and told Pa, "I'm going for a run."

After spending the whole day inside, I breathed in huge gulps of fresh air, while the conversation with Abuelita dogged my every step. Had I ever been in love? Was I falling in love with *Manuel*?

The thought tripped me midstride; I nearly tumbled to the pavement.

No way! I told myself, regaining my balance. *I am* not *falling in love with Manuel. Uh-uh. No, no, no!*

I ran harder against the cold wind, hoping to leave my thoughts behind. But in my heart I knew that my feelings for Manuel were growing. With each step I asked Jesus, *Am I falling in love with Manuel? Why?*

And even though it was Thanksgiving, I felt more confused than thankful.

21

THE SATURDAY FOLLOWING THANKSGIVING,

ANGIE AND I WENT ON OUR REGULAR DATE TO DINNER AND THE (S)MALL. WE WERE WALKING HAND IN HAND TOWARD THE MOVIE WHEN ANGIE SUDDENLY SHOUTED, "DAKOTA! MANUEL!"

"Angie!" Manuel yelled back, so loud that people turned to stare. Then he stretched his arms out, like in some corny romance, except he was laughing, and swooped her up off the floor, twirling her in a circle while she whooped.

As I watched them, a feeling that I couldn't identify nagged me. Then I recalled Angie sitting beside me in the car and asking, "Are you jealous of him?" Except it wasn't Manuel I was jealous of—it was Angie, being swung around. I wished that it was me in his arms.

I stood paralyzed by that realization as Manuel set Angie down, both of them still laughing.

"We're going to see the creature feature," Angie told Dakota, and gave me a look. After so many years with Angie, I knew what the look meant.

"Um, you guys want to join us?" I asked, coming back from my daze.

"Nah," Dakota replied. "We shouldn't barge in on you guys' date."

"It's okay," I told them, meaning it. Between Thanksgiving and Abuelita I hadn't seen Manuel for three days. I missed him.

As usual I paid for Angie's ticket, and she bought our drinks and popcorn. Dakota also bought a bag, and Manuel got their drinks.

As the four of us walked into the theater, we talked and joked about the tons of food we'd eaten for Thanksgiving. Halfway down the aisle I followed Dakota and Angie into a row, with Manuel trailing behind me.

"Do you want to sit next to Manuel?" Angie asked Dakota.

"That's okay," she replied. "Let the guys sit together."

That put Manuel on my left, Angie on my right, and me in the middle. We peeled off our coats, and when I reached into the popcorn bag I now shared with Manuel, our thumbs accidentally bumped.

"Um, sorry," I mumbled. Yet each time I reached into the bag, our fingers touched. "Sorry," I kept muttering.

Manuel laughed like it was hilarious.

"Hey!" Dakota peered over. "What're you two doing?"

Annoyed, I told Manuel, "You can have the rest."

I wiped the salt and butter from my fingers, and as the lights dimmed, Angie took hold of my hand. I started to lay my other hand on the armrest between Manuel and me, except . . . Manuel's was already there. I glanced anxiously at it and rested my hand in my lap.

Tonight's movie was a Halloween release that had only recently made its way to our town. It began with a newly married couple taking down the SOLD sign and moving into a picturesque—but isolated— country house. Almost immediately mysterious things began to happen. The phone went dead. Lights flickered on and off. Their car wouldn't start. A pitchfork disappeared.

All the while, Angie stroked my right hand, while on my left, Manuel's hand lurked on the armrest.

I tried to ignore it and focus on the movie, but my thoughts kept drifting. Why was it considered so wrong to hold another guy's hand? During my fourth-grade field trip to the Grace Museum in Abilene, everyone had paired up with a buddy. For the whole day I held a boy's hand, and no one had thought anything about it. At what age had it become sinful?

I struggled to rein in my thoughts, but the warmth emanating from Manuel didn't help any. Each time his shoulder brushed mine, it was as if a little zap of electricity sparked through my body. And when our naked elbows bumped, the hair on my arms practically jumped to attention.

On-screen, the couple awoke one stormy night to the sound of feet dragging through the hall outside their bedroom.

The woman clutched her husband. "What is it?"

"I don't know." The man wrapped his arms around his wife.

And I slowly lifted my forearm and let it rest casually against Manuel's, while my heart pounded like thunder. Sweat rained down my forehead. Why was I doing this? I should yank my lust-crazed arm away. *Do it! Now!*

But the touch of his bare skin excited me too much.

On-screen, the eerie scratching and rasping at the couple's bedroom door grew louder.

"Oh, God! It's trying to get in!" the woman explained, as if her husband might not realize that. But then the creepy sounds faded away . . . and the couple returned to sleep.

"Leave the house, you stupids!" I wanted to shout at the couple. But they stayed, and my arm remained on the armrest, pressed against Manuel's.

Annoyed and confused, I turned to look at him. The light from the screen shone across his eyes and mouth. And a feeling, different from the one in the lobby, tugged at me. It wasn't jealousy. It was something else, stirring from deep inside my chest. Unsettled, I quickly turned away.

"What's the matter?" Angie whispered.

"Um, nothing." I grabbed her hand more tightly and avoided turning to look at Manuel again. Instead, I tried to concentrate on the rest of the dumb movie, as the man and woman died gruesome deaths.

In the lobby afterward, Manuel annoyed the rest of us with scratching sounds while clawing with his hands. We all said good night, Manuel gave Dakota a ride, and I drove Angie home.

The night was clear, with no moon. As usual, I parked in front of Angie's and shut the engine off. Then I leaned over and gently pressed my lips to hers. Her kiss tasted like warm butter and salt, bringing back the memory of Manuel in the movie theater, our arms touching, making me both agitated and excited.

Angie's breath came heavily as well. Then, without warning, she took hold of my hand and urged it onto her breast.

My heart leaped with a jolt. It was my first time to ever touch a breast.

I froze, unsure what to do. I could imagine what some other boy might do, given such an opportunity. A little panicked, I withdrew my lips from hers. "Um . . . what are you doing?"

Angie blushed and let go of my hand. I briskly removed it from her breast and leaned back in my seat, worried. Had I hurt her feelings?

We sat silent for a while, as she stared out the window and I doubted myself. Should I have gone through the motions with her?

Then Angie turned to look at me, and her voice came out soft and unsure: "Can I ask you something? What exactly do you feel for me?"

My fingers tightened nervously around the steering wheel as my heart sped up. How could I tell her I wasn't sure? "Um, I love you."

"Yeah . . ." Her face relaxed a little. "I know you do, and I love you, too. But do you feel, like, *passion* for me?"

My heart rate whizzed up even faster. Angie's eyes were so wide and hopeful that I had to drop my gaze. I knew her question was opening the door for me, but I feared what might come out. My pulse throbbed in my temples as I mumbled, "What do you mean?"

"I mean:" She curled her ponytail between her fingers. "Are you sexually attracted to me?"

Little drops of sweat misted on my forehead. How could I admit that during all the years I'd known her I had *wanted* to feel that way, but hadn't? I was afraid to hurt her—or lose her. She meant the world to me.

"I, um, I thought—you know—we should wait till marriage . . . till we're both sure that's what we want."

Angie shook her head. "I'm not saying we *should* have sex now. I just need to know if you'll ever *want* to."

Her frankness made my stomach flutter. Could I admit that I didn't know if it would even be possible for me to have sex with her?

I cleared my throat to force a response. "If that's what God wants for us."

Angie frowned. Obviously, that wasn't the answer she expected. "Is there"—her voice caught, sounding hurt—"something you want to tell me?"

Her question took my breath away, as if two invisible hands were suddenly squeezing my windpipe to tell her the truth—or *not* to.

"No." I shook my head.

After that, we sat quietly for a long time, not saying much, each of us with our own thoughts, as I tried to calm down. Then I walked her to the door and said good night.

When I arrived home, Abuelita and my pa were already asleep. I crept quietly to my room, undressed, and began my prayers, reviewing the day's events. "Dear God . . ."

I hesitated a moment, thinking about the movie theater, Angie, and Manuel. Should I give thanks for the confusing thrill of pressing my arm against Manuel's? Or should I ask for God's forgiveness?

"I don't know what to pray to you any more. Every day I feel more and more confused. Please help me."

In the middle of sleeping that night I thought I heard a noise at my door. I woke up, startled, my mind racing back to the horror movie. Quickly I fumbled to turn on the light and looked around, but I saw nothing unusual. The only sound was my own frantic breathing. Still jittery, I closed my eyes, leaving the light on, and tried to get back to sleep.

22

SUNDAY MORNING PA AND I

HEADED TO CHURCH, WHILE ABUELITA STAYED HOME,
WAVING US ON OUR WAY. AS PART OF HER QUIRKY FAITH,
SHE REFUSED TO SET FOOT IN ANY CHURCH. ONCE, AS A
BOY, I HAD ASKED HER, "WHY?"

"It's like this . . ." She sat down at the kitchen table and leaned me
against her lap. "When I was a young woman, I found out that
your *abuelito* was not the good man he'd pretended to be. I realized
that I'd never be happy with a man who had lied and deceived me."
She stroked my hair gently with her fingertips. "But in those days,
really not so long ago, divorce was thought to be an almost unfor-
givable sin. Our priest said that if I divorced, I could never be part
of the church again."

Behind Abuelita's glasses, her eyes clouded with hurt.

"To be a divorced woman in a little Mexican town was a shame
beyond words. I took your papa, still only a baby, to Monterrey
with me to start a new life. There, too, the church was filled with
rules and bitterness. Catholics and Protestants didn't speak to
each other. And when I visited across the border to this country,
Mexicans weren't even allowed into the white churches. I think

that it's the same everywhere: The church preaches love, but too often it practices something else."

And yet Abuelita had managed to separate her resentment at the organized church from her faith in God. If anyone was a model for a personal relationship with the Lord, it was my grandma.

Since today was the Sunday after Thanksgiving, Pastor José began his sermon with a verse from St. Paul's first letter to the Thessalonians: "'Rejoice always, pray without ceasing, in everything give thanks; for this is the will of God in Christ Jesus for you.'"

"Let's be clear," Pastor said. "When St. Paul says 'in everything give thanks,' he means *everything*. Not just the turkey, gravy, sweet potato pie, and all those good things that the Lord brings our way, but also the heartburn and bad stuff. Give thanks for *everything*. Are we clear about that?"

He waited for the congregation to respond with the usual amens, although in this case they were hardly enthusiastic. Who wanted to give thanks for bad stuff?

"Now, some of you look like you're thinking, *But Pastor, how can I give thanks for my thorn-in-the-flesh mother-in-law who moved in when I never invited her in the first place?*"

Pastor laughed and the congregation joined him. But when the laughter quieted, Pastor turned serious. "Or you're thinking, *How can I give thanks when my daughter is diagnosed with cancer?*"

The congregation grew silent. We all knew that Pastor's daughter had died of leukemia only three years earlier.

"It's not always easy to give thanks . . ." Pastor's voice was solemn. "But that's what God calls us to do. Because those tough things are what break our hearts open and allow Jesus to come inside."

At Jesus' name, several church members cried out, "Amen! Yes, Jesus!" Many more swayed their arms in prayer. And I thought about my own "tough thing." How could I give thanks for *that*?

Pastor told us to turn our Bibles to St. Paul's Epistle to the Romans.

I withered in my seat. Chapter 1 contained the New Testament's most explicit condemnation of homosexuality, which Pastor often quoted when he preached against gays.

Much to my relief, today he read from Chapter 5 instead: "'We rejoice in our sufferings, knowing that suffering produces endurance, and endurance produces character, and character produces hope, and hope does not disappoint us, because God's love has been poured into our hearts through the Holy Spirit which has been given to us.'"

"Give thanks for the challenges the world presents you," Pastor encouraged us. "For if your problems bring you closer to Jesus, they have served their purpose."

I sat up, listening intently. Was *that* the purpose of my unwanted feelings? To bring me closer to Jesus? Could it be that simple?

After church Pa and I picked up Raquel at her house, and we drove home. For lunch Abuelita had made us chicken enchiladas, black beans, yellow rice, and for dessert, chocolate cheesecake.

I was helping to clear the table when my cell rang. Manuel's number appeared on the screen. I hesitated before answering, "'Sup?"

"Hey," Manuel said airily. "You want to come over?"

"Can't," I replied. "I'm about to drive my *abuelita* to the airport."

"You want me to go with you?" Manuel asked.

I thought it over for a moment, my heart thudding. Even though I'd seen him just the night before and ended up crazed with confusion, I wanted to see him again. But what would Abuelita think of him? What if he told her he was gay? Would she suspect me, too?

I covered the mike on my cell and whispered to Abuelita, "Is it all right if a friend comes with us? He's, um, a little weird."

"Of course it's all right." Abuelita wiped her eyeglasses with a dishcloth. "Weird people are more interesting."

I thought about that. "Okay," I told Manuel. "We'll pick you up."

While Abuelita hugged Pa and Raquel good-bye, I loaded her suitcase into the car. Then we stopped to get Manuel.

From the moment he climbed in the door, Abuelita's eyes lit up even brighter than usual. "Oh, I like the ring on your eyebrow."

"*Gracias, señora.* I like your necklace." She was wearing a colorful turquoise and silver chain that I could remember from the time I was young.

During the drive Manuel and Abuelita chattered back and forth over the seat, at times in Spanish and at other times in English, about flan recipes, immigration reform, Aztec history, places in Mexico that Manuel had visited, all sorts of stuff.

I braced myself on the steering wheel, nervous that he'd mention being gay. But he never did. By the time we reached the airport, he and Abuelita had become fast friends.

At the security gate Abuelita hugged me good-bye and said, "He's a very nice boy." Then she peered into my eyes and added, "Be true to your heart."

As she waddled toward the gate, I swallowed nervously. What had she meant by *that*?

23

ON THE DRIVE BACK FROM ABILENE

AIRPORT, IT WAS THE KIND OF PERFECT DAY THAT MAKES
YOU FEEL HAPPY FOR NO REASON. THE SKY WAS CLEAR AND
THE SUN FELT WARM LIKE SUMMER, WHILE THE AIR FELT
COOL LIKE FALL. WE ROLLED DOWN THE CAR WINDOWS
AND LISTENED TO THE STEREO, AND IN THE SEAT ACROSS
FROM ME, MANUEL'S HAIR BLEW ALL OVER THE PLACE.

As we passed our town limits sign, he asked, "You want to come
over awhile?"

I did. We baked some chocolate chip cookies and sat on the
carpet of his room, eating and listening to music.

"Aren't these amazing cookies?" He smiled, not in a boasting
way, just joyful. "I feel so good today. Hey, turn this song up!"

Whereas Angie and I mostly listened to Christian rock and
gospel, Manuel played all sorts of stuff: klezmer music, yodeling
cowboys, Latino hip-hop, Beethoven symphonies . . . Today: 1930s
big band.

I cranked the stereo while Manuel sprang up and started dancing in front of his dresser mirror. He twirled, first in one direction,
then the other. He was a great dancer—better than most guys I

knew. His shoulders remained level while his hips rolled in waves to the music's rhythm. And in my mind I pictured him dancing with his (ex-)boyfriend at prom.

Manuel's eyes caught mine in the mirror, watching him from behind. Quickly I glanced away.

"You were looking at my butt." He grinned.

"Shut up! I was not."

"Yes, you were. Admit it." He danced over to me and reached down, grabbing for my hand. "Come on, dance with me!"

I pulled my hand away. "No, thanks."

"Why not? 'Cause I'm a guy?"

"Duh, yeah!"

"So? What difference does that make? It's just dancing." He extended his hand again. "*Amigo*, if I were you, I'd take me up on this invitation. You never know in life if you'll get a second chance."

"*Amigo*," I mimicked back, "I'll risk it."

He kept dancing around the room, while I brooded and tried to ignore him. But out of the corner of my eye, I could see his body swaying and hips shaking. *What* would *it feel like to dance with him?*

I tugged nervously on my wristband, my thoughts returning to church that morning. "I've got a question for you," I told him. "What about St. Paul's letter to the Romans? Doesn't it clearly state that homosexuality is wrong?"

Manuel paused midstep and peered across the room at me. "You know . . ." A puckish smile played at the corners of his lips. "For someone who's supposedly straight, you sure do ask a lot of questions about being gay."

My face warmed with embarrassment. Obviously, Manuel suspected my doubts. "I want to understand it," I said defensively. But were our conversations actually helping or merely adding to my confusion? I wasn't sure.

"All right, here's the deal with St. Paul . . ." Manuel turned the music down and plopped down cross-legged on the carpet facing me, so close our knees bumped. "First of all, neither he nor anyone else in the Bible uses the word 'homosexuality,' at least not in any accurate translation. The fact that some people are naturally oriented toward the same sex wasn't even understood till the nineteenth century."

I scooted back from him against the bed, pondering that. "Yeah, but in Romans One, St. Paul talks about guys having sex with guys and women having sex with women. That's the same thing."

"No," Manuel argued back, "because the viewpoint is different. St. Paul wrote as a man living in the first century, who also thought that slaves should obey their masters, that women should wear veils to pray, and that the authority of governments was instituted by God. If you think St. Paul was infallible, that means he was right about all those things. Is that what you believe?"

Once again I thought back to my Sunday school teachers, who'd said we needed to view certain practices in the Bible in their historical-cultural context. But then how could those same teachers claim the Bible to be inerrant?

"St. Paul," Manuel continued, "saw same-sex behavior as part of idol worship. He didn't consider that God might possibly create some people oriented toward the same sex."

I squirmed on the floor. "But why would God *create* people gay?"

"Who knows? Why does she create some people left-handed and others right-handed? So we'll learn to love each other in spite of our differences? I don't know. But we do know this . . ." Manuel pointed his finger for emphasis. "The Creator *loves* diversity. Did you know that there are species that have neither male nor female, only hermaphrodites? And organisms that transform from one gender to the other during the course of their lives?"

I hadn't known that. And even if I had, I'd never have connected it with my worries about being gay.

Manuel thought to himself for a while, then gave me a searching look, like he was trying to pull the thoughts out of my head. "I've been thinking: Have you ever checked out porn sites?"

"No!" I sat up on the carpet, taken aback by the question. "I don't look at porn."

"Well, maybe you should." Manuel's tone was earnest. "Both gay and straight sites. See which turn you on more. That'll help you—"

"Whoa!" I held up my hand to stop him. "I'm *not* going to look at porn."

"Suit yourself." Manuel stood to change the CD.

I watched him from behind and tried to dismiss his idea from my thoughts. It rattled me how openly he was willing to question my sexuality.

"By the way . . ." Manuel turned to face me. "Angie asked me if I think you're gay."

"She *what*?" My heart almost stopped, as my mind flashed back to Angie in my car the night before. Was that why she'd put my hand on her breast? Was she testing me?

"What did you tell her?" I leaned forward, the blood pounding in my temples. "Did you tell her no?"

Manuel raised his eyebrows. "*Should* I have told her no?"

"Yes!"

Manuel waved me to calm down. "I told her she needs to ask you."

"I'm not gay!" I said firmly.

"Chill, *amigo*, it's no big deal. Just tell her."

No big deal? What was I supposed to tell her? That after all these years of going out with her, I wasn't sure if I was straight? And yet, what if I truly was gay? Was it fair to lead her on?

I slumped back against his bed, my heart sinking. "I don't want to hurt her."

"*Amigo* . . ." Manuel sighed. "You're already hurting her. How can you say you love somebody and lie to them?"

"I haven't *lied* to her."

"Yes, you have. What's the difference between lying and keeping a secret? Either way, you're not being honest."

My head felt like a dust storm had hit it, spinning my thoughts around. It seemed like whether I was open with Angie or not, I was hurting her.

I braced myself on the bed and got up. "I've got to go."

Manuel nodded understandingly and walked me to the door. I left his house, once again annoyed and angry. But this time I didn't bother swearing to myself that I'd never return. I knew I'd be back.

24

WHEN I ARRIVED HOME,

I THREW MY CAR KEYS ONTO MY DESK, STILL TROUBLED BY WHAT MANUEL HAD SAID. *WAS* I LYING TO ANGIE? I DIDN'T WANT TO. BUT WHAT IF I *WASN'T* GAY? WHAT IF I *COULD* CHANGE?

I got down on my knees and prayed harder than ever: "Jesus, you've got to help me. You know I don't want to hurt Angie. I want to change. I'm trying hard. But I need your help. Please? In your name. Amen."

I lay down in bed and stared at the crack in the ceiling that branched off in different directions. Eventually, my thoughts twist-and-turned back to St. Paul's Epistle to the Romans and the things that Manuel had said. From my nightstand I picked up my Bible.

In Bible studies I'd learned that St. Paul had written the letter to the church at Rome, which consisted of Christians from both Jewish and Gentile (non-Jewish) backgrounds, in part to try to get the two groups to stop judging each other harshly.

Chapter 1 began by affirming that the gospel was for every-one, including both Jews and Gentiles. Then, at verse 1:22, the letter began to condemn Gentiles who had turned to worshipping idols: *Claiming to be wise, they became fools, and exchanged the glory of the immortal God for images resembling mortal man or birds or animals or reptiles.*

Directly following that came the part that Pastor José and my other church teachers had used to preach against gays: *Therefore God gave them up in the lusts of their hearts to impurity, to the dishonoring of their bodies among themselves, because they exchanged the truth about God for a lie and worshiped and served the creature rather than the Creator. . . . For this reason God gave them up to dishonorable passions.*

I thought back to what Manuel had said. St. Paul seemed to think homosexual acts were the result ("Therefore . . . ," "For this reason . . .") of people turning away from God to idol worship. I'd never gotten that connection before, probably because I'd been so intimidated by the passage.

Now I wondered, *So how do these verses apply to Manuel—or to me?* I had never turned away from God to idol worship. Why had God given *me* up to dishonorable passions?

I kept reading: *Their women exchanged natural relations for unnatural, and the men likewise gave up natural relations with women and were consumed with passion for one another, men committing shameless acts with men and receiving in their own persons the due penalty for their error.*

I stopped and thought more about what Manuel had said. St. Paul didn't use the word "homosexuality." So exactly what types of same-sex relations was he referring to? Was he writing about sexual acts connected to idol worship? I knew from Bible commentaries that weird stuff like that used to happen in ancient times. This passage wasn't clear. But it certainly didn't sound like he was talking about two guys or two women in a loving relationship.

Could such a vague passage like this one be justified to condemn *any* and *all* sex between gay people? After all, the Bible cited all sorts of restrictions on heterosexual sex (362 according to Manuel's Lynn Lavner quote), and yet I'd never heard anyone suggest that those passages condemned any and all forms of *heterosexuality*.

In the passage St. Paul clearly stated that he thought same-sex acts were "unnatural." But what about what Manuel had said about same-sex behavior being found abundantly in nature? And if same-sex desires weren't "natural," then why had I had these feelings toward guys since middle school? True, I wasn't perfect, and I'd sinned many times, but I'd never turned away from loving God. Plus, how could I "give up" natural relations with women if I'd never felt the desire for them in the first place?

And what did St. Paul mean by "the due penalty of their error"? I knew the penalty couldn't be AIDS, since—as Manuel had pointed out—it affected straight people too, and wasn't even around in St. Paul's time. So, was he suggesting once again that homosexuality was the result (a penalty) for the error of worshipping idols?

To confuse things further, although St. Paul viewed the homosexual acts he referred to as impure, "dishonorable," and "shameless," he didn't say that they were evil or a sin.

I put down my Bible and pondered that. From Bible studies I knew that in Romans St. Paul was trying to respond to conflicts between the Jewish and Gentile Christians over obligations to observe Jewish law, which forbade certain acts as "unclean" and "impure," but not necessarily sinful. He differentiated between the Jewish law and the Gospel, insisting that a person is made right with God by faith in Christ, not by performing the works of the Law.

If St. Paul, a Jew who knew the Jewish law, thought same-sex acts were not merely impure or unclean but truly a sin, why hadn't he said so? Why didn't he include them in the succeeding verses,

1:28-32, where he listed *all manner of wickedness, evil, covetousness, malice*?

I heaved a sigh of exasperation and closed my Bible. Once again a passage that I had been led to believe clearly condemned gay people seemed confusingly unclear. The only thing the Romans passage *clearly* condemned was idol worship, and I'd never done that.

Was *every* Scripture verse supposedly against homosexuality so questionable? Wasn't there any Bible text that applied to someone like me, who didn't want to hurt anybody or worship idols, who just . . . had these feelings and dreams of . . . wanting to love and be loved by somebody who happened to be the same sex?

With renewed determination I decided to look up every other possible passage even remotely related to homosexuality. Since the Bible and my concordance didn't list the word "homosexual," I got up and walked to my computer. I clicked my browser open, and after some searching found a Christian website with a page titled "The Homosexual Deception" that claimed to list Bible verses dealing with homosexuality.

God doesn't want anyone to be gay, the site said. *With the Lord's help, anybody can become straight, if they are willing to follow Him.*

It seemed like Jesus was finally answering my prayers. Excitedly, I scrolled down the page to the Bible verses. But as I read the list, my heart sank. It included all the same verses I had already struggled with: the Genesis story of Sodom, the two verses from Leviticus, St. Paul's letter to the Romans . . .

Unwilling to give up, I kept reading. The references continued with 1 Corinthians 6:9-11, which contained a list of those who would not inherit the Kingdom of God, including "sexual perverts."

So, were gay people automatically considered perverts? Why? Who decided that? I looked up the same passage in the online King James Version. Instead of "sexual perverts" it said "abusers of themselves with mankind." What did that mean? I had never wanted to abuse either myself or anybody else.

The next reference was 1 Timothy 1:10, which listed the types of people who need to hear the Law, including "Sodomites." I sighed in disappointment. Once again the Sodom thing.

Last were references to Jude 7 and 2 Peter 2:6, both of which again referred to the destruction of Sodom.

From everything I could find, that was the sum of the Bible's allusions to homosexuality—none of the passages clear or specific. And not a single one addressed a loving same-sex relationship. Didn't this book I cherished have anything to say about that to someone who wanted God's guidance?

If God was truly so against homosexuality, why hadn't it made his Top Ten? And since the Bible wasn't clear, why did so many people use it so unequivocally to condemn gay people? Why had *I* been so willing to use it that way?

I closed my browser and flopped back into bed. My head ached as I pondered so many things I had simply accepted: that the Bible is the inerrant word of God, that the church is always right, that homosexuality is a sin, that being gay is a choice . . .

But if the church and its interpretation of the Bible were wrong about homosexuality, then what else might they be saying that wasn't true? How could I trust *anything* they said?

I pulled myself out of bed, changed my clothes, and went for another long, exhausting run.

25

WHEN I RETURNED TO SCHOOL

AFTER THANKSGIVING BREAK, I HAD A HARD TIME
CONCENTRATING. MY MIND CHURNED WITH DOUBTS ABOUT
THE BIBLE, ABOUT MY FUTURE WITH ANGIE, AND MOST OF ALL
ABOUT WHO I WAS. SO MANY THINGS I HAD IMAGINED FOR
MY LIFE — FALLING IN LOVE WITH THE RIGHT GIRL, GETTING
MARRIED, HAVING KIDS, BECOMING A MINISTER, AND
EVERYTHING I THOUGHT I BELIEVED IN — NOW SEEMED
CALLED INTO QUESTION.

In the midst of my confusion I kept thinking about Manuel's suggestion. Should I check out some porn sites? I was probably the
only seventeen-year-old boy on the planet who had never looked at
porn. Even Cliff and my other Christian guy friends had confessed
to viewing some. But I'd told myself that it definitely wasn't something Jesus would do.

Now Manuel's idea sort of felt like permission. Maybe he was
right. Maybe just a little peek could help me to resolve my sexuality once and for all.

One day after school, when I was home alone, I carefully
locked my bedroom door and turned my computer on. My heart

pounded with anticipation as I prayed, *Dear Jesus, please forgive me. I don't mean to sin. But I don't know what else to do. I need to find out. Can I ever be attracted to girls?*

My hand trembled as I opened the browser search engine and typed:

P . . . O . . . R . . . N

Within seconds, a page came up listing 154,368,529 entries. My breathing stopped. Where to start?

Taking a deep breath, I clicked on a link. The site that popped up taunted me: Choose either "Horny Babes" or "Hot Hunks." My eyes wavered back and forth between the two options. My rational mind told me, "Horny Babes." Instead, I clicked "Hot Hunks."

Instantly, an orgy of naked guys appeared on the screen, doing things I'd never even imagined. Up until that moment I had never really thought about precisely *how* guys had gay sex. My fantasies had never gotten that far. The mere thought of being in another guy's arms, my body pressed against his as we kissed, had been enough to propel me into ecstasy.

Now I gazed in open-jawed amazement. The chiseled guys on-screen were doing stuff with each other that made me nearly burst through my pants. Literally shaking, I closed the browser window and gasped for breath.

"Jesus, please forgive me," I prayed out loud this time, and waited for my excitement to die down. There was no denying my body's response to the naked hunks.

So, was I maybe . . . bisexual? At least that word didn't have the horrible connotations of the word "homosexual." Pastor José had never preached a sermon against *bi*sexuals.

But . . . if I was bi, that meant I was also attracted to women. So . . . *was* I?

"Please, Jesus," I prayed again. "Help me."

My palms damp with sweat, I once again opened the porn site, but this time I clicked "Horny Babes." A page full of beautiful naked women appeared. And as it did, my horniness further subsided. Better said, it ceased altogether.

It wasn't that the boobs and stuff were boring. Before that moment I had never actually seen a woman completely nude. And I definitely had never seen women doing the sorts of things these were doing. But rather than make me horny, the images made me a little nauseous. I felt kind of embarrassed for the girls, exposing themselves like that. And inside my pants I felt . . . nothing. Zip. Zero. Nada.

If I was truly bisexual, shouldn't I feel *something*? Maybe I'd just stopped feeling horny altogether. To check, I clicked back to the "Hot Hunks" site.

Instant wood. Quickly I closed the browser again.

I leaned back in my chair and took a huge breath, realizing the implications of my experiment. I was definitely turned on by guys, not girls.

I wiped my sweaty palms against my pants, more worried than ever. What if this wasn't a phase? What if I never became attracted to women and yet didn't want to sin by having sex with guys? Should I be celibate for all my life? Was that what God wanted for me? To never experience the warmth and love of someone else's body or feel their heart beat against mine?

I knew that St. Paul considered celibacy a noble calling, but he also realized how hard it was. I recalled 1 Corinthians 7, where he even said that it was "better to marry than to be aflame with passion." I didn't want to go through life alone and crazed with lust. I wanted to be loved and cared about like everyone else. I wanted someone to marry, to love, "to have and to hold till death do us part." So, why would it be so wrong for that person to be another guy? What if the two of us just didn't have sex?

Get real. I sighed. *How long would that last?*

Okay, then . . . So, what if I couldn't change, and neither celibacy nor marriage was an option, what other choice was there?

I adjusted my pants and glanced at my Bible. How could I choose between my sexuality and my spirituality, two of the most important parts that made me whole? It seemed so unfair, like some cruel joke.

"Why?" I asked Jesus. "I gave my heart to you before I even knew what sex was. I've always tried to follow you. Why has God given me up like this?"

Before, I had always believed that Jesus heard my prayers, even if he didn't respond. Now, for the first time in my life, I doubted. *Did* he hear me?

My doubts made me feel even guiltier. Maybe I needed to give my heart over to him again.

This time I wrote down my prayer, hoping to make it even more real, and I based it on everything I had learned in church and Sunday school:

> *Dear Jesus,*
>
> *I believe you are the Son of God and that you died for my sins. I accept you as my Lord and savior and give my life over to you. I believe that by your stripes we are healed. Please heal me. You know I don't want to be this way. I've tried and tried to change. I don't know what else you want me to do. Please forgive all my sins and come into my heart. Again. Thank you.*

I folded up the paper, opened the lid of my God Box, and surrendered it inside.

26

AFTER GIVING MY HEART

OVER TO JESUS AGAIN, I HOPED TO WAKE UP THE NEXT
MORNING FEELING CLEANSED AND RENEWED. INSTEAD —
MAYBE BECAUSE I'D LOOKED AT THE PORN, OR BECAUSE
I'D DOUBTED JESUS — WHEN THE SUN'S RAYS PRIED
THROUGH THE WINDOW BLINDS, I WANTED TO HIDE FROM
THE WORLD.

"You okay?" Pa asked, shaking my foot.

"Yeah." I pulled the blanket down from over my head and
hauled myself out of bed.

During homeroom I avoided looking at Manuel, afraid he'd
somehow know that I had taken up his idea about porn sites.

"Hey," he whispered, "are you ignoring me?"

I shrugged and didn't answer. Instead I glanced over at Angie,
recalling my lack of response to the porn pic women. How long
could I continue to withhold my secret from her?

In government class that morning the topic was the U.S.
Constitution. Almost immediately someone brought up the proposed amendment to make same-sex marriage unconstitutional. A
couple of guys on the football team said some pretty nasty things

about gay people, while other classmates uttered stupid stuff, like, "If two guys can get married, I should be able to marry my dog."

Big laughs, while Mr. Proctor simply smirked and allowed it.

I sat silently, taking it all in and wanting to crawl out of my skin. Then I noticed, a couple of seats away, Stephen Marten's lip begin to quiver.

I felt like I should do something: speak up and confront the jerks in class, comfort Stephen, show him he wasn't alone, do *something*!

"Aw . . ." Jude Maldonado saw Stephen and snickered. "The little faggot's going to cry."

At that point, Stephen stood up, his whole body shaking, and yelled at Mr. Proctor, "Why don't you stop this?"

Mr. Proctor looked blank, as if he didn't understand what Stephen was making a fuss about. "You're out of line, Stephen."

"No, *you're* out of line!" Stephen shouted, and ran out of class. And I slunk down in my seat, feeling even more ashamed for not having the guts to stand up for him—or myself.

The story of Stephen running out of class spread through the hallways.

"Did you hear about Stephen Marten? What a crybaby."

"He's such a fag."

With each comment my stomach turned—and yet I said nothing. At lunchtime Angie asked me, "Aren't you in his government class?"

"Yeah," I muttered. Not wanting to talk about it, I bit into my barbecue sandwich. Next to Angie's tray I noticed a library book. "What's that?"

"I was just telling Dakota. It's about a transsexual teenager."

Oh, great, I thought. *As if dealing with gay people isn't enough.*

"The story is so amazing!" Angie exclaimed, patting the book.

"Mrs. Ramirez is amazing," Dakota replied, "for having books like that in the library."

That was definitely true. The odd thing was: Mrs. R. didn't look like some freethinking radical who would read books about gays or transsexuals. She stood less than five feet tall, had graying hair, wore reading glasses on a silver chain around her neck, and dressed in boring-as-dirt clothes.

Suddenly, an idea occurred to me. "Hey, does the sponsor for the GSA have to be a teacher? Or can it be a staff member?"

Angie glanced at Dakota; then Dakota tossed her curls back, screaming at me: "Oh, my God! You're a genius!"

Hardly. I felt more like an idiot. If I didn't want the GSA, why had I said anything?

Angie pulled the club application from her notebook and hurriedly reread it. Then she gazed up with an ear-to-ear smile. "It says the sponsor can be any faculty *or staff* member."

"But do you think Mrs. R. would do it?" I asked, once again secretly hoping the club wouldn't happen.

"I'll find out," Angie replied, still smiling. And I pushed aside my soggy barbecue sandwich, too queasy to finish.

During afternoon classes, I barely paid attention. My thoughts swirled between porn sites, same-sex marriage, transsexuals, and the GSA.

When I arrived home after school, my pa's truck stood parked in the driveway. I strode in the front door and yelled, "I'm home!"

Pa replied from my room, "I'm in here."

He was sitting at my desk, using my computer—something he rarely did, since he had his own computer at work. My mind immediately rocketed to the porn sites I'd visited. I'd forgotten to erase my tracks. Had he seen my web pages history? Hardly able to breathe, I choked out, "Um, hi."

Pa turned from the computer, his dark eyes giving me a long serious look. "Hi."

"Um, I've got to go to the bathroom," I uttered and hurried down the hallway. I closed the bathroom door behind me, and as quietly as possible I threw up.

I guess the guilt was getting to me. I splashed cold water on my face, cleaning myself up, and realized how truly terrified I felt of Pa finding out about me. Would he be angry? Disappointed? What if he started to drink again?

During dinner I barely ate, waiting for him to mention my porn visits. But he never said anything. Maybe he hadn't noticed. Maybe I was just going wacko with paranoia.

I was taking out the trash when Angie phoned: "Guess what? Mrs. Ramirez thinks the GSA is a great idea. She'll do it! Isn't that awesome? Why didn't we think of her sooner?"

"Um, I don't know." Me and my big mouth. I tossed the trash in the can and slammed the lid.

"So," Angie continued, "she signed the application and I turned it in. The main office secretary saw it was for a gay-straight alliance and said, 'I think Mr. Arbuthnot will want to speak to you about this.'"

"Great," I mumbled. *Maybe he'll tear up the application.*

The following morning in homeroom Mr. Arbuthnot boomed over the loudspeaker: "The following students report to my office immediately: Dakota Sims, Stephen Marten, Angie Leon, and Manuel Cordero. *Immediately.*"

Angie and Manuel sat up in their seats. Classmates turned to stare. From the back row Jude and his goons hooted: "Uh-oh! What did you do? You're busted, man!"

"Quiet!" our homeroom teacher yelled. "Or I'll send you all down."

Boy, was that the wrong thing to say; the catcalls only got louder.

Manuel and Angie collected their books and headed out the

door, while I felt left behind. What would happen to them? I had to wait till lunch to find out.

When I got to the cafeteria, Angie and Dakota were sitting at our usual table, along with Manuel, Stephen Marten, and the rest of Manuel's crew: Maggie, Gerald, Rufus, and Janice.

Slowly I shuffled over. I didn't exactly relish being seen with that group.

Dakota was excitedly describing the meeting with Mr. Arbuthnot. "He said, 'We don't have any gay students at our school.'"

"So, I told him . . ." Manuel grinned proudly. "'Oh, yes, you do.'"

"And I explained," Angie interjected, "that our school also has a huge homophobia problem."

"So then Arbuthnot says . . ." Dakota lowered her voice to mimic him and banged her fist on the table. "'I won't allow a club that condones immorality to disrupt our school.'"

"Like Jude isn't disruptive," Stephen said sarcastically, "but our club would be? I told him about government class."

I averted my eyes, not wanting to recall that.

"And I told Arbuthnot," Dakota continued, "that because of the federal Equal Access Act, he *had* to allow our club, or we'd call the ACLU."

"He got quiet at that," Angie finished up, "and said he'd have to consult with the superintendent."

"We've won!" Dakota started a chain of high-fives around the table. "He's got to allow it!"

Seeing my friends' excitement, I wished that I had signed the GSA application. But when Angie patted my palm, her brown eyes gazed into mine, and I remembered why I hadn't.

27

AS WE GOT INTO DECEMBER,

THE WEATHER TURNED COOLER—AND SO DID MY
RELATIONSHIP WITH ANGIE. WE STILL IMED AND TALKED
ON THE PHONE, BUT I DIDN'T CALL HER AS MUCH. TOO
OFTEN, I NO LONGER KNEW WHAT TO SAY TO HER. IT WAS
ALL SO CONFUSING.

I was relieved when she told me, "Hey, I'm sorry I can't go out this
Saturday. I have to go visit my aunt in Amarillo."

"No problem," I told her. The real problem was inside me. I
had to talk to somebody about everything going on or I was going
to burst out of my skin. But who could I talk to?

The answer to my prayers came that Sunday at church. Pastor
José preached a sermon about how God needed to be the focus of
our lives and at the center of every Christian marriage. To give
examples, he described several couples that he'd counseled and
helped to get back on track.

I had never given much thought to that aspect of his pastoral
work. Now as I listened, I wondered, *Could he possibly help me with
Angie?* I still wanted for things to work out between us. But did I
dare open up to him? He was, after all, my pastor. Could he help get

me get back on the straight and narrow—especially the *straight*?

For several days I prayed for courage, until one afternoon, while at home alone, I picked up the phone. I knew our church's number from memory. Fingers trembling, I dialed.

"I Am the Way Church," answered Mrs. Tilly, our church secretary.

"Um, hi, this is Paul Mendoza. I'd like to know if, um, I could make an appointment to, um, come in and talk to Pastor?"

"Sure, hon." Mrs. Tilly always called me "honey" or "sweetie" or something. She'd known me since Pa and I had first joined the church. But today, as she scheduled my appointment, her cheer barely made a dent in my nervousness.

For the remainder of the week, my stomach gurgled constantly. At night, I could barely sleep. In school, I couldn't concentrate. On the drive to my meeting with Pastor, I gripped the steering wheel so hard that my knuckles turned white.

"Hi, honey," Mrs. Tilly greeted me, smiling. A half-joking sign on her desk read THE WAGES OF SIN IS DEATH. REPENT BEFORE PAY-DAY.

"Um, hi." I forced a smile back at her. "I think I'm, um, kind of early." (Half an hour early, in fact.)

"No problem, sweetheart. Oh, I've got a new one for you . . ." She was always telling jokes and now leaned forward eagerly. "The preacher's little boy asks, 'Papa, I notice that every Sunday before you preach, you bow your head. What are you doing?' And his papa explains, 'Well, son, I'm asking the Lord to give me a good sermon.' So, the little boy thinks about that a minute and asks, 'Then why don't he?'"

Mrs. Tilly burst out laughing. I tried to join her. Then I shuffled over to the sitting area and sank into the plush couch. While I waited, I glanced around at the inspirational signs on the wall. One read NO JESUS, NO PEACE. KNOW JESUS, KNOW PEACE.

The words failed to put me at ease. Should I leave while I still had the chance?

Jesus, I prayed silently. *Please give me your peace.*

The door to the study opened and Pastor José appeared, his big frame filling the doorway. "Hello, Paul. Come on in." As I stepped into his office he smiled and patted me on the back. "How are you? Have a seat."

I quickly dropped into a wing chair, hoping he wouldn't notice how badly I was shaking.

"So . . ." Pastor faced me in his big stuffed armchair. "I'm glad you came in. What's up?"

I stared at him, my mouth open. But no words came out. My tongue felt frozen.

Pastor gave me an encouraging nod. "You can talk to me about anything."

I took a deep breath and my voice slowly returned, though I stumbled over every word. "Um, I thought about what you said Sunday about the—you know—the, um, couples you've pastored? And, well, it has to do with Angie and me, sort of." As I spoke, I could feel the blood rushing into my face. "Um, I think, maybe, I don't know. I love her and I want to date her, but . . ." My voice trailed off.

Pastor peered at me in a friendly way, as though trying to understand. "But *what?*"

My head felt about to explode. I'd reached the point of no return. My next words would change Pastor's view of me forever.

"But, well, I'm, um, not attracted to Angie—or any girl. I don't know why. I just never have been. Ever."

Even though I didn't utter the word "gay," Pastor must have understood, because I suddenly broke down into uncontrollable tears.

For what seemed like forever, I gulped down my sobs, feeling as though every stitch of clothes had fallen off my body, leaving me exposed. I kept my eyes glued to the floor, waiting for Pastor to say something—that I was sick, or perverted, or condemned to hell. I had put my entire future into his hands. But he remained silent, quietly setting a box of tissues on the table beside me. Finally, as my tears subsided, I looked up at him.

His face wasn't scowling in rage or contorted in horror. To my amazement he seemed calm. That should have put me at ease, but a new worry came over me. Why was he so calm? Had he already suspected I was gay? How? For some reason, I recalled Manuel's story of coming out to his family and how "undramatic" it had been.

"It's good you came to see me," Pastor said reassuringly. "Now, Paul, I need you to be completely honest with me so that I can help you. Understand?"

"Yes, sir." I grabbed a tissue and blew my nose.

"Good." Pastor's face turned serious. "It's important for me to know: Have you ever had any sexual contact with another boy—or with any man?"

I shook my head vigorously. "No, sir."

"No kissing?" Pastor continued. "Or touching, or *anything*?"

My mind flashed to the night at the movie theater, how I'd pressed my arm against Manuel's and nearly burst through my skin from lust and excitement. Should I mention that? I wanted to be fully truthful.

"Um, at the movies," I confessed, "I pressed my arm against another guy's."

Pastor leaned forward with a quizzical look. "And . . . ? Did anything else happen?"

His reaction surprised me. Wasn't that *enough*? Even now the mere memory of it made me lightheaded. "Um, nothing else."

"That's good." Pastor sounded relieved, and I wondered: Did he think that maybe I wasn't gay?

"But I've *thought* about guys," I insisted. "And I've looked at—you know—some websites. Do you think I'm gay?"

Pastor ran a hand thoughtfully across his jowl. "Only you and God know what's in your heart. The important thing is for you not to fall prey to sin. If you stay chaste, I believe the Lord will forgive you."

His words gave me a momentary reprieve. My minister, from a conservative church, was telling me that if I was gay, that in itself wasn't a sin.

"But," he added, and my anxiety returned, "you may have to deal with these feelings all your life."

All my life? I cringed as though a church bus had just crashed into me. "Then you don't think I can change?"

Pastor crossed his long thick legs and quoted Matthew: "'With God, all things are possible.' You're still young. You might become attracted to a woman."

His reassurance reminded me of the Christian website's promise: With the Lord's help, anybody can become straight.

"But then again . . ." Pastor uncrossed his legs. "You might not. It's up to God."

I was starting to feel confused again. Wasn't he saying two opposing things? "So, then, you don't think being gay is a choice?"

"I think . . ." Pastor drummed his bulky fingers on his armrest. "I think that these feelings are usually caused by trauma in early life. In your case, perhaps your mom's death."

I sat up, even more confused. My ma's death had made me gay? How?

"Whatever the cause"—Pastor waved a hand as though dismissing what he'd just said—"you have to choose what to do with your feelings—whether to follow Jesus or turn to sin."

I tried hard to understand what Pastor was saying. But if my gay feelings had been caused by some trauma I hadn't chosen, then how could they be sinful?

"You're going to need help." Pastor walked to his cabinet and brought me several glossy pamphlets. One was titled *No Longer Gay* and another *God's Love Won Out*.

Teen and adult faces smiled proudly from the shiny covers. Each brochure contained a testimonial from somebody who had successfully "walked away from homosexuality." Although that sounded good, I wasn't quite sure what it meant. If for whatever reason I truly was gay, then how could I walk away from myself?

On the back of one pamphlet was the toll-free number of a national organization whose ministry was "to preach the Good News of the ex-gay community."

"If you truly want God to change you," Pastor said firmly, "I want you to take the responsibility of calling them. Can you do that?"

I nodded respectfully. "Um, yes, sir."

"Good. They can arrange for someone to come and talk with you here at church. Okay?"

Again I nodded obediently, and Pastor gave me a warm, kind smile. I felt like he really cared about me and understood my troubled heart.

"You've shown God your faith by coming to speak to me." Pastor reached across and patted my arm. His words made me feel closer to Jesus than I had all week. And when Pastor proceeded to pray with me, his voice rang with confidence.

"Lord Jesus, you told us that when two or more are gathered in your name, you are in our midst, and that if two of us agree about anything we ask, it will be done by our Father in heaven . . ."

As Pastor spoke those words, I wondered, was *that* why my prayers to change had gone unanswered? Because I hadn't opened up about my secret and prayed with another believer? Maybe Jesus had been waiting for me to reach out.

THE GOD BOX 133

"We ask you now," Pastor continued, "to cleanse Paul of the lust in his heart, rid him of his sinful desires, heal him with the purity of your love, and set him free on your righteous path toward salvation and eternal life. We ask this in your name, Jesus. Amen."

I emerged from Pastor's office into the sunny afternoon, brimming with new hope. Not only had I admitted my long-buried secret to my very own pastor, he had accepted me anyway, in spite of it.

When I got home, I flipped eagerly through the brochures he'd given me. One testimonial, written under a pseudonym, told the success story of a man who'd rejected his choice of being a homosexual, married a beautiful, good-hearted Christian woman, had two wonderful children, and now lived a happy righteous life.

That's exactly what I wanted. And the pamphlets promised that with God's help I could have it.

28

DESPITE THE ENCOURAGEMENT

OF PASTOR JOSÉ AND THE PAMPHLETS, I PUT OFF PHONING
THE EX-GAY ORGANIZATION — MAYBE BECAUSE THEY WERE
STRANGERS. BUT EACH DAY I PRAYED FOR COURAGE TO
CALL. MEANWHILE, THINGS AT SCHOOL GOT WORSE.

Jude had begun making life hell for Manuel in any and every way he
could: spitting on his seat in class, bodychecking him in the hallway, or "accidentally" squirting him with ketchup at lunchtime.
Even though the teachers and lunch patrol saw what was happening (they'd have been blind not to), none of them did anything to
stop it. And when Manuel reported the incidents, Mr. Arbuthnot
blamed Manuel for having "provoked" Jude with his "disruptive
announcements" about being gay.

It infuriated me, but Manuel seemed almost resigned: "I
shouldn't have teased him that time about flirting with me.
Sometimes I wish I could keep my mouth shut. I think I set something off in him."

"That doesn't excuse his attacks," I argued.

"Well, what can I do besides turn the other cheek? I already
pray for him."

Manuel's words stopped me cold. I had never thought to include Jude in my prayers. I hadn't wanted to think about him. Instead, I steered clear, blocking him from my thoughts. Obviously, Manuel couldn't do that.

One day, in the cafeteria serving line, I found myself stuck behind Jude as he complained about the food to the cafeteria ladies. To make his point, he burped loud enough for the entire line to hear. *Ignore him,* I told myself.

I was trailing behind him into the lunchroom when I noticed Manuel walking from the ketchup counter in our direction. As if watching two approaching cars set to collide, I sensed what was about to happen. Next thing I knew, Jude body-slammed Manuel.

Manuel lost his balance, stumbling. His tray sailed into the air. Dishes clattered to the floor. Chicken nuggets, French fries, ketchup, and Jell-O flew in all directions. And Manuel crashed onto the tile.

At the commotion the entire lunchroom went silent. Then Jude sneered, "Why'd you bump me, faggot?"

Unable to ignore the incident, cafeteria monitors rushed over, but incredibly, they did nothing to stop Jude as he started away.

"You jerk!" I shouted after him, without thinking.

He whirled around. "What are you, like, his *boyfriend?*" The question was loud enough for the entire lunchroom to hear.

I cringed, as blood surged into my head from anger—and embarrassment.

Jude swaggered away, and I glanced down at Manuel, sprawled on the floor. I couldn't just leave him. I set my tray down and helped him up.

People resumed their conversations. Manuel stood, his shirt smeared with food and his mouth cut from the fall. "Your lip is bleeding," I mumbled.

"Crap." Manuel glared across the lunchroom at Jude. "You

think I should keep trying to turn the other cheek?"

"I don't know," I replied. And for the first time *I* prayed for Jude, asking Jesus, *Please soften his heart. . . . And also mine—toward him.*

I helped Manuel collect his scattered dishes. He didn't feel like getting anything else to eat. I wasn't hungry either. As I got to my table, I wondered if Angie had heard Jude's question to me. If she had, she didn't say anything. But all afternoon I thought about it.

After school I took my homework over to Manuel's house, still worried about him. When he answered the door, his lip was swollen.

"Did you put something on that?" I asked.

"Like what?" He gave me a suggestive grin, glancing at my own lips. Apparently he wasn't so hurt that he had forgotten how to annoy me.

"Like *ointment*." I brushed past him.

"Oh." On the way to his room he stopped by the bathroom and got some antibiotic. "Can you put it on for me?"

I dropped my backpack onto his bedroom carpet and glanced between the tube and his mouth. "You're not helpless."

"Please?" He puckered his lips into a pout, making him look like a little boy.

I don't know why I gave in. "Stand still." I took the tube and squeezed some ointment onto my finger. As I dabbed it across the cut, the tenderness of his lips surprised me. I guess I assumed that a guy's lips would somehow feel different from a girl's.

Manuel stood only inches away, staring at me. "You're really cute," he said softly. "You know that?"

Although Angie had often told me I was cute, I'd never really liked how I looked.

"Shut up," I grumbled, and avoided Manuel's eyes.

"Yeah." His lips stretched into a smile beneath my fingertip. "You are."

I capped the ointment and shoved the tube into his hand. "I think your mouth is back to normal now."

I plunked down onto the carpet and pulled my homework out of my backpack. When Manuel sat down beside me, his knee grazed mine. The touch set off a spark in my body. I wanted to move away, and yet I couldn't. It felt as if Manuel was pulling at me again.

"What's the matter?" he asked.

"Nothing." I flipped through my math book.

"Yeah, there is." Manuel nodded. "You've been acting weird lately. I mean, even more so than usual."

I frowned at him. Then I thought about the porn sites and my talk with Pastor. Should I tell Manuel about all that? I gazed down at my math book and confided in a low voice, "I, um, looked at some—you know—some websites . . ."

Manuel's voice shot up. "You mean *porn?*"

"Um, yeah." I shrugged like it was no big deal.

"And . . . ?" Manuel asked hopefully—at least that's how I interpreted it.

"And . . ." My throat clenched as I tried to swallow. Was I really ready to be fully honest with Manuel? "I think, um, maybe, I might be . . . bi."

I knew that in truth I had failed the bi test. The "Horny Babes" page had proven that. But Pastor José and the ex-gay brochures had renewed my hope that I might possibly *become* attracted to women.

"Bi, huh?" Manuel scratched his chin. "Well, at least that's a step."

"A step toward what?"

"Toward accepting yourself."

I glanced up at Manuel's wavy, good-smelling hair and recalled my idea about a close relationship with another guy *without* sex. Manuel was a Christian. He'd told me that he and his family had joined a church across town. Could he and I both eventually get married to women and still have a special friendship, bonded by our righteous desire to not fall prey to sin?

"I, um, talked to my pastor about—you know—stuff."

"That's good." Manuel sounded sincere. "What did he say?"

"Um, he said that so long as a person stays chaste, it's not a sin. He told me to call this group and meet with someone."

I pulled from my backpack the pamphlet about the man who had kicked the gay habit.

Manuel looked it over. "Why did the guy write it under a fake name?"

"Um, I don't know. To protect his privacy, I guess."

"You mean like the witness protection program? If the guy believes what he's written, why not be open about it?"

Manuel's skepticism annoyed me. "You just don't believe people can change."

"I believe people can change *some* things." Manuel tossed the pamphlet back to me. "But not how you're sexually hard-wired. Maybe you can avoid sex with guys, and *maybe* you can even perform with a girl, but that won't change the fact that you're gay. It's like wanting to change from being left-handed." Manuel grabbed hold of my hand, sending a tingle up my arm. "You can avoid using your left hand and learn to use your right, but you'll still be left-handed. So what's the point? To please other people?"

"Because . . ." I pulled my hand away. "Being gay is wrong."

"No," Manuel said firmly. "Gay isn't wrong *or* right. It just *is*. What's wrong is hating yourself because of it. You're going to spend more time with yourself than with anyone else in your life. You want to spend that whole time fighting who you are? Do you really think that's what God wants? If she didn't want people to be gay, then why were we born that way?"

Manuel was messing with my mind again.

"Being gay is usually caused by some childhood trauma," I argued.

"Is *that* what your preacher told you?" Manuel shook his head in obvious dismay. "Why do some people always try to find something to blame being gay on? I suggest you do a little Web search on the so-called ex-gay thing. See if you can find any scientific evidence that it works or locate even one legit professional organization that believes in it. Why can't you just stop buying into the story that God condemns gay people?"

I clamped my jaw, not knowing what to answer. Once again I wanted to get up and leave Manuel. But why bother? I knew I'd come back.

"Can we change the subject? Please?"

Manuel sighed and stared at me, as if considering what he wanted to say, before he spoke again. "I think you *should* meet with an ex-gay. I'll be curious what he tells you. And that's the last I'll say about it."

True to his word, Manuel pulled out his government book and rested it on his lap. In the process his knee once again bumped mine. Even though it was only for an instant, I nearly melted at his touch. And although I knew I should move my knee away, I let it rest there.

When Manuel's parents arrived home, they were pretty upset about his cut lip. During dinner they said they were going to talk with Mr. Arbuthnot. But I doubted it would do any good.

Later that evening, when I went home, my pa and his girlfriend were in the living room, watching TV.

"*Mijo!*" Pa waved me over, and Raquel smiled. "Come sit with us a while."

They were watching *Will & Grace*, the show about the gay guy and his chick friend. My stomach wobbled as my pa and Raquel laughed at Will's effeminate friend swishing his hips and flailing his wrists.

When the show switched to a commercial, Raquel told Pa, "You know Harold at my office? Last week his daughter told him she's a lesbian."

My pa shook his head. "Poor guy."

Suddenly I felt like I might be sick again, and I excused myself. Upon reaching my room, I took a deep breath, and my stomach settled. Was the whole world turning gay? I dropped my backpack and pulled my jacket off, catching my reflection in the mirror.

For a long moment I stared at myself. How could Manuel possibly think I was cute? My eyes were too dark, my nose too flat, my lips too big. Was he just teasing? Or could he be feeling the same for me as I was for him?

I turned away from the mirror, quickly changed my clothes, and went for a run.

Later that week, after Pastor José asked me at church if I'd called the ex-gay group, I finally dialed the toll-free number—and immediately tossed my cell phone back down, unable to go through with it.

"Jesus," I prayed in a trembling voice, "you know how confused and scared I am. Please give me courage." Once more I dialed, and this time I was able to stay on the line. It rang about a million times. I was about to hang up when an old lady answered—not at all what I expected.

"Thank you for calling New Life Ministries . . ." She sounded warm and friendly, like Mrs. Tilly. "Spreading the Good News of the ex-gay community. How may I help you?"

"Um . . ." My voice quavered. "My pastor said to call you . . ."

"Well, I'm glad he did," the lady said cheerily.

Still a little uneasy, I had to force my words out: "He asked me to, um, set up a meeting at my church with—you know—somebody from your group?"

The lady asked what part of the country I lived in and told me they had a group in Abilene. "We'd be happy to send someone from that fellowship to meet with you."

"Um, okay."

She said she'd call me back to confirm a date and time.

After hanging up, I collapsed into bed and whispered, "Thank you, Jesus."

29

FOR THE REMAINDER OF THE WEEK

I WAITED ANXIOUSLY FOR THE EX-GAY MINISTRY TO CALL.
EACH TIME MY CELL RANG, MY HEART JUMPED, TILL
FINALLY, THE OLD LADY PHONED AND SAID THEY HAD
SET UP A MEETING AT MY CHURCH. THEN I WAITED EVEN
MORE ANXIOUSLY, HARDLY ABLE TO EAT OR SLEEP, UNTIL
THE DAY OF MY APPOINTMENT. ONCE AGAIN I ARRIVED AT
CHURCH WAY TOO EARLY.

"Hi, sweetie," Mrs. Tilly greeted me.

"Hi, um . . . I'm supposed to be, um, meeting someone here?"

"I know, honey." She nodded understandingly. Had Pastor José told her why I was here today? She leaned forward as if to tell me a secret. "I've got a new joke for you. The preacher's little boy watched his papa write a sermon and asked, 'How do you know what to say?' His papa replied, 'Why, God tells me.' So, the little boy thinks about that a moment and says, 'Then why do you keep crossing things out?'"

Mrs. Tilly burst out laughing. I politely tried to join her. Then I trudged over to the couch and waited. A sign on the wall stared back at me: BELIEVE AND RECEIVE. DOUBT AND LOSE OUT.

After what seemed like centuries, the front door opened, and a guy in his late twenties walked over to Mrs. Tilly. Instinctively I knew he was the ex-gay. He wore crisp khakis, polished loafers, a tweed jacket, and a striped tie—a preppy look unusual for our west Texas town, except for going to church. But I guess technically we were in church.

"Paul?" Mrs. Tilly called to me, and I walked over. "This is Eric Smith."

Eric smiled politely and gave me a firm handshake, though his palm felt almost as clammy as mine.

"Pastor is away." Mrs. Tilly opened the door to his office. "So you can use his study."

It felt a little awkward to be in Pastor's room without him there. Eric sat in the wing chair where I had sat last time, but I didn't feel right sitting in Pastor's chair. Instead, I sat on the couch.

"So, um . . ." Eric cleared his throat. "I'd like to witness to you about my own life. Okay?"

"Sure," I said, clasping my hands to keep them still.

"Ever since I was a boy," Eric began, "I always felt different. In school, other kids called me names, and I bought into the lie that I'm gay."

"You're not?" I blurted out. I guess I'd assumed the group would send someone gay.

"Well," he clarified, "we don't believe anyone is truly gay. We're just broken, wounded, and have deep-seated gender-identity confusion—GIC—which is usually the result of broken relationships with our parents, sexual abuse, rejection from peers, or childhood trauma causing same-sex attraction, SSA."

Even though Eric had barely started speaking, my thoughts already began to scramble. *Do I have deep-seated GIC?* But I'd never felt confused about my gender identity. I'd always wanted to be a guy, not a girl. And I'd never been sexually abused. Furthermore, I knew lots of people at school who had broken relationships with their parents. *How come they don't have SSA? Besides, according to Pastor José's sermons, aren't we all broken and wounded?*

I had so many questions I wanted to ask, but I forced myself to sit still and listen.

"In high school," Eric continued, "I tried dating girls, but I kept being attracted to guys. Every night I dreamed about them. You know, sex dreams. I knew it was wrong and hated myself for it, but I couldn't stop my feelings. I felt like the loneliest boy on earth."

I sat up excitedly, knowing exactly what he meant. He was telling *my* story!

But then he continued: "Until I couldn't take it any longer. Junior year, I started drinking and doing drugs."

That part I definitely did *not* identify with. After seeing what alcohol had done to my pa, I'd stayed clear of even a sip of beer and steered miles away from drugs.

"For college," Eric continued, "I went to Austin and immediately fell into the gay scene. At first I thought I'd gone to heaven, with all these cute guys coming on to me. I went home with a new one every night. But inside I started feeling even more lonely than before."

So, why didn't you get a boyfriend? I wondered. Eric was good-looking and seemed nice. Hadn't he wanted one?

As Eric spoke, his leg jiggled fretfully. He appeared even more nervous than I was, if such a thing was possible.

"The crowd just bounced from guy to guy." Eric frowned and looked sad. "Gay love is a lie. It doesn't exist. Being gay is really about being a slave to sex and desire. The lifestyle is all about partying hearty and getting off."

But what about someone like Manuel? That wasn't his "lifestyle." Actually, it sounded more like some of the *straight* guys at my school, with their parties, drinking, drugs, and girls. As Eric talked, it seemed like he wanted to blame all his problems on being gay.

"My grades crashed and I got put on academic probation," Eric continued. "Then I got a DUI for driving drunk."

So, did you go to AA or rehab? I was about to ask, but Eric pressed on. "I didn't want to be gay, and yet I couldn't stop myself. Then I found out that a guy I'd had sex with had HIV, and we hadn't used a condom. I freaked out."

I edged back in my seat, a little wigged out myself. Why hadn't they used a condom? Didn't they know about safe sex? Was Eric now HIV positive? I'd never met anyone like that. And even though I knew you couldn't get AIDS from shaking hands, I casually wiped my palm on the sofa's armrest.

"I got tested," Eric continued, "promising myself that I'd never have gay sex again. But when my test turned out negative, I was back at the bar, partying to celebrate. The next morning I woke up with a new guy whose name I couldn't even remember."

I squirmed uneasily on the sofa. Even though I admired Eric's honesty, the more he talked, the more his testimony seemed way different from my life. I had no desire to drink, do drugs, or have sex with different guys.

"In my soul . . ." Eric gave a sigh. "I started to feel desperate, you know? Hopeless. I no longer wanted to live. My mom knew something was wrong. She sent me a Bible, but I didn't read it. I had stopped going to church, believing my religion didn't want me. But out of desperation, I prayed for the first time in years. 'God, help me.' A week later, I met a guy outside a bar. And instead of asking me to go home, he invited me for coffee. *That's different,* I thought, so I went with him."

Eric wiped his brow and seemed to calm down a little. "Over coffee, my new friend told me about his struggle with homosexuality and how his life changed when he invited Jesus Christ into his heart. For the first time I heard about the life-changing power of the Gospel. Before that, I'd never known people who struggled to live Christ-like lives."

But what about a case like mine? I wondered. *I do know Christians. I know Christ. I've tried to live a Christ-like life. And I've invited Jesus into my heart—twice.*

"God answered my call for help." Eric's voice rang with certainty. "He led me to ex-gay people who, like me, had learned the hard way how empty and destructive the gay lifestyle is. They helped me get through the lies I'd bought into. I now understand that homosexuality is simply a form of idolatry—worshiping the male body as a god."

That rang a bell. Was that what St. Paul meant by his passage in Romans against idolatry? But then what about straight people? Were heterosexuals turning away from God to worship the opposite sex's body as a god?

"What you're going through is a test," Eric told me. "Simply because you have SSA doesn't mean you're gay. A lot of young people have same-sex crushes, but they grow out of it."

I recalled my middle school health book saying that. Yet I *hadn't* grown out of it. And it sounded like he hadn't either.

Eric gripped the arms of his chair. "My desire for guys is now one percent of what it was before. You've got to have faith. God works miracles. With help, he can change you, too."

One percent didn't sound so bad . . . and yet the thought of wrestling with these feelings all my life made me wonder, *Why?*

"Do you have any questions?" Eric said.

My head was throbbing with about a million questions. To start, I asked, "Are you in AA?"

"No," he replied. "But our recovery program is based on the twelve steps. You see, homosexuality is like alcoholism. You've got to resist the lie—like an alcoholic fights his desire to drink."

Hmm. That wasn't what my pa said. He'd explained to me that by accepting he was an alcoholic, he had *ceased* fighting. He often said that acceptance was the answer to all of life's problems.

Another thing: Eric seemed to keep repeating that being gay was a lie, and yet . . . hadn't he said he'd had gay feelings since he was a kid? The things he was saying seemed almost more confusing than helpful. In spite of all the questions I had, I hesitated to ask him anything more.

"I know it's a lot to think about," Eric said, nodding. "I want to invite you to our fellowship and support group in Abilene, so you can meet other members. We have meetings twice a week with worship, teaching, and prayer."

I pressed back in my seat. After hearing Eric, I wasn't ready to face a whole group of other people like him.

"Would you pray with me before I go?" Eric asked.

I nodded, relieved to shift my focus to God.

"Dear Jesus," Eric prayed, "please forgive Paul. Don't let him be ensnared in sin. Strengthen him to fight the sinful deception of homosexuality. And give him faith to believe he can be healed. In your name. Amen."

"Amen," I echoed, and suddenly asked one more question: "Are you married now?"

Eric's brow furrowed. "No." His Adam's apple bobbed as he swallowed, and his leg started to jiggle again. "I have a girlfriend, but . . . well . . . um, we've decided to take a break for a while, to be sure about what God wants for us." Eric shifted in his seat and glanced down at his hands. "Relationships are complicated. People are complicated." He gazed up, returning from his thoughts. "But I'm happier now than when I thought I was gay."

Although Eric *said* he was happy, his words didn't match the rest of him. His face was serious and his body stiff, and his tone wasn't exactly cheerful. During the entire time he had hardly smiled at all.

I recalled Galatians 5:22: *The fruit of the Spirit is joy.* I didn't feel much joy coming from Eric. He seemed nice, but . . . what had I expected? I wasn't sure. Maybe someone genuinely joyful, despite being gay—somebody more like . . . Manuel.

30

IN SPITE OF MY DOUBTS,

I WANTED TO BELIEVE ERIC. I TOLD HIM I'D SEE WHEN I
COULD GO TO THE EX-GAY MEETING AND WE EXCHANGED
CELL NUMBERS. I STILL HOPED THAT I COULD CHANGE.
AND YET, WHEN I LEFT THE CHURCH THAT AFTERNOON,
I FOUND MYSELF DRIVING TO MANUEL'S.

He was folding laundry in the wash room, wearing a pair of old torn-up jeans and a T-shirt with the sleeves cut off. It was the first time I'd seen his arms fully bare, and even though he wasn't "Hot Hunk" buff, each time he folded a piece of laundry, my gaze wandered to his naked biceps.

"What?" He gave me an impish smile, like he knew I was checking him out.

"Nothing," I felt my face turn red. To calm down, I grabbed a pair of socks and folded them. "So, um, I met with the guy this afternoon—you know—the ex-gay?"

"Oh, yeah?" Manuel asked casually. "How'd it go?"

"Um, okay. He seems nice."

"That's good," Manuel said, and continued folding laundry.

His calm response threw me. I'd expected one our usual

arguments. Had he given up? Wasn't he interested anymore?

When we finished folding, Manuel grabbed the basket full of clothes, and led me to his bedroom. As I watched him put his stuff away, I noticed a rip in back of his jeans. Like a little window, it revealed his thigh, sleek and smooth.

"Want something to eat?" Manuel asked.

"Sure." I nodded, anxious to shift my attention.

We wandered to the kitchen, and Manuel brought out a pack of popcorn. "So . . ." He tossed the bag into the microwave. "The guy seems happy now?"

"Um . . ." I listened to the corn pop in the oven and recalled how Eric hadn't really sounded very happy. But he'd *said* he was. "Yeah. Mostly."

"Hmm." Manuel gave me a sidelong glance. When the oven timer chimed, he pulled the popcorn out. "You don't sound very convinced."

I frowned, knowing I wasn't very convinced. We carried the steaming hot popcorn back to Manuel's room.

"Well," I insisted, "he said his desire is ninety-nine percent gone. He said homosexuality is like alcoholism."

"Oh, really?" Manuel plopped down on the carpet, setting the popcorn bag in front of him. "I don't get that. Does it mean everyone who drinks alcohol is an alcoholic?"

"Um, no." I sat down facing him.

"Then, is everyone gay some sort of addict?"

"No."

"Then I don't get how being gay is like being an alcoholic."

Actually, I didn't either. It suddenly struck me that maybe Manuel and I were arguing less because I was agreeing with him more, even if I didn't want to.

While we munched popcorn, I tried not to stare at his tan,

sinewy arms. Every time I reached into the bag and our fingers bumped, I recalled pressing against him in the movie theater. Now, I was feeling confused again. Did I want to change or didn't I?

"If somebody is unhappy being gay," Manuel proceeded, "they can try to get involved with the opposite sex, or just not have sex at all. But why judge and try to 'save' others rather than just accept that everyone is different? Even if sexual orientation *were* a choice, aren't we a country where we're supposed to be free to pursue our happiness, whether we're hetero-, homo-, bi-, trans-, or even *a*-sexual? To use your friend's alcohol analogy, being antigay is like Prohibition, when a small group of busybodies thought *no one* should be allowed to drink."

I had learned about Prohibition in American history. Old Mr. Oglethorpe had told us, "That was the only time when our nation's constitution was amended to curtail people's rights rather than expand them."

Now, I recalled our government class discussion about a proposed amendment to ban same-sex marriage. Wasn't that trying to curtail people's rights, too?

"You know that Prohibition failed," Manuel continued, "don't you? It had to be repealed. So, maybe alcoholism isn't a good analogy to being gay."

"Okay," I gave in. "What *is* a good analogy?"

Manuel immediately replied, "Being *straight*."

I should have predicted that.

"But what if it's just a phase?" I insisted. "Eric said a lot of teens have same-sex attraction but they grow out of it."

"If they'll grow out of it," Manuel said matter-of-factly, "then why do they need ex-gay conversion?"

I considered that, with no idea what to answer.

"In my ideal world," Manuel pressed on, "a world without

152 ALEX SANCHEZ

homophobia, kids could explore their crushes with *either* gender and figure out who they are without being told their feelings are wrong or sinful."

As he described that ideal world, I had an image of little kids pecking kisses with either gender and not getting called names because of it.

"But gay relationships don't last," I argued.

"Oh, really?" Manuel said. "Did you know that the first San Francisco gay marriage was between two women who'd been together for fifty-one years? Hel-lo! Half of all *straight* marriages end in divorce. Like that's a stellar track record? But are churches just as outraged at promiscuity and adultery in heteros? No, because that doesn't draw in crowds, and more importantly people don't donate money to combat it. Slap the gays around, though, and watch the money pour in . . ."

As Manuel spoke, he seemed a lot more sure of himself than Eric had been. And even though I didn't accept everything Manuel said, I admired the strength of his spiritual conviction. I wished I could be that certain.

As I listened to him, I found myself staring at his mouth and wondering: *What would it feel like to kiss him?* That may have been a very weird thought to have while chomping popcorn and discussing religion. But there was something that kept pulling me toward Manuel, no matter when or where or what we were doing. I wanted him in a way I'd never wanted anyone; in a way I couldn't understand or stop.

"Did Jesus ever say," Manuel continued, "'I have come so that you can live life in a box?' Or did he say, 'I have come that they may have life, and that they may have it more abundantly'?" Manuel stopped abruptly and gave me a curious look. "Hey, are you listening?"

I realized I had zoned out. "Yeah, I'm listening." I wiped the salt and butter from my fingers. In the past, I would have been set to leave by this point, feeling too confused and agitated to stay any longer. But tonight, in spite of my confusion, I didn't want to go. I wanted to be with Manuel. So, I merely said, "I don't want to talk about this anymore. Can we drop it?"

"Sure." Manuel nodded. "Okay."

We played a couple of video games after that and I forgot about my talk with ex-gay Eric. Sitting side by side with Manuel, every once in a while my arm pressed against his and made it hard for me to concentrate. He totally clobbered my on-screen player, winning every game, but I didn't care. I felt more happy and confused than ever.

31

HAVING MET WITH ERIC,

I STOPPED CARRYING AROUND THE EX-GAY BROCHURE AND
PUT IT AT THE BOTTOM OF MY SOCK DRAWER. AND WHEN
PASTOR ASKED ME AT CHURCH ABOUT THE MEETING,
I MERELY MUMBLED, "UM, IT WENT FINE." I HAD TOO
MANY OTHER THINGS TO THINK ABOUT — SCHOOL,
CHOIR PRACTICE FOR OUR BIG UPCOMING CHRISTMAS
PERFORMANCE, ANGIE, MANUEL . . .

I was hurrying down the crowded school hallway between
classes when Cliff tugged at my arm. "Hey! You coming to
Bible Club today?"

Aaron Esposito had told me about the scheduled meeting, but
after the last two runaway Bible studies, I wasn't exactly chomping
at the bit to go — especially with Cliff bearing down on me.

"Um, I'm not really up for a Bible study. Besides, I've got
choir practice."

"It's not a Bible study," Cliff said, his lip curling into a crooked
smile. "It's a club admin meeting. I think you'll want to be there."

Club admin meeting? What did that mean?

At lunchtime, when I set my tray down at our table, Dakota

informed me, "Cliff and Elizabeth heard we're starting a GSA."

"So . . ." Angie stopped eating her cheese ravioli. "They're try-ing to block it."

"Even though they can't," Dakota argued.

"You're coming to the Bible Club meeting," Angie said, "aren't you?"

"You've got to come," Dakota agreed.

"Um . . ." Why hadn't Cliff been more forthright with me about the meeting? It aggravated me, and I still didn't want to go. "We've got choir practice, remember?"

"I know." Angie nodded. "But this is important. Even if we just go for a little while. Please?"

I really didn't want to go, but her brown eyes begged me. "All right. But just for a while."

During afternoon classes a sense of dread nagged at me. Would the Bible meeting get into a shouting match again? Or might it be even worse?

After the final bell I slowly jostled through the hall toward the meeting. From the classroom came a commotion of voices, laugh-ter, and grunts—not the sounds of our usual Bible studies. I leaned guardedly into the doorway and peered inside.

Almost the entire football team had packed the room (no doubt persuaded by Cliff), along with other students. Altogether, there were about thirty people, a record for our little Bible Club.

Angie, Dakota, and Aaron Esposito huddled together, sitting up straight and defiant, although their faces seemed a little tense and pale. Who could blame them? As I walked over and sat beside Angie, Cliff's leveled gaze tracked me.

"Let's get started," he told the group, and asked Elizabeth, "Will you lead us in prayer?"

"Certainly." She closed her eyes and I did too. "Heavenly

Father," she began, but the football players kept yakking and cutting up. Elizabeth paused, and I looked up to see her eyes narrow into icy slits. "*Excuse me!*" she roared at the boys. "We're praying!"

"Yeah, guys," Cliff backed her up. "Shut it!"

One guy punched a teammate. Others snickered. Then they all got quiet, more or less.

"Heavenly Father," Elizabeth began again, "guide us this afternoon as we prepare to fight for your glory and righteousness, so that we can share your hope and salvation with all who need it. In Jesus' name, amen."

"Amen!" The football team cheered and clapped. Did they think this was a pep rally?

"Thanks," Cliff told Elizabeth, and announced to the group, "As you've all heard, a club on our school campus is being formed for homosexuals."

The football players burst into boos and hisses, banged on their desks, and stomped their feet. I shifted uneasily in my chair, but Angie and Dakota merely rolled their eyes.

"As Christians," Cliff continued, "it's our duty to speak out against sin . . ."

As he spoke, Elizabeth passed around anti-homosexuality tracts with titles like *Sin City of Sodom* and *Triumph Over Homosexuality*, along with *No Longer Gay*, the ex-gay title I had buried at the bottom of my sock drawer.

A battle of feelings collided inside me, making me want to disappear.

Dakota spoke up, interrupting Cliff: "Why are you doing this?"

"You used to read the Bible," Elizabeth retorted. "You know being gay is wrong."

With the football team stacked against us, it didn't seem too bright to get into a debate about that, but a clear response rang inside my head: *Maybe being gay isn't wrong* or *right. Maybe it just* is.

In the midst of the commotion, Angie said, "Just as this Bible Club has a right to exist, so does any other school group, including a gay—*and straight*—alliance."

Cliff scowled at our little opposition team, his eyes on fire. "You'd better turn or burn."

His teammates jumped on that, turning it into a chant: "Turn or burn! Turn or burn!" Soon they were pounding their fists and stomping their feet.

In the past, threats of eternal hellfire would have rattled me. Now, instead, I mostly just wanted to get the heck away from this crazy meeting.

"I'm going to choir practice," I told Angie, and walked out.

32

THAT DAY WAS MY WORST

CHOIR PRACTICE EVER. EVEN THOUGH I KNEW THE
HYMNS BY HEART, I KEPT BLANKING ON THE WORDS
WHILE MY MIND GALLOPED BACK TO THE BIBLE MEETING
GONE BERSERK. WHAT WAS MAKING CLIFF AND
ELIZABETH SO CRAZY AGAINST GAY PEOPLE? WHY WERE
THEY WHIPPING UP THE FOOTBALL TEAM? SHOULD I
OPEN UP TO THEM ABOUT MY OWN STRUGGLE? BUT HOW
COULD I, WHEN I HADN'T EVEN OPENED UP TO ANGIE?

As the week went on, I became determined to tell her *something*
about what was going on inside me. I had no idea what to say, but
I knew I couldn't keep on this way. It wasn't fair to her, and I was
feeling worse and worse about myself.

On Saturday night I helped her with the usual evening feeding
of the critters. Then we once again went to dinner at the Chinese
place. While we ate our stir-fried spinach and tofu Buddhist
Delight, we talked about Elizabeth, Cliff, and the bonkers Bible
meeting. Angie told me, "Dakota is writing an article about
Manuel and the GSA for the school paper."

I recalled that Dakota had originally proposed interviewing Manuel the first time she'd met him. Now that seemed like eons ago. "But the GSA hasn't been approved yet," I pointed out.

"So?" Angie gave an unconcerned shrug. Meanwhile, my conscience nagged me more than ever. When we broke open our fortune cookies, mine seemed eerily on target for the situation: *Everybody does better with the truth.* But Angie's didn't exactly seem to apply: *If you're angry, count to ten. If you're really angry, count to a hundred.*

After dinner we went, as usual, to the movie—a formulaic action pic in which practically everything and everybody got blasted away by the hero. I didn't get how destroying everything made him a hero. In any case, I didn't pay much attention to the film. While Angie held my hand, I pondered what to tell her—and how?

After the movie we drove to her house and parked outside. It was a clear, cold night, with the moon nearly full.

Angie leaned across the seat and rested her head on my chest, her breath warm on my Adam's apple. She slipped her fingers beneath my wristband, playfully tugging on it.

I recalled the previous time, when without warning she'd taken my hand and pressed it onto her breast. Was she thinking the same thing?

I leaned over and pressed my lips to hers. Next thing I knew, the buttery-sweet taste of popcorn was reminding me of Manuel, at his house, and wanting to kiss him. Even though I hadn't kissed him, I had wanted to, and I felt I was betraying Angie—if not in the flesh, at least in my heart.

I *had* to say something to her about what was going on. But what? I didn't want to hurt her feelings.

Jesus, I prayed. *Please help me.*

As though in answer to my prayer, ex-gay Eric popped into my mind—and what he had said about "taking a break" from his girlfriend. Could I propose the same thing to Angie? It seemed a lot easier than trying to explain everything going on inside me. But would she understand? Or would she get angry?

When she pulled away from our kiss, I leaned back in the seat and took hold of her hand. "Um, I've been thinking . . ." My voice trembled as I spoke. "Maybe we should, um . . . take a break?"

Angie peered across the seat. She didn't show surprise, but when she spoke, she sounded kind of upset. "You mean from dating?"

"Um, yeah. You know, maybe just for a while."

One corner of Angie's mouth turned down, sadlike. "Can you tell me what's going on?"

The truth practically jabbed at my throat, wanting to come out, but I wouldn't let it. "No . . ." My voice rose guiltily. "I mean, I want to, but I can't."

"Why not?" She pulled her hand away from mine. "Why can't you tell me?"

I shook my head silently, wishing I *could* tell her. Maybe I should take back my suggestion of a break. But my throat felt too tight to speak.

She glared at me, her brow furrowed with frustration, and took about ten deep breaths. Then she asked me, "Are you sure?"

I nodded, biting my lip so hard I could almost taste the blood.

"You can be so stubborn!" She swatted my shoulder with a light pat. "Well, whatever is going on, can we at least pray?"

She reached out for my hand. I took hold of it, thanking God that at least Angie hadn't stormed out of the car, or broken down in sobs, or said she hated me.

"Dear Jesus . . ." Her voice became soft and low. "You know what Paul is going through. You understand what's in his heart. Please guide and help him . . . and remind him that you love him, no matter what."

As she prayed, I felt my throat choking up. It almost seemed as if she already knew what I couldn't tell her. Little tears welled up in my eyes, but I fought them back. It wouldn't take much for me to pour everything out to her. Yet as much as I wanted to, I wasn't ready for that.

"In your name, Lord," Angie concluded. "Amen."

"Amen," I echoed, squeezing her hand and quickly letting go. "Thanks."

"Sure," she said, reaching for the door handle.

I started to get out to walk her, like I always did, but she stopped me.

"No, that's okay. Good night."

My heart wrenched as I watched her stride up the sidewalk by herself. She went inside and turned off the porch light. Then I drove home, staring through misty eyes at the road ahead.

33

AT CHURCH THE NEXT MORNING

ANGIE SMILED AND SAID HI, BUT HER EYES SEEMED MORE
SAD THAN FRIENDLY. SHE DIDN'T CALL OR IM ME THE REST
OF THE DAY, LIKE SHE USUALLY DID. I PULLED MY CELL
OUT OF MY POCKET, THEN PUT IT BACK AGAIN, WANTING
TO TAKE BACK WHAT I HAD TOLD HER, THOUGH I KNEW
THAT WOULDN'T BE RIGHT.

During school on Monday we still talked and sat together at
lunch, but the distance between us stretched like some uncross-
able canyon.

On Tuesday Dakota's school newspaper interview with
Manuel, which Angie had mentioned, was supposed to appear. But
Mr. Arbuthnot found out about the article and canned it.

At lunchtime Dakota slammed her tray down onto our table,
her freckled face redder and angrier than ever. "He says it's 'inappropriate' and 'too controversial' for a school paper."

"That's censorship!" Angie exclaimed, almost equally angry.

I was curious to know what the article had said, but also felt a
little relieved. Wouldn't it only create more trouble for Manuel?

Meanwhile, across the cafeteria Cliff and Elizabeth handed out their antigay tracts unimpeded. Apparently, *that* wasn't inappropriate and controversial.

Dakota stabbed a fork into her meat loaf, and Angie suggested, "Maybe you should publish your article as a tract."

I laughed, but Dakota didn't. Instead, her mouth turned up into a thoughtful smile. "Maybe you're right."

The following day Dakota asked Angie, me, and everyone we knew to help pass out tracts with a simple but effective message: *Read the article BANNED from the school paper!*

Below that was the URL for a website she had created.

By the time Mr. Arbuthnot got the news, it was too late. According to Dakota the site had already counted over a thousand unique visitors.

"That's probably more than would have read it in the paper!" Dakota giggled proudly.

One of those thousand readers was me, on my home computer after school. The article was titled "Hoping to Help Others."

When Manuel Cordero, a seventeen-year-old senior, transferred from Dallas to Longhorn High this September, he came with a mission.

"By being openly gay, I hope to help people become more accepting, both of themselves and others," says the Mexican-American teen with a winning smile.

But so far Manuel's efforts have been fraught with hardship. While diversity is supposed to be celebrated in America, teens know that real life can be a different story. Since arriving at Longhorn, Manuel has been called names, tripped, and knocked down, and has had his locker vandalized. Although he's reported the harassment to the school administration, nothing has been done.

One way that Manuel hopes to help others is by starting a gay-straight

alliance. "In more than three thousand schools across America," Manuel
proudly explains, "straight and gay students are joining forces to promote
tolerance and fight homophobic prejudice." The organizers of the club are
still awaiting approval from the Longhorn H.S. administration.

Manuel explains his philosophy this way: "Every person is different in
some way. That's what makes us each special. I want to urge other gay and
bi students to come out. Even if it's just to one friend, letting out that huge
secret is such a freeing feeling. Like Jesus said in John's Gospel, 'The truth
shall make you free.'"

It was no wonder Mr. Arbuthnot had banned the article. His
administration came off seeming pretty lame, whereas Manuel
sounded like a hero.

I closed the web page and tried to do some homework, but my
mind kept drifting back to the article. I didn't hear Pa come home.
When he tapped on my doorway, I jumped.

"Can you go shopping with me, *mijo*? I need your help to buy
a new shirt." Pa often asked me to shop with him, telling me, "You
know how to pick stuff out better than I do."

"Sure," I now agreed, even though I had homework to do.

As we wandered around the (s)mall, I continued thinking
about the newspaper article. *How would Pa react if I told him my
secret?* I didn't want to hurt him—or set him to drinking again.

At the store where Pa and I looked at shirts, a mom was buying
clothes for her son. She pulled a shirt from the stacks and held it against
his chest. "This one looks nice on you." As I watched them, it struck
me that with Pa, our parent/child roles were often reversed—not just
in terms of shopping, but with lots of things: cooking, cleaning, worrying . . . Ever since Ma's death, so many times *I* was the one who took
care of *him*. Was my not coming out just one more example? Why
should I have to hide in order for him to stay sober?

"Here!" I shoved a shirt at Pa. "Get this one!"

He reeled back, startled by my gruffness.

"Sorry." I turned away, annoyed at myself for snapping at him. "I've got homework to do. I'll wait for you in the truck, okay?"

But I didn't get much work done that night. Manuel's interview kept haunting me. What would it be like to feel free, to not be hiding from anyone? What would happen to Manuel now that he was undeniably out to the entire school?

I arrived at homeroom the next day more worried than ever. Yet surprisingly, Manuel didn't get hassled any more than before. I guess the people who wanted to harass him were already doing so. Or maybe his being open made it redundant to call him names. For example:

Homophobe jerk in hallway shouts, "Hey, fag!"

Manuel answers back, "That's right. I'm glad you can read."

I began to worry that Dakota's article could have a bigger impact on *me* than on Manuel. From now on, anybody who spotted me hanging out with him would know for certain I was hanging out with someone gay.

When school let out for the holidays, I hurried out the door, desperate for the break.

34

THE SATURDAY BEFORE CHRISTMAS

I DROVE TO ABILENE AIRPORT TO PICK UP ABUELITA.
SHE GREETED ME WITH A HUG AND MY FAVORITE KIND
OF CHOCOLATE: A BRAND YOU CAN ONLY GET IN MEXICO.
WHILE WE WAITED FOR HER BAGGAGE, SHE ASKED ABOUT
PA AND RAQUEL, AND DURING THE DRIVE HOME SHE SAID,
"AND HOW IS ANGIE?"

"Um . . ." My throat tightened a little. "She's okay."

Across the seat Abuelita adjusted her glasses at me. Somehow, she could always tell when something was troubling me. "Is everything all right?"

"Sure." I gave an evasive shrug, knowing that wouldn't be the end of it. But for now I put the discussion off and ate my chocolate.

Traditionally, my family had our big holiday meal on Christmas Eve. While Pa ran last-minute errands, I helped set the table for dinner, and Abuelita asked me, "What time is Angie coming over? I have a present for her."

Angie had joined my family for every Christmas Eve since I'd known her, but after our "take a break" conversation, neither of us had mentioned it for this year.

"Um . . ." I gulped to swallow the lump in my throat. "She might not come over."

"*Mi amor*." Abuelita stared me down from behind her boxy glasses. "What's going on?"

"Nothing," I said, dropping a fork that bounced across the carpet. "Nothing. Everything is fine." Hurriedly, I finished setting the table.

For our feast Pa had invited Raquel and some friends. And, as always, Abuelita laid out an extra place setting, to remind us of those who didn't have enough to eat—and of the Lord. But tonight the vacant space reminded me mostly of how much I missed Angie. After I'd finished helping clear the dinner dishes, I decided to phone her.

"Um, hi." My voice trembled. "Merry Christmas Eve."

"Hi!" Angie sounded surprised. "Merry Christmas Eve to you too. I'm happy you called."

"You are?" I let out a sigh, relieved that she didn't sound hurt.

"Yeah," she said. "How was your dinner?"

"It was fine . . . Um, I missed you."

The line was silent till Angie said, "That's good. I missed you, too. Hey, I have a present for you."

"Really? I got you one too." After all, it was Christmas, and even though we weren't dating, I still considered her my best friend.

We agreed to exchange gifts after our choir concert on Sunday. It felt so good to be talking with her, and it made me wish things could go back to how they used to be between us—before Manuel. But could they ever again? That doubt made me even sadder than before.

After bedtime prayers I flopped into bed, still feeling kind of down, till my cell phone chirped with a text message from Manuel: *Feliz Navidad!*

I texted him back: *Merry Christmas to you too!*

Then I went to sleep, feeling a tiny bit better.

35

THE SUNDAY AFTER CHRISTMAS

WAS OUR CHURCH'S CELEBRATION OF JESUS' BIRTH — THE
BIG EVENT MY YOUTH CHOIR HAD BEEN REHEARSING FOR
SINCE OUR LAST CONCERT. WE LIT SPARKLERS OF HOPE,
WAVED FLAGS FROM COUNTRIES WHERE WE HELPED
MISSIONARIES, UNFURLED RED AND GREEN BANNERS — AND
I NEARLY SANG MY LUNGS OUT.

After the service Pastor José stopped by the choir room to tell us,
"You made the Lord proud today." Then he patted my shoulder.
"How's it going, Paul?"

"Good." I tried to smile, while squirming inside my shoes.
How could I begin to explain how it was really going?

That afternoon Angie came over to my house to exchange
gifts and see Abuelita. And for the first time in Angie's nearly million visits, I felt a little awkward. What should we talk about?
Should we sit next to each other—or across?

Abuelita peered at the two of us and scratched her head, like
she knew something was up. Then she gave Angie a silver flower
pin. Angie gave her a shimmering turquoise-colored shawl. And I
gave Angie a pink cotton sweater.

"I love it!" She pulled it on. It looked great on her. In turn, she gave me a pair of Thinsulate gloves (made without harming any animals) that I really liked.

I'd hoped Angie would hang out for a while like she usually did, but after only a few minutes she said, "I wish I could stay, but I've got to go to the mall with Mom."

Did she really have to go? I wondered. Or did she just feel too uncomfortable?

I walked her to the door and said good-bye. Then I returned to the kitchen, where Abuelita had started to make a pot of chicken stew for supper.

"I'm so happy she came over," Abuelita said. "Can you help me cut up some vegetables?"

As I began to chop up some carrots, I expected Abuelita to say more about Angie. But instead she asked, "How is your friend I met last time, Manuel?"

What had made her think of him? "Um . . . he's fine."

Abuelita stirred the stew pot and gazed over at me. "Does he have a boyfriend?"

I nearly chopped my finger off. Why had she asked that? What made her suspect that Manuel was gay?

"Um, he used to, but . . ." My throat felt like a chicken bone had caught in it. "They broke up."

"Well, that's too bad. He seems like such a nice boy. He should have someone."

I peered cautiously across the kitchen at her. Didn't it bother her that Manuel was gay?

"But homosexuality is a sin," I told her.

She gave me a stern look. "You know, when I was growing up, I never even knew the word 'homosexual'—not till I left your *abuelito* and moved to Monterrey with your papa, and tried to find a job. No one would hire me"—she wiped her hands on her apron—"except the owner of a hair salon. I was so grateful to him. Then I began to hear gossip that he was a homosexual—and how supposedly sinful that was. But I thought, *If this man is so bad, why was he the only one willing to help me?*" She tapped the old, seasoned wooden spoon on the stew pot. "I think that unless people are told to believe homosexuality and God are in conflict, there is no conflict."

As I listened to her, I sliced some celery—carefully, so as not to cut myself. "But what about what the Bible says?"

"Pablito, the Bible was meant to be a bridge, not a wedge." Abuelita nodded her head at me. "It's the greatest love story ever told, about God's enduring and unconditional love for his creation—love beyond all reason. To understand it, you have to read it with love as the standard. Love God. Love your neighbor. Love yourself. Always remember that."

My nervousness eased a little as she spoke, and, emboldened, I ventured another question: "Then, you don't think, um, gay people should try to change?"

"Change?" Abuelita snorted, pulling a big red onion out of the fridge. "Anyone who expects a person to change something as private and personal as who they hold in their arms at night needs to change their own judgmental attitude." She slammed the fridge door. "The Bible says a lot more against judging others than against homosexuality. Remember First Samuel Sixteen?"

"Yeah." I knew she meant 16:7, one of my favorite verses in the entire Bible: *The LORD sees not as man sees; man looks on the outward appearance, but the LORD looks on the heart.*

I had never thought of it in terms of the gay debate. Now my mind bubbled over with confusion. How had Abuelita known Manuel was gay? And more importantly, did she think I might be gay too?

If she did, she didn't seem terribly troubled by the possibility. But I still was—though maybe a tiny bit less than before.

36

WHEN I INVITED MANUEL OVER

TO MY HOUSE THAT WEEK, ABUELITA GREETED HIM
ALMOST AS HAPPILY AS SHE HAD ME, WITH A HUG AND A
CHOCOLATE BAR. "CALL ME ABUELITA," SHE TOLD HIM,
AND THEY TALKED IN SPANISH LIKE THEY'D KNOWN EACH
OTHER FOR YEARS.

Manuel and I hung out several times over the holidays. One afternoon he and I drove to a skating rink in Abilene with his brother,
Jaime, who was home from college.

For a Christmas present, Manuel gave me a battery-operated
desktop cactus that waved its arms while its body danced to mariachi
music. It was pretty funny. I gave him a key chain with a miniature
license plate that said MANUEL.

"Is this for the key to your heart?" Manuel grinned slyly.

"You wish." I pretended to be annoyed, not knowing how
else to react. No one had ever flirted with me so directly, not even
Angie, and definitely not any guy. Even though it made me uncomfortable, it also felt good. My feelings for Manuel were continuing
to grow, but I had no idea how to handle them. Should I push him
away? But even though he riled me, I wanted to be with him.

"Hey." Manuel phoned one evening. "Want to go to the (s)mall?"

My skin prickled at the thought. Being seen with him in public in my own town still made me wary.

"Why don't you just come over to my house?" I suggested.

"Nah. I'm sick of being cooped up. I want to go somewhere, and there's nowhere else to go. Come on!"

Should I risk it? I flipped the switch to the cactus on my desk and it began to dance.

"Okay," I agreed against my better judgment. "I'll meet you at the music store."

As I drove to the mall, another norther was blowing in, and it started to sprinkle a little rain. When I got to the parking lot, I turned my jacket collar up to keep the wind out before climbing from the car. Then I shoved my hands into my pockets, realizing I had forgotten the gloves Angie had given me.

As I started across the parking lot, a pickup truck rumbled past me, blasting its horn. It was Jude and one of his goon friends, Terry Skidmore. I avoided eye contact, kept walking, and whispered a prayer for them—and for me.

At the music-and-movies store, I found Manuel browsing DVDs in the comedy section. He had told me that he liked over-the-top goofy movies, the kind where everybody acts totally stupid. "There's a new one showing at the theater," he said.

"Oh, yeah?" I replied, not paying much attention.

We listened to sample CDs and then walked through the mall, looking in store windows. Each time I spotted somebody from school, I ducked beneath my jacket collar, hoping they wouldn't see us.

"Are you okay?" Manuel said, noticing me.

"I wish we could go somewhere else," I mumbled.

"Okay. Where?"

"I don't know." There really wasn't anywhere else to go.

As we strode past the theater, Manuel paused in front of the poster for the movie he'd mentioned. "Hey, you want to see it?"

I recalled our last time at the movies and how I'd pressed my arm against his. My heart stirred at the thought, while a voice in my head whispered, *Danger!*

"Nah." I buried my hands in my jean pockets and kept walking.

"Why?" Manuel's eyes glimmered with mischief. "You afraid someone will think we're on a date?"

"No." I glanced over my shoulder.

"Then why not?"

"Because, I don't want to."

"Oh, come on!" Manuel tugged at my jacket sleeve, like a little boy wanting to play. "It's Christmastime. I'll treat."

I tried to pull away, but his touch melted my resistance. He could have suggested we run away to Mexico in that moment, and I would have said yes.

"All right," I agreed. At least it would be dark inside, so people wouldn't see us.

The lights were dimming as we entered the theatre. In our small conservative town, if two guys went to a movie together without dates, they always left an empty seat between them, so they wouldn't get called "queer." But tonight when I tried to leave a space between us, Manuel stood again and moved into the seat beside me.

Not wanting to get into a discussion about it, I merely gritted my teeth. Besides, the fact was: I *wanted* him to sit next to me. My heart sped up as I pulled my jacket off and smelled the clean scent of his hair.

The film began, and my gaze kept shifting to the armrest

separating us. I expected Manuel to lay his hand on it, like last time, and press against my arm. But he didn't. Instead, he watched the movie and laughed.

I pretended to laugh too, while inside my head I debated what to do. Should I lay my own hand between us? No! Why couldn't I just calm down?

Slowly, I laid my hand on the vacant armrest.

An instant later, as if he'd been waiting for me to make the first move, Manuel raised his hand . . . and without a word of explanation he brought it to rest on the back of mine.

I fought the urge to leap out of my seat. Was he joking? Or serious? Or crazy? Pressing arms was one thing; holding hands was another.

My pulse quickened as I glanced around the dark theater. Everybody was laughing, though fortunately not at us. I should pull my hand away. *Now!* But it might as well have been bolted to the chair.

Sweat trickled down my back, and Manuel's fingers gently stroked mine. His touch felt softer than I had expected. And, as though my hand had a mind of its own, it turned over. Our palms touched, and my heart beat so loud I thought certain everyone in the theater would hear it. Nervously, I looked over at Manuel.

The screen light flickered across his face, giving it a warm glow. His bangs dangled carelessly toward his mischief-filled eyes and their long, curly lashes, while his lips curved into a laugh. I'd always liked his laugh—both playful and earnest. He was everything I could want in a guy—smart, with good looks, a kind, joyful heart, and a passion for God.

I remembered being in his bedroom and wishing we'd kissed. Now, as I looked at his mouth, I wished it again.

As if reading my mind, Manuel gazed back at me, his mouth

open a little. Our eyes met and held, just like the first morning I'd seen him. And, like that time, every part of me felt drawn to him by a force stronger than my own. My skin tingled beneath his touch, and my stomach quivered as he leaned toward me.

Then it happened. His hand brushed my wristband, and something snapped inside me. I'm not sure what—maybe all those messages of sin and threats of hellfire. Or was it fear of what I felt toward him? For whatever reason my excitement abruptly spiraled into panic. What was I doing? Was I nuts? I yanked my hand away from his, fumbled for my jacket, and sprang to my feet.

"Hey, what's the matter?" Manuel leaped up after me.

I stumbled across the dark row and up the theater aisle. As I burst out the door into the lobby, Manuel trailed behind me. "Wait! What's going on?"

I bounded toward the mall exit, wanting more than anything to get outside to the fresh air.

"Whoa, are you all right?" Manuel tried to grab hold of my arm, but I shook him off and threw open the door to the parking lot.

It had started to rain harder. Jude and his friend were hovering beneath the entrance awning, smoking cigarettes and jabbering. Upon seeing us, Jude called out, "Faggots!"

I wanted to punch him, but instead I cringed and hurried toward my car.

"Wait up!" Manuel chased after me. "What the hell's the matter with you?"

As I fished out my keys, I turned to him. "Why did you do that?"

"Do *what*?" Manuel stared blankly at me.

"You know what."

"Hold your hand?" Manuel's face crinkled in confusion. "Because I wanted to. You didn't exactly seem to mind. If you didn't want to, you could have said no."

I snapped a look at him, annoyed, though of course he was right. I tried to jam my keys into the car door, but they fell onto the wet pavement.

Manuel bent down and picked them up. For an instant I thought he might not give them back. I didn't care. I'd walk home—rain or not.

"Hey, come on . . ." Manuel's voice softened as he handed me the key chain. "Lighten up, *amigo*."

I couldn't lighten up. It was all too confusing. "What do you want?" I asked.

Manuel cocked his head at an angle. "What do you mean?"

"I mean, what do you want from me?"

Manuel wiped a raindrop from his face and gave me a long look. "I want *you*. I like you. A lot. Isn't that obvious?"

My heart gave a lurch as I gazed at his damp cheeks. I liked him, too. Maybe I was even in love with him. Why couldn't I accept that?

"It's wrong!"

"No." Manuel's tone was firm. "What's wrong is you putting yourself into a box that you won't let yourself out of, or me into."

I turned away, not wanting to listen, and feeling cornered.

"All your talk about what the Bible says . . ." Manuel stepped around to face me. "What about Jesus' second commandment? 'Love your neighbor as yourself.' You think that love means using a girl to pretend you're something you're not?"

I leaned back against the car, getting pelted by rain and withering with every word. Was he right? Had I *used* Angie? Even though I wasn't attracted to her, I *did* love her . . . didn't I?

"And what about the 'yourself' part?" Manuel pushed his wet bangs from his forehead. "Don't you get that letting Jesus into your heart means letting *yourself* in too?"

My thoughts were swimming. "I've got to go." I jammed my key into the door, trying not to drop it again, while Manuel's voice grew louder: "You talk about God, but you don't know a thing about love. You don't even know *how* to love. You've got no idea."

I climbed in and slammed the door, too confused to listen any further. As I pulled forward out of the parking space, I glanced in the rearview mirror.

Manuel stood in the middle of the wet pavement while the rain fell harder. Why didn't he get to his car? It was just like him, to act crazy like that.

I braked for a moment, feeling that tug again—like he was pulling at me. I sensed I was about to lose something but wasn't sure what. Maybe I ought to turn around.

But I didn't. Instead, I jammed the accelerator. And as I drove out of the parking lot, I watched him grow smaller, till I turned the corner and lost him from sight.

37

WHEN I ARRIVED HOME,

ABUELITA AND PA WERE ALREADY ASLEEP. NOT WANTING TO
WAKE THEM AND HAVE TO ANSWER ANY QUESTIONS,
I TIPTOED DOWN THE HALL.

In my room, I tossed my jacket on top of Manuel's dancing cactus, still angry about the movie theater—and mad at myself. As I undressed for bed, I muttered to God: "I'm so confused. I don't know anything anymore. I *do* love Angie . . . don't I? Or have I been using her?"

I flung myself beneath the covers and tried to review the day's events. But it was all so jumbled. Was Manuel right? Did I even know how to love?

"Help me, Lord," I asked, and flicked off my nightstand lamp.

It seemed as if I had barely drifted to sleep when the overhead light suddenly shone into my eyes. I blinked awake as Pa shook my foot, hard.

He extended the cordless phone toward me, his forehead etched with worry lines. "It's about your friend Manuel."

I glanced at the clock: 1:47 a.m. I took the receiver, expecting to talk with Manuel. "Hey, what's up?"

"Paul? This is Jaime, Manuel's brother. Something happened to him tonight."

Jaime's words spiked into my groggy brain, together with the background sounds of an intercom, ringing phones, and people talking.

"Is he okay?" I bolted upright in bed. "What happened?"

"He's bashed up pretty bad. Some guys attacked him. You'd better come down here to the hospital. The police want to talk to you."

The *police*? Exactly how badly had Manuel been hurt?

"Okay, um, I'll be right there." A million questions jammed my head as I leaped from bed, handing the phone back to Pa. "I've got to go see him."

"You want me to go with you?" Pa's offer kind of surprised me. I'd thought he didn't like Manuel ever since his *"maricón"* comment. Maybe I was mistaken.

"No, that's okay." I yanked my pants and shoes on.

As Pa walked me to the door, I checked to make sure I had my cell. I wanted to phone Angie after I got to the hospital and found out more.

"Let me know what happens," Pa said as I raced out the door.

38

RAIN WAS STILL DRIZZLING AS I DROVE

TO THE HOSPITAL, PRAYING THE ENTIRE WAY: "PLEASE,
JESUS. PLEASE, PLEASE, PLEASE, LET HIM BE OKAY."
I hadn't been to the hospital since Ma died. Now, as I parked in the
lot, memories of that time came flooding back: the endless hours
spent beneath the bright waiting-room lights, the bitter smell of
alcohol and antiseptic, eating in the snack bar with Pa, sitting
beside Ma's metal-framed bed as she died . . .

As I hurried inside the hospital doors, all I could think was,
This can't be happening again. Please God, don't let Manuel die.

In the visitors' lounge, Mr. Cordero was talking on his cell
phone, while Mrs. Cordero sat on the vinyl couch with Manuel's
little sister asleep beside her. Two police officers stood speaking to
Jaime. One was writing notes on a pad.

"How is he?" I asked Jaime. "Is he all right? What happened?"

"We're not sure. All we know is he got jumped walking home."

The officer with the notepad narrowed his gaze at me. "Were
you the one with Cordero? What time did you last see him?"

"Um, maybe ten, ten thirty. We went to the movie. But why
was he walking home? Didn't he drive?"

"No." Jaime frowned. "I dropped him off. He told me he'd get a ride home with you."

My mind flashed to Manuel standing in the parking lot, the rain splattering on him. "Why didn't he tell me he needed a ride home?"

Then again, why hadn't I asked? Why hadn't I turned the car around and driven back to him?

The second policeman eyed me guardedly. "Did you leave the movie theater together?"

"Yeah." I swallowed, feeling like I needed to cough, and tried to compose myself. "I mean, I left. Manuel followed. And we, um, had a . . . fight."

The officer darted a glance at his partner, then returned his gaze to me. "What kind of fight?"

"Not a fight." My voice rose nervously. "An argument. Not even that. I just told him I was going home. He didn't say he needed a ride."

"A fight about what?" The second policeman's gaze cut through me.

"Nothing . . ." I remembered Manuel's hand on the armrest, holding mine, and how I'd wanted to kiss him. "It *wasn't* a fight. I just wanted to go home."

The two officers exchanged a look, and the one with the pad told me, "Have a seat. You need to answer some more questions."

I sat beside Jaime and tried to answer the police truthfully as a picture emerged of what had happened: After I left Manuel in the parking lot, he started walking home. A couple of blocks from the mall, a lady heard shouts outside her house. She peered through the blinds and saw two guys jump out of a pickup truck and strike a third boy with what looked like a tire iron, hitting and kicking him.

She phoned 911, but because of the dark and the rain she hadn't been able to see the license plate as the truck sped off.

Paramedics had rushed Manuel to the emergency room. His left knee was shattered and three ribs were broken from being struck by the tire iron. One rib punctured his right lung, and a chest tube had to be inserted to reinflate the lung. Most seriously of all, his skull had a fracture that had left him unconscious and may have caused brain damage. His right eye had also been hurt, so badly that he might lose vision in it, perhaps even need to have it removed.

As Jaime described the injuries, I felt sick. How could anyone do that to Manuel? "So what's happening to him now?"

"They're trying to stabilize him," Jaime explained. "Once they do, they'll transfer him to Abilene Regional to do an MRI and start operating—hopefully in the next few hours."

"Do you have any idea who might have attacked him?" the second officer asked me.

Immediately, I pictured Jude and Terry at the mall. A chill shivered up my spine as I recalled Jude's comment at school: "If I saw two guys walk down the street holding hands, I'd take a baseball bat and kill them." Why hadn't I remembered that when I left Manuel alone in the parking lot?

I told the cops about Jude and how he harassed Manuel at school. After the police finally finished their questions, Jaime and I walked over to his parents.

"Um, hi." I buried my hands in my pockets, not sure what to say, and feeling like this was all my fault. "How are you?"

"Not so good, and you?"

"Yeah, not so good."

Our small talk sounded so stupid, but Mr. and Mrs. Cordero smiled politely. There was so much more I wanted to say, and yet I felt helpless to say any of it. After a few minutes, I excused myself to phone Angie.

By then it was three in the morning, and it took several rings before she answered her cell. "Paul?" Her voice was low and sleepy. "Is everything all right?"

"Um, no. Not really." I told her about Manuel.

"Oh, Paul!" Angie gasped. "Hold on. I'll be right there."

"That's okay. You don't have to." I hadn't expected her to actually come to the hospital, but she insisted. While waiting for her, I snapped my band against my wrist, wishing I could go back in time. Why hadn't I foreseen this? What if Manuel died?

When Angie rushed into the visitors' lounge, I leaped up from the couch. Her arms felt so comforting.

"How are you?" she asked.

I exhaled a deep, long sigh. "In shock, I think."

Angie nodded. "I was afraid something like this would happen. I prayed every day for God to keep him safe."

So had I. But at the moment I felt too confused to think about God's role in any of this.

Angie said hello to Manuel's family and talked with them awhile. Then she and I sat down nearby. "Let's pray," she whispered, and I let her take hold of my hands. My palms felt so sweaty compared to hers.

"Jesus," she said softly, "please heal Manuel. You know how much we care about him. And especially help his family. You understand their hurt and what they're going through. Please guide the doctors as they try to help Manuel. And lead the police to figure out what happened. In your name, amen."

"Amen," I echoed, though I didn't feel very connected to God. I was too numb.

After her prayer Angie and I walked to the snack bar where

I'd eaten countless meals with Pa when Ma was sick. Although the counter was now closed for the night, Angie and I got some vending machine hot chocolate and sat down in one of the red Formica booths. I hoped the drink would help calm me, but it was too hot. When I took a sip, the liquid seared my tongue.

"Damn it!" I quickly put the cup down and my face grew warm—not from the chocolate, but from swearing. "Sorry," I told Angie.

"Don't worry about it. You're upset."

That was an understatement. "I shouldn't have left Manuel; then this wouldn't have happened."

"You can't blame yourself." Angie rested her hand on top of mine. Then she asked, "What did you guys fight about?"

I'd mentioned that Manuel and I had argued, but not about what. How could I admit that I'd freaked out because we'd held hands and I was afraid to kiss him? Or that we'd argued because I couldn't accept my feelings toward him?

"Um . . ." I picked up my chocolate and blew on it, but it was still too hot. "I can't remember."

Angie's mouth turned down as though she didn't believe me.

"Let's go back," I said, and got up.

While we waited in the visitors' lounge, we talked with Manuel's parents some more.

Mr. Cordero kept saying optimistic things like, "He'll pull through. He always does." He told us a story of how one time as a boy Manuel had tried to skateboard down a playground slide and wiped out.

"He had to have six stitches," Mrs. Cordero added, clutching her hands worriedly.

Angie and I debated whether to phone Dakota and tell her about Manuel. But since there was nothing anyone could do right now but wait, we decided to hold off. At six a.m. my pa phoned, and I filled him in.

"I'm sorry to hear it," Pa replied. "Why don't you come home and get some rest?"

"I want to wait," I told him. "When he goes to Abilene, I want to go with him."

"*Mijo*, you can't drive without having slept."

"But I've *got* to go." I felt too responsible for what had happened. More than ever, I felt as if Manuel was pulling at me, like I *had* to be with him.

"Tell him I'll go with you," Angie whispered.

"Angie will go with me."

The line was quiet a moment. Then Pa said, "All right."

After I hung up, Angie and I decided to call Dakota and tell her the news.

"Why didn't you phone me sooner?" Dakota protested. In seeming minutes she was hurrying into the visitors' lounge. "I could have come and been with you guys. You two look like hell, you know that?"

Dakota said hello to Manuel's family. Then, she, Angie, and I went to the snack bar, which had opened for breakfast. Over powdered donuts I told Dakota everything that had happened to Manuel, including the fact that "I thought he had his car."

"That's like the hundredth time you've said that," Dakota observed.

Was it? I felt the color rise in my cheeks.

We returned to the visitors' lounge, and one of the doctors informed the Corderos, "We're ready to transport him." A few minutes later several hospital staff rushed past us, wheeling a gurney toward an ambulance in the driveway.

Manuel was hardly recognizable. Bandages covered his face and head. IVs protruded from his arms. Tubes to a ventilator projected from beneath the gurney sheets.

I watched silently, too stunned to breathe. Could that really be Manuel? There had to be some mistake. In my mind I saw him striding through the ER doors, healthy and strong, smiling with mischief, and asking, "Hey, what's all the hoopla?" We'd all feel relieved from the scare we'd gone through and embrace him like the prodigal son.

"Paul?" Angie's voice called beside me.

"Huh?"

She rested her hand on my arm. "Ready to go?"

We said good-bye to Dakota, who had to go to the job she had gotten for the holidays, and I followed Angie to her car.

Angie and I didn't talk much on the drive to Abilene, past fast-food places, gas stations, and gray winter pastures. I stared aimlessly out the rain-streaked window and held tight to Angie's hand.

Manuel's family arrived at the medical center ahead of us. Once again we joined them in the visitors' lounge and waited while Manuel was taken into the operating room. For the rest of the day Angie and I mostly prayed and watched TV. I dozed a little but felt too restless to sleep. At 5:45 that afternoon, after nine long hours, Manuel was finally brought out of surgery.

"We managed to save his right eye," the doctor announced. "But he's lost all vision in it. He'll probably be able to see light, but he won't see shapes or movement. His knee and ribs will have to mend on their own. We'll keep him on a respirator for several days, but he should be breathing on his own by the end of the week. He's still unconscious, so we don't know about brain damage. The longer he remains in a coma, the greater the risk."

My stomach got a hollow feeling as I watched Manuel being wheeled into the intensive care room. Although his face was visible now, he looked nothing like the person I had left in the parking lot. His cheeks were bruised and purple, his lips swollen, his face scraped raw and crusted with blood. A patch covered his right eye. Bandages clothed his scalp. The very life seemed beaten out of him. Would—*could*—he ever be the same?

"We should get some rest," Angie told me.

I didn't want to leave Manuel, even though I felt exhausted.

"Come on," she whispered, gently pulling me away from the ICU window, as the respirator eased air in and out of his lungs.

She drove us back from Abilene through the rain, and I tried to stay awake, but it had already turned dark outside. As the car cruised down the highway, the steady flick of the windshield wipers quickly lulled me to sleep.

I was barely aware when Angie dropped me off at home. Abuelita asked about Manuel, but I don't know what I answered. I can't even remember crashing onto my bed to sleep.

39

THE NEXT DAY,

WHEN I SLOWLY EMERGED FROM SLEEP, IT WAS LIKE
ANY OTHER MORNING. BUT AS I GAZED DOWN AT MY
SLEPT-IN CLOTHES FROM THE NIGHT BEFORE, THE
MEMORY OF WHAT HAD HAPPENED TO MANUEL SEEPED
INTO MY BRAIN LIKE POISON.

I lay still, hardly breathing, as though a heavy weight were bearing
down on me, while my mind replayed the sight of Manuel in the
movie, the parking lot, the hospital . . .

Dear Jesus, I prayed. *Heal Manuel. Please? And help me to deal
with all this.*

Only by praying was I able to finally pull myself out of bed.
When I shuffled into the kitchen, Abuelita was sitting at the
breakfast table, reading the morning paper. Immediately, she got
up and embraced me. *"Buenos días, mi amor."*

It felt so good to be held by her. She gestured to the paper on
the table. "It's in the news." I grabbed the *Reporter-News* and read
the article, headlined TWO ARRESTED FOR ATTEMPTED MURDER.

*Two seventeen-year-old males were arrested and charged with
attempted murder yesterday for the near-fatal attack of Manuel Cordero.
Police have withheld their names due to their ages.*

While walking home on December 29 at approximately 10 p.m., Cordero, 17, a senior at Longhorn High, was attacked and severely beaten with a tire iron. He is currently in critical condition at Abilene Regional Medical Center.

Attempted murder? My stomach wrenched. Were the two seventeen-year-olds in fact Jude and Terry? What would happen to them?

Abuelita set a plate of eggs and crisp bacon in front of me, but I told her I wasn't hungry. More than anything I wanted to get back to Abilene and see Manuel. Although there was nothing I could do besides pray and wait, I wanted to be with him—even if he didn't know I was there.

Abuelita wiped her glasses with her apron and sighed. "Pablito, you have to eat. Come on."

I must have been hungrier than I thought, because I ate everything on the plate. I had finished brushing my teeth when Pa phoned from work: "Did you get some sleep?"

"Yeah, but I'm going back to see him. He's in ICU."

Pa became quiet, as if thinking. "Okay, but I want you home early. It's New Year's Eve—too many drunks on the road. Understand?"

"Yes, sir."

It was still raining off and on during my drive to Abilene. I tried to keep to the speed limit, though I wanted to hurry. I was thinking about Manuel's parents and what I wanted to tell them, when suddenly my cell rang.

"Thank God you're okay," said Eric. He was the last person I expected a call from, especially since I had never phoned him about the ex-gay meeting. "I heard on TV that a boy from your town was attacked. I was afraid it might've been you."

"No. He's a friend of mine."

"Oh, yeah? Was he gay?"

It made me feel creepy that Eric said "was"—as if Manuel had died. Maybe I just heard it that way. I braced my arms against the steering wheel and replied, "Yeah, he's gay."

"The lifestyle isn't safe." Eric exhaled an audible sigh. "If you want God's protection, you've got to get right with him."

I should have predicted that response. Would he have said the same if Manuel had been straight? Why wasn't he blaming the attackers instead of Manuel? I clenched my jaw, wanting to tell Eric, "Go screw yourself."

"When are you coming to our fellowship?" he asked.

"I don't know." That was the farthest thing from my mind right now. "Look, I've got to go."

"Okay," Eric said. "Call me if you want to talk."

"Yeah, sure," I said, and hung up. I had no intention of calling. And even though it was cold outside, I turned on the AC to help cool my anger.

By the time I arrived at the hospital, I'd managed to get Eric's phone call out of my mind, and I hurried into the visitors' lounge, eager to find out about Manuel.

"How's he doing?" I asked his parents. "Any news?"

"No . . ." His mom forced her lips into a pale smile, as if trying to be hopeful.

"But the doctors say it's good that he's stable," Mr. Cordero offered.

I nodded in agreement and fidgeted with my wristband, thinking what I had rehearsed to tell them. "Um, I'm really sorry . . . for not giving him a ride home. I thought he had his car."

Mrs. Cordero nodded forgivingly. "I know. He could have called us."

"He's always been so headstrong," Mr. Cordero said. "We've had our share of arguments because of it."

Mrs. Cordero smiled a little more easily to me. "He said once he wished he could be more like you . . . accepting and patient."

Accepting and patient? Me? I sure didn't think of myself that way. More than anything I wanted Manuel to wake from the coma and be well *now*! Today! This instant!

"He cares a lot about you," Mr. Cordero added.

"I care about him, too," I said feebly, feeling like a fake. If I truly cared so much about Manuel, why had I freaked out when he turned to kiss me in the theater? If I'd kissed him like I'd wanted to, would we even be in the hospital now?

The remainder of the day I stood looking through the ICU window at Manuel lying bruised and broken.

I tried to picture his mischievous brown eyes beneath the bandages. In my mind I traced my fingers across his cut and swollen lips, remembering how tender they'd felt when I dabbed them with ointment. Once again I now imagined kissing them, but this time I tasted the dried blood on his face, bitter, like acid.

Over and over that day I prayed, *God, Jesus, please make him well.*

During my drive home that night I felt so exhausted that I rolled down the windows to keep me alert. The cold winter air blasted into the car, whipping around my head. Thunder rumbled far off in the west, along with low flashes of lightning, and my thoughts returned to God. Why had he allowed Manuel to get hurt so badly? How could he allow such suffering and still claim to be loving and good?

It wasn't the first time I'd had such doubts—or at least started to. Sometimes, while watching news reports of wars or disasters, I'd asked myself, *Why does God allow it?* But I changed the TV channel or turned the page, not wanting to dwell on it too long. It was simpler to accept Pastor José's response: "It isn't our place to question God's wrath; instead, be grateful for his kindness and mercy." That was a lot harder to do when the hurt and confusion hit so close to home—as with Manuel . . . or with my ma's illness and death. Except that then I had been a child. As a boy I accepted what adults told me.

Now, as I looked out over the vastness of the empty plains, I prayed, "Why do you allow it, God? Help me to understand. Where are you in all this, Jesus? Where *are* you?"

Only the wind answered, whistling in through the windows. By the time I reached our town limits sign, I was nearly frozen.

On Main Street the cross atop the church I'd gone to as a child caught my attention, lit up for the holidays. I slowed the car and pulled over to stare at the faded stucco building. The place seemed a lot smaller than when I was little.

Without any particular plan I turned the engine off and got out of the car. I strode up the walkway, climbed the front steps, and tried the church doors. Naturally, they were locked. I walked back down the steps and over to the Sunday school building. Cupping my hands on the window of my boyhood classroom, I peered inside.

The light from the streetlamp barely illuminated the room. Across the child-sized desks and chairs the once larger-than-life Jesus mural now looked small and dim. He seemed so distant.

In my memory I pictured a Sunday morning long ago, the room crowded with kids. Sunlight streamed in the windows. My ma waited patiently in the classroom doorway for me until I ran to take her hand, excited to tell her the Bible story I'd learned that day.

Now a million questions taunted me. *What if all those Bible stories are merely that, just stories? What if all the miracles were made up? What if Jesus was a mere mortal, or just another made-up story? What if there is no eternal life? What if it's all a lie? What if my prayers are just talking to myself? What if there is no God?*

I folded my arms tight against my jacket, thinking back over my life since the days in that classroom: the loss of my ma; how much I'd missed her; my frustration at my dad's drinking; having to be strong for him when I was the one who needed him; my shame over the attraction I felt toward other boys; my loneliness, year after year, unable to voice my secret; my guilt with Angie; and now all my confusion about Manuel . . .

As I stood in the cold dark night, peering into that building, something broke inside me. Maybe it was the hope I had tried so hard to sustain all those years: that I could be different from what I was. Or perhaps it was my heart, which I had given so trustingly to Jesus.

What would become of me? Should I be honest about who I was—and end up like Manuel, in a hospital bed and possibly destined to hell for giving in to sin? Or should I continue living a lie, feigning unquestioning faith and happiness outside while fighting and hating who I was inside?

Neither choice seemed fair. Was there another possibility, one that I had never dared consider?

I had always been taught that the mere thought of suicide was a sin. God gave us life, and it was only for him to take it away. But now I no longer cared if I went to hell for it. How much worse could it be than the torment and despair I'd felt all these years? Wasn't I *already* in hell?

I recalled a schoolmate during freshman year who had done it. Late one night he sat in his car in the garage with the engine running, till he asphyxiated. I could do that. Nobody had ever found out what made him do it. Should I leave a note? Would I have the guts to admit my reason? What about Angie, and Pa, and Abuelita? Could I do that to them?

I turned my collar up against the wind, but it didn't stop the dark chill that pierced through me. Slowly I returned to my car and climbed inside. Bending my head over the steering wheel, I told Jesus, "I'm begging you. If you truly exist, you've got to help me. Because I can't do this anymore."

Then I turned the ignition and drove home.

40

EVEN THOUGH IT WAS NEW YEAR'S EVE,

I COLLAPSED INTO BED, TOO WIPED OUT AND DEPRESSED
TO DO ANYTHING BESIDES SLEEP. IN THE MIDDLE OF THE
NIGHT, MY CELL RANG.

"Happy New Year," Angie said.

"Um, you too," I mumbled, barely awake. "Thanks."

At some time the following morning, I was still half asleep
when Pa came into the room. He stood at the foot of my bed,
but he never said anything; he just looked at me. I guess he figured I needed the rest, because he went back out, and I returned
to sleep.

The sound of more rain finally woke me up at nearly noon. But
for all my sleeping, I felt more empty than rested. The only thing
that drew me out of bed was Manuel. Even in a coma he was still
pulling at me.

When I got to the kitchen, Abuelita wrapped her arms around
me. "Happy New Year! I was about to wake you."

"Happy New Year," I said, noticing her suitcase by the door.
I'd forgotten she had to leave today. Now I wished I'd spent more
time with her.

Abuelita asked about Manuel while making me a breakfast of chorizo, piping hot eggs, and beans. Pa had already said good-bye to her and gone to run errands. After I finished eating, I carried her suitcase to the car, stepping over dark pools of water on the pavement. They seemed like mirrors of the mood I felt inside.

Halfway down the highway to Abilene I turned to Abuelita. "Can I ask you something? Have you ever wondered if God exists?"

"Of course." She shrugged, as though it was the most natural question on earth. "But what difference does it make? What matters is the courage and strength that I get from believing in him. Whether he exists or not, he's real to me today."

I didn't think her answer made much sense. "How can you believe in him if you doubt he exists?"

"*Mi amor*, we have to believe in something—in some power—otherwise we'd have no hope. Believing gives us hope. God *is* hope."

I pondered that, feeling my own lack of hope.

"I've had days," Abuelita continued, "when I didn't think I could go on." She gave me a long, searching look, as if she'd guessed the thoughts I'd had last night at the church. But how could she? I hadn't told her about it.

"Days when that power, that hope for something better, was the only thing that got me out of bed in the morning."

Was hope the pull I had felt from Manuel since first seeing him? Hope in answer to all my confusion?

Abuelita let out a weary sigh. "And besides, if there was no God, who would I get mad at? Better to turn that ire at God than at myself."

I laughed a little nervously, recalling the times I'd come home and found Abuelita shouting at God. I had never allowed myself to get angry at him. Maybe I had felt too guilty.

"God is great, Pablito. Don't be afraid to be angry with him. Let him know what's in your heart—all of it. He can take it. He can take more than you could ever give him. Just don't give up."

I stared out at the roadway, not exactly comprehending everything she said, but what mattered was that she seemed to understand—even the things I hadn't told her.

At the airport I carried her bag to check-in and said good-bye, hugging her tightly, and watched till she passed through security. Then I drove to the hospital.

As the hours went by that day, I sat outside Manuel's room, and my mind rambled all over. I thought a lot about how much it would hurt Abuelita, Pa, and Angie if I did give up, if I ended my life. But what if I just couldn't go on?

It felt like the only thing keeping me going was the hope that Manuel would recover. Yet, what if he didn't? I remembered the afternoon we'd been in his room, listening to his big band music, and he'd reached for my hand, inviting me to dance. "If I were you," he'd said, "I'd take me up on this invitation. You never know in life if you'll get a second chance."

If only I'd known then how true his words were and I had taken him in my arms, like I'd wanted to.

I thought about the stuff he'd said to me in the mall parking lot, about putting myself in a box. Was he right? Had I? Was I even capable of love?

"Please don't die," I now whispered to him from behind the glass of the ICU window. "I need you so much. I want to love, but what if I can't? What if I don't know how? You've got to teach me. I need you to teach me."

I let my forehead drop onto the window as tears trickled down my cheeks.

41

ON JANUARY 2, CLASSES STARTED AGAIN.

I DIDN'T WANT TO GO. I WANTED TO BE WITH MANUEL.
BUT PA TOLD ME, "YOU CAN WAIT TILL AFTER SCHOOL."
I DIDN'T HAVE THE STRENGTH TO ARGUE.

On campus everyone knew about Manuel. Although the newspapers hadn't published the attackers' names, Jude and Terry hadn't returned to school and word spread that they were the ones who had been arrested. The attack seemed like the only thing people were talking about:

"Did you hear about the gay guy? Supposedly brain mush now."

"Can you imagine beating somebody with a tire iron? How sick is that?"

"Like, big surprise? Jude always gave me the creeps."

On my way to lunch Elizabeth came up close to me, sporting new clothes. "Hi. I'm sorry to hear about Manuel."

Her tone sounded sincere, but given her past attitude I asked, "Are you really?"

"Yes, *really*." She clenched her teeth into a frown.

I felt bad for misjudging her. But then she added, "Even though he did bring it upon himself. You can't walk around boasting your sin and think nothing will happen to you. 'Pride goeth before a fall.'"

I immediately stepped back from her, seething with fury.

"I'll pray for you." She turned away, smiling scornfully.

"And I'll pray for you," I muttered. When I got to my lunch table, I slammed my tray down.

"What's wrong?" Angie stared at me, alarmed.

Dakota's gray eyes widened. "It's not about Manuel, is it?"

"No, he's the same." I jabbed my fork into my turkey and told them about Elizabeth's comment.

"So much for Jesus softening her heart," Dakota remarked.

Angie nodded. "I remember Manuel once said, 'Some people's minds will never change, no matter what.'"

I tossed my fork aside, too upset to eat. "It's like everyone wants to blame Manuel for what happened."

"Who else said something?" Angie asked.

"Eric," I replied, and immediately realized my error.

Dakota gave me a confused look. "Who is Eric?"

"Um . . ." I picked up my fork again. "Just someone I know."

Angie stared expectantly. "Are you going to tell us who?"

"Just somebody I met through church. Do either of you want my dessert?"

I tried to change the subject, while at the same time I wanted to climb atop the cafeteria table and just yell the truth to every-one—get it over with. I was getting sick of hiding and covering up. Who cared what other people might think? But I stayed seated, remembering what had happened to Manuel.

After school, I once again drove the seventy-nine miles to Abilene. The wind off the plains shoved my car all over the road, and waves of emotion pitched through me. I had been thinking a lot about what Abuelita had said about getting angry at God. Although I had spent years mad at myself for not being able to get rid of my secret feelings, the thought of expressing my anger at God had never really crossed my mind. If I couldn't stop my shameful feelings, that was my fault, not God's. Who was I to challenge him?

And yet hadn't I wondered how a good and loving God could allow such a cruel joke to be played on me? And now that I thought about it, hadn't almost every Bible hero, from Moses to Jonah, to Job, to St. Paul, to Jesus on the cross, questioned and challenged God? Not to compare myself to them, but hadn't I wanted to be like them when I was a boy listening to their stories in Sunday school?

Besides, now that I no longer even believed for certain that God existed, and since I was probably bound for hell anyway, why not unleash my anger at him? I gripped my hands on the steering wheel, and in the solitude of my car I prayed in a way I never had before: "Jesus, I'm really angry . . ." I hesitated, a little nervous. "At you and at God."

Unwittingly, I ducked down in my seat, glancing up at the sky and into the rearview mirror. Even though I knew it was silly, I sort of half expected a thunderclap, a lightning bolt, or something.

When nothing happened, I felt emboldened. "I'm angry," I repeated, "really, really, really mad." With each word my voice grew stronger, and I started to realize how deeply furious I was.

"Mad that you let all this happen to me—that you let my ma die, that you let me have these gay feelings, that you let Manuel get hurt so bad." I began shouting. "You promised that anything asked in your name would be done—and it wasn't. Why should I believe *anything* you say?"

Every time a car passed on the road, they must have thought I was crazy, ranting like some mad man. But I didn't care. It's a wonder I didn't run off the road; I could barely see clearly.

By the time I reached the hospital, my voice was hoarse from shouting.

42

I'M NOT SURE THAT MY SHOUTING

ACCOMPLISHED MUCH, OTHER THAN TO HELP ME
REALIZE HOW ANGRY I'D BEEN WITH GOD FOR A VERY
LONG TIME — AT LEAST SINCE MA HAD DIED. AS A BOY I
HAD FELT TOO SCARED BY HER DEATH TO RISK BEING
ANGRY. NOT ANYMORE. AND YET WHAT GOOD DID IT DO?
IT WAS LIKE OPENING UP THE PROVERBIAL WOUND.

Now, as I stared through the glass of the ICU window, Manuel's weak and broken body seemed to reflect how broken I felt inside myself.

As I waited for hours, I made empty small-talk with his mom and dad, and the nurses, or on the phone with Angie, Dakota, my pa . . . Otherwise, I simply waited—and prayed.

Please, God, I repeated over and over, *if you truly exist, heal Manuel. In your name, Jesus, please heal him.*

I knew that praying made no sense. Why turn to a being I was furious at, especially when I no longer trusted he even existed? And yet, just as some unseen force kept drawing me to Manuel, some power continued to pull me toward God.

And each night, when visiting hours ended and Manuel's condition remained the same, I drove home shouting at the Lord, louder and stronger.

At school I mostly went through the motions, barely paying attention, counting the minutes till I could drive back to Abilene. Yet once I got there, I could do little except wait.

One evening, after spending hours watching Manuel and praying for him, I picked up a Bible somebody had left on the windowsill and halfheartedly flipped through it, first to the Psalms, and then to Romans—but not to the vague and confusing passage in Chapter 1. Instead, I turned to one of my favorites, Romans 8:38-39, where St. Paul said:

For I am sure that neither death, nor life, nor angels, nor principalities, nor things present, nor things to come, nor powers, nor height, nor depth, nor anything else in all creation, will be able to separate us from the love of God in Christ Jesus our Lord.

I had often read that promise when I worried why God wasn't taking away my secret feelings. Now it reminded me of what Abuelita had said about the Bible being the greatest love story ever told. Could I truly trust the Word of God that his love was so boundless and unconditional that *nothing* could separate me from that love? Not even doubts of his existence? Or all my unbridled fury at him? Or my gay feelings?

What if my secret feelings didn't go away and I failed to change, as I believed he wanted? Would he still love me? Could Jesus, who prayed for those who drove nails into him and forgave those who denied and forsook him, still forgive me—and save me from hell?

I lay the Bible down on my lap and thought about that for a long while, gazing at Manuel and recalling the things he'd said that night in the parking lot, about love. Was he right? Had I put myself in a box, unable to love and be loved? If St. Paul's promise was true, and God's love was so unshakeable, then wasn't *I* the only thing separating me from God's love—me and my own unwillingness to accept his love?

My mind struggled to absorb that. Had I actually been resisting God's love all these years by not accepting who I was? I picked up the Bible again, leafing through it a little further, to St. Paul's second letter to the Corinthians, chapter 12:

. . . to keep me from being too elated by the abundance of revelations, a thorn was given me in the flesh, a messenger of Satan, to harass me, to keep me from being too elated. Three times I besought the Lord about this, that it should leave me . . .

I had read that passage a million times, asking God to remove my own thorn of unwanted feelings. But St. Paul's words had never spoken to me quite so clearly as they did now. I guess I hadn't been ready to accept the response that came next:

. . . but [the Lord] said to me, "My grace is sufficient for you, for my power is made perfect in weakness."

That reminded me of the Serenity Prayer, and what it said about God granting me "the serenity to accept the things I cannot change."

I had tried so hard to change and be straight, certain that it was God's will for me. And yet I hadn't changed one single bit. So, was my thorn really my secret feelings? Or was it my own stubborn refusal to accept them? I returned to the epistle, trying to make sense of it all.

I will all the more gladly boast of my weaknesses that the power of Christ may rest upon me.

Reading that, something struck me for the first time: even though St. Paul said he'd boast of his weaknesses, he never did reveal to us what his thorn was. What exactly was his secret thorn, so shameful that he never specified it? Could it have been any worse than mine?

For the sake of Christ, then, I am content with weaknesses, insults, hardships, persecutions, and calamities; for when I am weak, then I am strong.

Could *I* also be content to accept that the Lord might not want to change me, or he would have done so by now? Could I admit that it might possibly be the Lord's will for me to love and accept myself as . . . gay?

Romans 8 had made it clear that nothing could stop God's love for me. But could I love and accept myself as I was, with all my confused and thorny feelings, along with all the "insults, hardships, persecutions, and calamities" that it might bring? Or would I spend the rest of my life fighting who I was, feeling sorry for myself, and being angry at God about it?

When I left the hospital that night, Manuel's condition continued the same, but inside me a seismic shift was occurring.

43

WHEN I DROVE FROM THE HOSPITAL

TOWARD HOME THAT NIGHT, I DIDN'T FEEL LIKE
SHOUTING AT GOD ANYMORE. I LOOKED ACROSS
THE MOONLIT PLAINS AND THOUGHT ABOUT WHAT
ABUELITA HAD SAID ABOUT GIVING MY ANGER UP
TO THE LORD. IT ALMOST FELT AS IF HIS HAND
HAD REACHED DOWN AND LIFTED MY FURY AWAY—
TAKING ALONG WITH IT MY DESPAIR
AND THOUGHTS OF SUICIDE.

I also thought about things Manuel had tried to tell me about
being honest and real, no matter what the cost. Was I finally ready
to believe him? Could I take that risk? As the lights of my town
approached, I knew what I had to do.

When I reached Angie's house, the porch light was on. I
shut off the engine and stared at the open arms of the St. Francis
statue on the front lawn, summoning my nerve, until at last I got
out.

"Come in." Angie answered the door, her face lined with worry. "How is he?" Obviously, she feared bad news about Manuel.

"The same," I said, stepping inside the living room.

"Well . . ." She tried to smile. "At least he's not worse. You want some hot chocolate?"

"No, thanks. I need to talk to you."

She nodded understandingly, and led me to her room. Closing the door behind her, she sat down on the carpet and patted the spot next to her. "Come sit."

I slid down, and she asked, "How are *you* holding up?"

"Um, all right . . ." I fidgeted with my wristband, feeling my resolve wane. "I need to tell you something."

"Okay." She looped her ponytail around her fingertips, and her eyebrows arched with curiosity. "I'm listening."

I sucked in a huge breath of air. "I'm really scared to tell you."

She reached out for my trembling hands and whispered, "I know."

At that, my heart paused. What did she mean? I glanced at her face, searching. Did she already know what I was about to say? Or was she simply reassuring me?

"I don't want to hurt you," I mumbled, shifting my gaze toward the carpet.

She grabbed hold of my chin, her fingers gentle and warm, and she tipped my head up to look at her again. "Paul, I *know*."

Tears welled up in my eyes, and, unable to contain my anxiety an instant more, I whispered, "I'm gay." I felt like a criminal admitting it to Angie and yet at the same time like a prisoner released. "I'm sorry, Angie. I'm really sorry. I wanted to tell you. I truly did. I never meant to hurt you."

"It's okay." Angie shook her head as a slow stream of tears began to roll down her cheeks too. "It's not your fault."

I nodded, though uncertain. Did she mean my being gay? Or my not telling her?

"I just wish you'd told me sooner." She wiped her cheek and then hit my shoulder with a little punch.

I kind of wished she'd hit me harder. Clearly, she was upset. "Go ahead," I told her. "I deserve it."

"No, you don't." She sniffled, but then she suddenly raised her other fist, and *smack!* She struck my chest, hard. Maybe I shouldn't have encouraged her. I winced, and she leaned over and wrapped her arms around me. "I'm sorry.

She rested her head on my shoulder, like so many times before. And I leaned back against the bed, holding onto her as if I were one of her wounded critters.

"So, you knew?" I asked.

"Not for sure." Her voice was raspy and sad. "I think I always sort of suspected. You're so different from other boys—in lots of ways. That's part of what I love about you."

I noticed she said "love" in the present tense. I let out a breath, relieved, though I still felt a little guilty for all those years I'd spent hiding from her.

"Maybe I should have said something to you," Angie continued. "But what could I have said? I didn't want to hurt you, either. You've always been so hard on yourself. I prayed about it a lot. Maybe I didn't want to know for sure—or I thought I could save you, so you wouldn't go to hell."

As she spoke, I thought, *How weird. It's like the two of us have been living secret lives with each other, both too scared to talk.* And yet, she *had* saved me. I had needed her so much. How could I have made it through without her?

"When Manuel came," Angie pressed on, "I started to question if being gay was really such a horrible thing."

"Then you don't think it's wrong?" I sat up a little. "You don't think I'll go to hell?"

"How can it be wrong to love?" She shook her head slowly. "God is love. How can you be sent to hell for loving someone?"

I chewed at the corner of my mouth, thinking about that, and started to feel guilty again. "You don't feel like I wasted your time?"

"Don't be silly." She looked at me straight on, and I thought she might punch me again. But instead she planted a tiny kiss on my tear-wet cheek. "I cherish every moment we've spent together."

I wanted to believe her, and for a long time we held each other, quiet—just being with our tears and each other.

It had been so scary to tell her, "I'm gay"—like I was casting off a mask I'd worn for years and finally letting someone see the real me. And yet I felt oddly stronger now, as though I'd finally stepped into my own skin instead of wanting to crawl out of it.

"I want to ask you something," I said, sitting up straight and wiping my cheeks. "I'm thinking of telling Pa. You think I should?"

Angie sat up beside me. "Do you want to?"

I nodded, a little uncertain. "But what if he starts drinking again?"

"Well, that's why he goes to AA, isn't it?" She was right, of course. Why hadn't I thought of that? We talked about my doubts and worries a little more, but I knew that I wanted to tell him, and Angie suggested we pray.

"Dear Jesus . . ." she started slowly. I kept my eyes open, gazing at her. "Please guide Paul and help him make the right decision about his dad. Help him to trust that no matter what happens, you'll be there for him . . ."

As Angie prayed, I recalled St. Paul's passage about how nothing could separate us from God's love. Listening to her, I felt closer to that love than I had in a long time.

As I was leaving, she said, "I'm here for you, whenever you need me."

I kissed her on the cheek and walked to my car. When I drove away, she waved to me from the front doorway, like she had so many times before. Except tonight she left the porch light on.

44

WHEN I ARRIVED HOME FROM ANGIE'S,

PA WAS ASLEEP IN FRONT OF THE TV, SNORING. AN EMPTY
BUTTERMILK GLASS STOOD ON THE END TABLE BESIDE THE
COUCH. I WATCHED HIM FOR AWHILE, AND WONDERED,
CAN I REALLY TELL HIM?

I knew I *had* to tell him. I didn't want to hide anymore, and I didn't
want him finding out from someone else. But first I needed to eat.
Talking to Angie had left me drained and starved.

Ever since Manuel had gone into the hospital, Pa had been leaving dinner for me on the stove, knowing I'd be home late. Tonight
he had made chopped steak, rice, and pinto beans. I warmed it up,
trying to be quiet. I was mixing a glass of chocolate milk when I
heard the TV shut off. A moment later Pa stood in the kitchen
doorway, rubbing the sleep from his eyes.

"Hi." He yawned, covering his mouth. "How is your friend?
Any better?"

"No, the same." I sat down at the kitchen table with my dinner and started to eat.

Pa pulled a chair up and watched me quietly, his thoughts
seeming years away. "Every day when you drive to the hospital," he
said softly, "I think of your ma."

I stopped chewing a moment. Pa hardly ever mentioned Ma. I
had followed his example, figuring that it hurt him to talk about her.
I now set my fork down and admitted, "So do I. I miss her a lot."

Pa nodded across the table, his eyes clouded, and we both sat quietly again.

Maybe now wasn't the best time to tell him about me. But then, when would be?

I took a swig of milk to fortify myself. "Pa? I need to tell you something." I tried to keep my voice steady as I looked at him. "I'm gay."

The words seemed to hang in the air between us. I waited as Pa sat silently, his face showing no emotion, his eyes getting that miles-away look again. What was going on inside him now? Was he angry? Disappointed? What was *ever* going on inside him?

Unable to stand the silence, I asked, "Are you going to say anything?"

He raised a hand to rub his wrinkled forehead, his fingers shaking a little. "I promised your ma I'd take care of you."

I shifted in my chair. Did that mean he would accept me being gay? Or that he thought he'd screwed up?

"Well, you have taken care of me."

"No." He brought his hand down from his brow, across his graying mustache. "Not very well. I should have paid more attention to you."

What was he implying? That I was gay because he hadn't paid enough attention? I recalled Manuel once asking, "Why do some people always try to find something to blame being gay on?"

"Pa, this isn't about you—or anything you did or didn't do."

Pa shook his head as if seeing things differently. "I'm sorry, *mijo*."

"Sorry for *what*?" I had feared he might be angry, but *I* was the one getting mad. "There's nothing to feel sorry about. It's just how I am. It doesn't matter why."

I got up and carried my half-eaten dinner to the sink, no longer hungry, and scraped the remains into the garbage disposal. After shoving my plate into the dishwasher, I turned to face Pa. "Are you going to get drunk again?"

He flinched. "What?"

I felt a little crass for having asked, but wasn't that a big chunk of the reason I'd been so scared to come out to him?

"I said, are you going to start drinking again?"

"No." He shook his head as though he still didn't understand why I was asking that.

"Good!" I folded my arms. Why was I so angry at him? He had taken my coming out much better than I'd expected and said he wasn't going to drink again. What more did I want?

His dark eyes stared back at me, as unreadable as ever. Would he always be a mystery to me? When he spoke again, he simply said, "*Te quiero, mijo.*"

"I love you too," I muttered, meaning it, though I didn't feel it very much right now.

That's all we said that night. I felt like there were volumes more we needed to say, but I didn't know what. Maybe he didn't either.

I went to my room, kicked my shoes off, and fell onto the bed.

"Well, I did it," I told Jesus. "I don't know if it was your will or not, but I did it."

I stared at the crack in the ceiling, waiting for some sort of reaction to my prayer, but there wasn't any. Sometimes God seemed as mysterious as my pa.

45

WHEN I AWOKE THE FOLLOWING MORNING,

WELL BEFORE MY ALARM, THE SKY WAS STILL DARK. I SAT
UP IN BED, RECALLING DAKOTA'S NEWSPAPER ARTICLE.
MANUEL HAD SAID WHAT A FREEING FEELING COMING OUT
WOULD BE. IT WAS TRUE: I FELT STRONGER AND MORE
FULL OF ENERGY THAN I HAD SINCE MANUEL'S ATTACK.

I got up, dressed, pulled my sneakers on, and tiptoed down the
hall. Not even Pa was awake yet. I bounded out the front door, and
while the sun rose, bright and orange, I jogged down the empty
early morning streets and prayed. "Thank you, Jesus, for giving me
the strength and courage to be honest." I still wasn't convinced it
was God's will for me to be gay, but I felt set free.

When I got to homeroom that morning, I whispered to Angie,
"I told Pa."

"How'd it go?" she said brightly. "You don't look devastated."

"I guess it went okay. I'm not sure." I told her about it and she
nodded reassuringly.

"Well, give him time. Just remember how long it took for you
to accept it."

I thought about that a lot during the remainder of that day. I
didn't tell Dakota or anyone else about me. I wasn't quite ready for
that yet.

After school I drove to the hospital to see Manuel, wishing I could communicate to him what I had done. I knew he would be so proud of me. But then I had a disturbing notion: What if he never came out of his coma, like in one of those news cases? I shook my head, not wanting to think about it. Now that he'd stepped into my world, I couldn't imagine it without him.

"Please Jesus," I prayed. "Don't let that happen to him. Please heal him. *Please*."

And yet, what if Manuel was never healed and his condition never changed? Because he'd come into my world, *I* had been healed and changed. And nothing could ever undo that.

When I arrived at the medical center, I was relieved—actually more like ecstatic—to hear that Manuel had in fact improved, even if it was only a tiny bit. He was now able to breathe without a respirator and had gotten moved out of ICU. Although the staff warned Manuel's family and me to keep our expectations in check, I prayed over and over and over, "Thank you, Lord. Thank you."

During my visits to the hospital I had been gradually getting to know the staff. As one of the nurses said, "You come here as much as his family."

One afternoon she had asked me to help bathe Manuel. At first I felt a little embarrassed at the thought of seeing him naked, especially when I recalled how lust-crazed I'd gotten from merely seeing his bare arms. But when I saw the full impact of the attack on his still-bruised body, I had to swallow hard to fight back my tears.

How could anybody have hurt someone so much? How could anyone be so full of hate? I had to pray hard and long after that to not feel the same hatred toward Jude and Terry.

There were other afternoons when I helped to clean and change him after he had soiled himself. That was hardly something I'd ever foreseen doing for anyone. Not that I was becoming a saint or anything, and I didn't do it to score points in heaven. I did it for Manuel, and for all he'd done for me.

Several days after he'd been moved out of ICU, when I walked into his room, a nurse was there, and Manuel's mom brightened at the sight of me. "He almost came out of it for a few minutes this morning."

"It's still too early to say," the nurse cautioned, "but the doctors think he may be regaining consciousness, though there is still the question of brain damage. Let's keep hoping for the best."

I stayed with Manuel's mom till visiting hours ended. The entire time I prayed and hoped Manuel would awaken. But he didn't.

For the next Saturday both Angie and Dakota had planned to come to the hospital, and they'd mentioned it to Manuel's group. Stephen Marten offered to take everyone in his family's mini-van. At ten a.m. we all met at his house. As Stephen drove, I found myself avoiding his gaze in the rearview mirror. I guess I still felt guilty about never helping him.

It was the first time I'd really hung out with anyone from that group. Gerald, the atheist Goth guy, brought a whoopee cushion that cut a fart sound every time someone sat on it. It was kind of gross but hilarious, and it helped to cheer everybody up. I never would have expected that from somebody who once wore a black trench coat to school every day.

As we all rode to Abilene together, talking, I realized there was more to everyone than I had pegged them for. We spent the whole morning together at the hospital, with Manuel's family, waiting and hoping.

After lunch I went to the men's room. When the door swung closed behind me, I saw Stephen at the washbasin, rinsing his con-tact lens with saline solution.

"Hi," I mumbled, and slipped into a stall, not wanting to face him. While peeing, I listened for the hallway door to open, hoping he'd leave. Instead, I kept hearing him at the washbasin.

I stepped out from the stall and he explained, "They're new contacts."

"Yeah," I replied, and washed my hands. I knew what I needed to tell him. My heart pumped hard and I scrubbed my hands way longer than necessary, until finally I sputtered, "I'm sorry."

"Huh?" He gazed over at me.

I made myself look at him. "For never saying anything and turning away. I'm sorry."

Stephen nodded, and his voice came out soft and sad: "You have no idea how hard it was, how scared I was coming to school every day, and feeling so alone."

I stood quietly beside him, listening to his hurt and feeling more humble than ever in my life.

"No one ever did anything," he continued, "until Manuel."

"I'm sorry," I repeated a third time.

Stephen gave a shrug. "It's past.

I wasn't sure exactly what he meant by that, but I hoped he was forgiving me.

We rejoined the others in the hospital room, and I continued to pray that Manuel would come to again . . . but nothing.

During the drive home that night, each time Stephen's eyes caught mine in the rearview mirror, I still felt a twinge of shame about the past, but I no longer looked away.

46

ON SUNDAY MORNING WHEN MY

ALARM RANG, I HIT THE OFF BUTTON AND ROLLED OVER.
FOR THE FIRST TIME I COULD REMEMBER, I DIDN'T FEEL
LIKE GOING TO CHURCH. MAYBE IT HAD TO DO WITH
BECOMING MORE HONEST AND OPEN — OR MAYBE I WAS
JUST TOO EXHAUSTED.

I had drifted back to sleep when I felt Pa shaking my foot. "*Mijo*, get up."

"Would you stop doing that?" I yanked my foot away and blinked my eyes open, glaring at him. "I don't like it!"

"Sorry." Pa lifted his hand from my foot, looking stricken. We stared at each other a moment. "Well," he said, "are you coming to church?"

"Yeah," I grumbled, not wanting to get into a discussion.

On the drive to the service neither Pa nor I said much. We each looked out our separate sides of the windshield at our different sides of the road. The bleak winter landscape seemed so cold, and inside the truck it hardly felt any warmer.

Ever since the night I had come out to Pa, we had been like strangers sharing the same house. Neither of us said any more about my announcement, but the memory of it was always there. It was as if everything had changed between Pa and me, even though we were still the same people.

When we arrived at church, the usher found us seats only a few rows from the front. As I sat down, I spotted Angie sitting with her mom several rows back. We waved. The service began as usual, with singing and praying till it came time for Pastor José's sermon.

He stood before the congregation, his head bowed in silent prayer for what seemed like a very long time. When at last he began to speak, his voice was somber, not at all his normal cheery tenor: "Brothers and sisters in Christ, this morning my heart is heavy."

Somehow I knew what he was going to preach about. My chest tightened as I braced myself.

"I have learned," Pastor announced, "that some students at our very own Longhorn High are forming a club for homosexuals." A wave of gasps and whispers rustled through the pews—and beside me, my pa grew rigid.

I had figured that Pastor would eventually have to say something about the group—especially after Dakota's website article. I glanced over my shoulder at Angie. She nodded as if she, too, had expected this.

"Now," Pastor continued, propping himself against the pulpit, "I'm going to tell you something else that may shock you . . ."

His sullen gaze scanned his congregation, as we waited for his revelation.

"I know people," he confessed, "who practice the homosexual lifestyle. I'm not ashamed to admit that I've reached out to them. Because I believe that the power of love, as demonstrated in the life and teachings of Jesus Christ, compels us to extend his holy love to all our brothers and sisters, even those who choose to turn their backs on him."

Around me people shifted in their seats, anxious about where this was going—as was I.

"There is so much pain"—Pastor shook his head sadly—"among those lost souls who choose homosexuality: promiscuity . . . alcoholism . . . drug abuse . . . AIDS . . . all the result of hearts closed to the love of Jesus."

Throughout our congregation heads nodded in agreement.

"Some of these people," Pastor pressed on, "I've helped to change . . . restoring them to a healthy, wholesome, and *holy* heterosexual life."

Several people called out, "Praise Jesus," and "Amen."

"Unfortunately," Pastor announced sternly, "others have refused the call to repent." He paused to exhale a sorrowful sigh. "But that's how it goes sometimes. Some people don't want help. Remember what Jesus asked the man who had been sick for thirty-eight years? We, too, must ask those we try to help, 'Do you *want* to be healed?'"

As I listened to my pastor—a man I liked, trusted, and admired, who seemed to truly care about people—doubts began to churn again in my mind. Had *I* truly wanted to be healed? Maybe I hadn't tried hard enough.

"We cannot turn our backs on our brothers and sisters . . ." Pastor's voice rose with passion. "But neither can we allow a sinful school club to seduce our children into a destructive lifestyle that can only lead to death and damnation."

My doubts of a moment before vanished abruptly. Was he talking about the same little club that Angie, Dakota, Manuel, and I had discussed at our lunch table?

"What's next?" Pastor's voice grew angrier. "An incest, bestiality, and pornography club? Is that what we want for our children?"

All around me people responded at full voice: "No!"

I squirmed, as little blisters of sweat burst upon my forehead.

"Just as almighty God destroyed Sodom for its wickedness," Pastor continued, "today Jesus calls on us"—His hand swept over the audience—"to speak out and stop this vile and profane homosexual club."

I should have known the Sodom reference was coming, once again equating gay people with violent rapists. I wanted to correct Pastor. But how could I stand up in front of two thousand people and say that he, our minister whom we all believed in, was misrepresenting Scripture?

As if he could read my mind, Pastor José paused and stared down at me. Pa followed his gaze and whispered, "Are you part of that club?"

I shrank in my seat, knowing how much Pa respected Pastor. "Yeah. But the group isn't what he says. It's not true. He's wrong."

Pa gave me a hard look, his dark eyes drilling into me. Was he angry or trying to believe me? Without warning he bolted to his feet, tugging at my arm. "Let's go!"

I hesitated. Go where? No one ever got up in the middle of Pastor's sermon unless they were going for the altar call or having a coughing fit. I grabbed my jacket and scrambled after Pa, jostling past the people seated in our row.

Pastor's gaze followed Pa and me. He had stopped preaching, almost as if he wanted to draw attention to us.

I hunched down in my collar as the entire congregation stared. Would Pastor use me as an example of a homosexual who'd turned his back on Christ? Maybe he thought Pa and I were retreating in shame. In fact I kind of was. And I figured Pa was too—ashamed of *me*.

But when Pa reached the aisle, he stopped and drew himself up. My pa, who hated speaking in front of even small groups, said in a voice loud enough for all to hear, "Pastor, you're wrong."

Then he turned toward the front entrance. I stood dumb-struck. Instinctively, I looked toward Angie. She was gazing at my pa and smiling bright as the sun. I hurried after him, past the whispers and blank stares of the congregation and out the front door, asking myself, *What just happened?*

As Pa drove out of the parking lot, he pulled his tie off and carefully folded it onto the seat. I glanced over at him, waiting, but he didn't offer any explanation for walking out of church.

Rather than wait forever, I asked, "Why'd you do that?"

His brow wrinkled as if he were baffled by my question. "Because I believe in you. You're my son."

Apparently, he didn't feel the need to explain any more than that. I wished he would have, but he didn't. I leaned back in my seat, glancing at his rough gardener's hands and not knowing what else to say.

47

DURING SUNDAY LUNCH

AT RAQUEL'S PA DIDN'T SAY ANYTHING TO HER ABOUT THE
INCIDENT AT CHURCH, THOUGH I SUSPECTED HE MIGHT
MENTION IT LATER. SHE HAD A WAY OF GENTLY GETTING
HIM TO TALK. I DIDN'T MENTION IT EITHER, BUT I KEPT
THINKING ABOUT IT.

During my drive to Abilene, Angie phoned. "Wow! Your dad's my
new hero. Wasn't he amazing?"

"Yeah," I replied, though not quite as enthusiastically. To me,
there still seemed so much that Pa and I needed to sort out.

"My mom and I," Angie continued, "had a long talk about the
GSA—what it is and what it *isn't*. When I explained to her the
truth about it, she was totally annoyed with Pastor."

While I drove, Angie and I talked about whether or not we
would return to church—at least to *that* one. Angie suggested, "We
should try Manuel's church." But after this morning I wasn't sure I
wanted to go to *any* church. Maybe I'd just talk to God on my own,
like Abuelita did.

When I arrived at the medical center, Mr. and Mrs. Cordero
were sitting at Manuel's bedside. As we talked, I asked about their

church and learned that on several mornings, while I was at school, their minister had come to pray for Manuel.

I wondered if Pastor José had ever even considered praying for him. Instead of preaching against the GSA and the sinful lifestyle of homosexuals, why didn't he preach about the destructive lifestyle of homophobia? Surely he knew that Jude and Terry had been charged with attempted murder.

After chatting some more with Manuel's parents, I pulled out my books to try to do some homework. I had begun falling behind in school. But as I glanced across the room at Manuel, it suddenly seemed like he shifted a little.

"Did he just move?" I said to Manuel's parents, and tossed my books down. It was the first time since he'd been hospitalized that I'd seen him move more than a twitch.

His parents and I crowded around the bed as Manuel groaned softly. My pulse quickened as his eyelids fluttered. I grabbed the call button, ringing for the nurse.

For an instant Manuel's unpatched eye flickered open and he gazed at us. My heart nearly zoomed from my chest. But then his eye closed, and he was gone again.

The nurse hurried into the room. "What happened?"

"He opened his eye!"

"That's good." She checked his IV and pulse. "A real good sign. I'll let the doctor know."

For the rest of the day Manuel's parents and I stayed glued to his bedside—well into dinnertime, till his dad offered to get us food from the snack bar.

"Um, I'll go," I volunteered, not really wanting to leave Manuel, but I figured Mr. Cordero didn't want to either. When I returned to the room, I nearly dropped the tray. Manuel was stirring again.

I set the food down and rushed over as he blinked his left eye open.

He stared blankly at his parents and me. Could he recall who we were? I waited, breathless, remembering the possibility of brain damage.

"Manuel?" his mom said, as a hopeful smile worked its way onto her face.

"Yeah?" His voice was scratchy after days of not speaking.

Then his gaze moved over to me, as though he wasn't sure who I was and was straining to remember.

I got a hollow feeling in my stomach. All this time I had been thinking only of him, and he couldn't recall me. I clenched my jaw, trying to hide my disappointment.

But he kept his eye fixed on me, and in a clear voice he asked, "So, now will you kiss me?"

My jaw dropped slightly, and my face warmed with embarrassment. His question was the last thing I expected. Was he delirious? Why was he asking that? Then I recalled the movie theater and our near-kiss. But if he had brain damage, how on earth could he remember that?

I stared at him open-mouthed, not sure how to respond, especially with his parents there, staring at me.

"Well?" Manuel insisted.

There was no doubt from his tone that he was sincere. But could I actually do what I wanted?

Bracing myself on the silver bed rail, I leaned over and touched my lips to his. It wasn't a hard kiss, or very long, but it held my whole heart. And with that gentle kiss, all my doubts, guilt, and uncertainties vanished for a moment, replaced by a million possibilities. This was how it was supposed to feel: natural and real. It was how *I* was supposed to feel—to have life and have it more abundantly.

When I leaned back up, Manuel's one good eye was twinkling at me with mischief. And all I could think was, *Thank you, God.*

48

WHILE HIS MOM AND DAD

TALKED WITH MANUEL, I PHONED ANGIE TO TELL HER THE
GREAT NEWS. SHE AND DAKOTA STARTED FOR THE
HOSPITAL IMMEDIATELY, ARRIVING AS FAST AS THEY
COULD.

Even though Manuel struggled to talk, he remained conscious—
and lucid. "So, did you guys start the GSA yet?"

"I bug Arbuthnot about it every day." Dakota smiled proudly.
"He says he'll let us know by the end of the week."

"Remind him that the ACLU says he's got to allow it." A smile
crinkled at the corners of Manuel's mouth. "Or we'll sue."

If that comment didn't prove Manuel had escaped brain damage, I didn't know what would.

It was hard to leave him that night. I was scared he might slip
back into a coma, but he didn't. He progressed quickly after that,
and every day I gave thanks. Within a week he got released from
the hospital and moved to a rehabilitation center, where I continued to visit him. Each afternoon I brought him schoolwork to
catch up on. But although his mind was clear, he tired easily. So,
oftentimes I merely sat beside him while he rested, and I caught up

on my own homework. At other times we just talked.

One evening I asked out of curiosity, "Do you remember anything from being unconscious?"

"Yeah . . ." His forehead wrinkled, like he was thinking. "I remember hanging out with J. C."

"Sure, right." It annoyed me when anyone called Jesus "J. C." It seemed sort of irreverent. But that was Manuel.

"It's true." Manuel nodded earnestly. "I felt a peace I can't express. He doesn't look anything like his pictures."

"Shut up!"

"No, really." Manuel grinned, but his voice was serious. "He said he wanted me to go with him, but I argued I wasn't ready yet, that I still needed more time to work on you."

My annoyance faded and I turned quiet, recalling the afternoon in the hospital when I had told Manuel I needed him and begged him not to die.

"So?" Manuel asked. "How's your battle going?"

"I've, um . . ." I cleared my throat and tried to stay composed. "I've stopped fighting."

"Praise Jesus." Manuel said, his tone sincere. "You know he loves you—no matter what."

I was beginning to believe that, and I had to clench my throat to hold back my tears.

One thing still weighed heavy on me. I drew in a long, deep breath so I could tell him: "I'm really sorry that I left you alone in the parking lot that night. If I hadn't, then maybe—"

He quickly raised his hand to my lips, shaking his head and shutting me up. "Let that go, *amigo*. I was stupid to *let* you leave me."

Then he reached for my hand, and my tears just flowed, no matter how hard I tried to stop them. I had never cried in front of him before, and I grabbed his hand tight, whispering, "I need you to teach me how to love."

"You already know that," he whispered back, tears running down his own cheeks. "You're born knowing that. You just needed to learn to let it out."

I tried not to hold his hand too hard, though I wanted to never let go.

49

WITHIN TWO WEEKS

MANUEL HAD GOTTEN STRONG ENOUGH TO BE RELEASED
FROM THE REHAB CENTER. TO WELCOME HIM HOME,
ANGIE, DAKOTA, AND I WENT OVER AFTER SCHOOL,
TOGETHER WITH STEPHEN, GERALD, MAGGIE, AND RUFUS.
THEN JANICE JOINED US WITH A SURPRISE — NOT A
WHOOPEE CUSHION, BUT HER LITTLE GIRL.

Even though she apologized for having to bring the baby, it
seemed like a perfect gesture. Manuel loved the kid, making faces
and cooing as it giggled. Each time I hung out with his crew, the
more I liked them.

Now that Manuel was home, I drove him to physical therapy
twice a week, and in between sessions I helped him with his exercises. His knee injury was the hardest, making it difficult for him
to stand up or walk, and pretty much confining him to a wheelchair. But the PT exercises helped, and as the weeks passed, he
kept getting stronger.

The best news was that his right eye healed better than
expected, recovering 95 percent of its vision. The doctor said that
that was a miracle.

Meanwhile, the winter winds started letting up, and the spring days got warmer. Pa and I still weren't getting along exactly great, but we had begun talking more about Ma, and I told him how really hard it had been for me when he'd started getting drunk.

It took a lot for me to tell him that. I think it was hard for him to hear it too, because he got really sad for several days afterward. But I'd needed to tell him, and I was glad I did.

50

AS EASTER BREAK APPROACHED,

I COULDN'T WAIT FOR ABUELITA TO COME STAY WITH
US AGAIN. EVER SINCE HER LAST VISIT I HAD KEPT HER
POSTED OVER THE PHONE ABOUT MANUEL. SHE WOULD
ALWAYS TELL ME, "DON'T GIVE UP ON HIM." AND SHE HAD
BEEN RIGHT.

"I want to come out to her when she comes," I told Pa one night
during dinner.

He kept eating quietly, thinking to himself, until he said, "It's
up to you, *mijo*. Let me know if you want my help."

On Palm Sunday I drove to Abilene Airport, psyching myself
up for my big announcement. But when I finally saw Abuelita, I
wasn't sure how to tell her. Every morning during her stay I looked
at myself in the mirror and said, "Okay, I'm going to tell her." But
then I chickened out.

I don't know why it was so scary for me, given all the tolerant
things she had said about love, homosexuality, and being in love.
But it was. Abuelita held such a special place in my world. And the
possibility that she might reject me—even if it was all in my head—
still petrified me.

"Just tell her!" Manuel encouraged me after I took her to visit him.

"She loves you more than anything," Angie reminded me.

I felt like such a wuss. When Easter Sunday arrived, the last day of her visit, I still hadn't told her. I watched the minutes tick by all through lunch, while helping her to clean up afterward, and during the drive to the airport. As we approached the security gate, I knew it was my last chance.

"Um, there's something I want to tell you."

She cocked her head and peered at me, her eyes huge and bright behind her glasses. "Then tell me."

My nerves were a wreck and my knees wobbled beneath me, but—who knows how—my words came out clear and steady: "I'm in love . . . with Manuel."

Abuelita nodded slowly, showing no surprise. She reached out with her frail arms and hugged me. "*Mi amor*, I'm so happy for you." Then with her finger she gently poked at my heart. "Now let yourself be happy too."

She kissed my cheek. And as she waddled away, I had this odd thought, about how Manuel sometimes called God "she."

Maybe he was right.

51

DURING THE WEEKS THAT FOLLOWED

PASTOR JOSÉ'S SERMON ABOUT OUR GSA, HE HAD
RALLIED OTHER CHURCHES TO OPPOSE THE CLUB. THE
SUPERINTENDENT TOOK THE ISSUE TO THE SCHOOL BOARD
FOR THEIR NEXT MEETING. LETTERS TO THE EDITOR
APPEARED IN THE *ABILENE REPORTER-NEWS*, DECRYING THE
CLUB AS "AN INSTRUMENT OF THE HOMOSEXUAL AGENDA,"
"A THREAT TO FAMILY VALUES," AND "A CHALLENGE TO
CHRISTIAN FAITH."

I had to agree on the last point. This whole experience had definitely challenged my faith—and made it stronger.

Dakota downloaded a letter from the ACLU website and presented it to the school board at the meeting, informing them that under federal law they *had* to allow the GSA or ban *all* non-curricular clubs. Only after that did the board finally approve the group.

That evening, Angie, Dakota, Manuel's crew, and I gathered at his house to celebrate. His mom had made a rainbow-icing cake. The only bad part was that Manuel still wasn't strong enough to come to school and attend the GSA's first meeting.

On that day my arteries pumped hard with anticipation—and anxiety. I still hadn't come out to anyone at school besides Angie, and, more recently, Dakota. (That had been a nonevent. I was beginning to think the entire planet had suspected me.) Nevertheless, when the lunch bell rang, I shuffled apprehensively toward the library, where the GSA would meet. Mrs. Ramirez had said we could bring food, but my stomach felt too knotted-up to eat.

"Are you excited?" Angie asked, catching up to me in the hall.

"Um, a little." My voice quavered. "Or a lot."

She patted my shoulder gently, as though reassuring some frightened pup, and we walked together.

In the hallway outside the library a crowd of students had gathered. On one side of the door Cliff and Elizabeth were leading a group in prayer against the GSA.

On the other side, Dakota, Stephen, and Gerald were chanting, "Pray, pray, pray, pray! It won't change people being gay. Jesus loves them anyway!"

The sight was both comical and unnerving. "Who's going to walk through that?" I asked.

"We are." Angie took hold of my hand and led me toward the door.

Fortunately, Mr. Arbuthnot arrived on our heels, yelling at both sides, "That's enough! Either get inside or go to lunch. Now!" I exhaled relief as the crowd disbanded, and Angie and I stepped into the library.

Maggie, Janice, and Rufus were already there, dragging chairs across the carpet to form a circle. "How many do you think we'll need?" Maggie asked me.

"Um, I don't know. Maybe ten?"

Mr. Arbuthnot strode in, eyeing us like he expected some sort of satanic ritual. Behind him trailed Dr. Lamar, the superintendent, and Mrs. Driscoll, the president of the PTA.

Then two girls shuffled in, giggling. One of them, wearing a T-shirt with a sequin heart, whispered to Angie, "Is this the you-know-what group?"

"Yeah, hi. Help yourself to some cookies."

The girls slinked over to the soft drinks and snacks Mrs. Ramirez had set up, looking ready to sneak out if no one else showed up. But then another girl strode in, followed by a jock-looking boy who mumbled hi to Janice and veered nervously toward the refreshments.

Gerald and Rufus scrambled for more chairs, widening the circle, as six more students came in. I'd never imagined so many people would be interested.

When we reached twenty-three, Mrs. Ramirez told us, "You'd better get started."

Dakota led the meeting in a discussion about homophobia and things the club could do to help create more tolerance and understanding.

"We should invite teachers," Maggie suggested. "We need to tell them how much name-calling hurts and to not just look away."

"I heard about this thing called the Day of Silence," Stephen said. "Students spend the entire day being silent and draw attention to how we can't talk about who we really are 'cause we risk being bullied."

"Can't we do something fun?" Rufus proposed. "Maybe sponsor a movie night? Like with *Dead Poets Society*? I mean, I know that's not about being gay, but it's about being yourself. I mean, I'm not gay, but dude—I got so much crap just for coming here. It's, like, homophobia hurts everybody."

That was the most I had ever heard him say.

Dr. Lamar and Mrs. Driscoll both took notes, and with each passing minute they seemed to relax a little more. When the end-of-lunch bell rang, Mr. Arbuthnot announced, "I've learned a lot today and want to applaud your efforts to foster a safer school environment."

Yeah, right. Why hadn't he applauded Manuel the times he reported Jude?

Nevertheless, we all left smiling. In spite of our little meeting, afternoon classes proceeded normal as pie. School didn't descend into chaos, the sanctity of marriage remained intact, and Western civilization survived—maybe even improved.

During the time we had been organizing our GSA, Jude had gone to court, and his charge of attempted murder had been plea-bargained down to aggravated assault. But because of the seriousness of the original charge and the fact that he had now turned eighteen, he was sentenced as an adult to seven years at state prison, with eligibility for parole after only four. Terry merely received a two-year sentence.

"That's all the time they got?" My chest swelled with anger. "After they nearly killed you and scarred you *for life?*"

Manuel took it better than I did. "It doesn't matter if it's two or twelve years. They need help, not punishment. What good is sitting in jail going to do?"

"It'll make them think," I argued. "And maybe think twice next time."

"Maybe." Manuel shrugged. "Or they might come out even more hard-hearted and angry."

I gritted my teeth, not knowing what to respond. Manuel never ceased to make me wonder.

52

IN LATE APRIL

MANUEL FINALLY HAD THE STRENGTH TO RETURN TO SCHOOL — IN A WHEELCHAIR. OUR GSA GREETED HIM OUTSIDE THE FRONT DOOR WITH CHEERS AND A "WELCOME BACK" BANNER.

I felt kind of edgy. What if someone else tried to hurt him? But most students kept at a distance, like he was a leper or something. And as the days passed, he didn't get harassed much anymore. Maybe the brutality of what had happened to him had shaken people up.

In early May the prom committee began putting up posters and selling tickets at lunchtime. One afternoon, as I drove Manuel to PT, he asked, "So, will you be my date?"

I forced a chuckle. He couldn't possibly be serious. "You're joking, right?"

"Nope." A smile danced across his lips. "I want you to go with me."

"Are you crazy? It's not safe!" I wasn't so much concerned about myself as about him. He was a sitting duck in that wheelchair, and I didn't want to risk anything happening to him again. I'd screwed up once. I wasn't going to twice. "No way."

"Oh, come on!" Manuel gently punched my shoulder. "Who's going to beat up a crippled guy and his manservant?"

"Forget it." I shook my head, refusing to give in.

"*Amigo*," Manuel insisted. "Are you ever going to stop living in fear?" He raised his finger and wagged it at me, preaching: "'For God hath *not* given us the spirit of fear; but of power, and of love, and of a sound mind.'"

"I think you're ignoring the 'sound mind,'" I grumbled.

Actually, there was another part to all this: During the years that Angie and I had dated, we had often talked about going to senior prom together. Even though we were no longer a couple, how would she feel if I went with Manuel?

"Jesus, please guide me," I prayed, before I phoned and told her about Manuel's crazy idea.

"Of course you should go with him," she encouraged me. "Why not?"

"Because we might, um, *get killed*?"

"I doubt it," she said calmly. "After everything that's happened? We'll make it a GSA project."

I gripped the phone more tightly. "But what about you? I mean—you know—like, you wouldn't mind if I went with him?"

Angie was quiet a moment, as if thinking; then she exhaled a long, audible breath. "Paul, I appreciate that, but . . . I'm trying to move on. And so should you. I will still love you. You'll always live in my heart. But I believe that if you truly love someone, that means you want them to be happy, no matter who they're with. And I want you to be happy."

As I listened to her, my eyes started going blurry again. I thought I heard her sniffle too.

"Look, why don't we go as a group?" she suggested. "That would totally confuse people."

To say the least, I thought. But it also made a lot of sense: There was safety in numbers.

After hanging up, I stared at the photo of Angie and me at junior prom. Then I glanced at the dancing cactus Manuel had given me. The past year had turned out nothing like I'd expected.

53

ON PROM NIGHT

I DRESSED IN MY TUX, LOOKED AT MYSELF IN THE
BEDROOM MIRROR, AND LAUGHED, UNABLE TO DECIDE IF
I LOOKED REALLY GOOD OR TOTALLY GOOFY. I HAD BEEN
LAUGHING A LOT MORE THE PAST FEW WEEKS —
OFTENTIMES AT MYSELF.

Then I noticed my bright red WWJD wristband poking out from
beneath my sleeve. It looked a little out of place with the formal tux.

Wait, when had I stopped snapping it against my wrist? I tried
to remember but couldn't. I guess that wasn't really the purpose of
it anyway. Gently I tucked the wristband beneath my sleeve and
let it stay there.

In the living room Pa and Raquel were watching TV.

"*Ay, que guapo!*" Raquel exclaimed at the sight of me. "So
handsome!"

"You look good," Pa agreed, turning the TV off and standing to gaze at me. "Photos!" he told me. "I want photos! Where's
your camera?"

I already had it in my tux pocket to carry along.

"Take one of him and me together," Pa told Raquel, and put his arm around me. Then he gave me a fifty that I hadn't expected, but it was standing alongside him that meant the most to me.

When I went to pick Manuel up at his house, his little sister answered the door, hopping up and down with excitement. She giggled uproariously while I leaned over Manuel's wheelchair so we could pin on each other's boutonnieres.

More photos flashed—of Manuel and me, Manuel with his family, and all of us together. Then Manuel and I headed to the Chinese restaurant, where we'd arranged for dinner with Angie, Dakota, and the others in Manuel's group. They had sort of become my group too.

Angie was already there, wearing a shimmering ivory strapless gown, in which she looked beyond beautiful. She gave Manuel a kiss on the cheek and whispered something into his ear.

Manuel nodded, softly squeezed her hand, and grinned over at me. She looked over too, admiring me from head to toe, and threw her arms around me.

"You look so awesome!" I told her.

"And so do you." Her brown eyes smiled.

Our dinner was spiced with jokes, laughter, and more photos. Afterward, we all opened fortune cookies.

Manuel's was: *Make plans, and God laughs.*

Angie's was: *A person who makes no mistakes probably won't make anything.*

And mine was: *The journey of a thousand miles begins with a single step.*

Even though I'd heard that one a gazillion times, it seemed more true than ever.

When we arrived at the lodge where prom was being held, I wheeled Manuel across the parking lot toward the music blaring from inside. As we entered, a cloud of perfume and cologne wafted over us.

Cliques circled the edges of the dance floor, chattering and checking out each other's outfits, while other schoolmates bounced beneath the twinkling reflection of the mirror ball.

"So . . ." Dakota turned to Manuel and me with a devilish glint in her eye. "Are you guys going to dance together?"

"Absolutely!" Manuel shouted over the music.

I knew he was kidding. He had to be; he could barely even stand.

As couples brushed past us onto the dance floor, I pushed his wheelchair out of the way. But when the music changed to a slow set, Manuel clamped the brake.

"Help me up!" He braced himself on the chair and clutched my arm.

I was thunderstruck. Hadn't we pressed our luck enough?

"You're going to hurt yourself," I protested, wrapping my arms beneath his shoulders to keep him from falling.

All around us couples stopped dancing to stare, and I felt more exposed than ever.

"Come on." Manuel must have been in tremendous pain, and yet he whispered, "Dance with me? Please?"

Our eyes met and locked, taking me back to that first morning in homeroom. Suddenly I understood the pull I had felt that day—and ever since. It was love, beyond all reason.

That was the only way I could explain how I gathered the courage to take one step, followed by another, in front of all those people, pressing my chest to his so close that I could feel his heart beat. And as I breathed in the scent of his hair, we danced beneath the twirling mirror ball.

Some people gaped and pointed. A couple of guys from the football team raised their fists and yelled something.

At that, Angie, Dakota, and the others in our group

formed a circle around Manuel and me, spreading their arms like angel wings.

"Thanks," Manuel whispered to me, even though we actually only lasted a few steps together. His clenched jaw betrayed how much pain he was in. When I eased him back into the wheelchair, he exclaimed, "I think I'm ready for a double shot of painkiller."

The remainder of the evening we talked and joked with the others. I danced with Angie, Dakota, Janice, and Maggie and watched our other schoolmates holding one another close, each couple in their own world this special night. My dream had been prom with the people I loved. And it had happened, just not exactly how I had planned.

At one in the morning everyone said good night. I took Manuel to his house and gave him a prom-night kiss. Then I drove home, praying more earnestly than I had in weeks. "Thank you, Jesus, for Manuel, for Angie, for *everything* . . ."

On the late-night radio some 1930s big-band tune was playing, taking my mind away from my prayers, back to that afternoon in Manuel's bedroom when he had reached for my hand, inviting me to dance . . .

And I gave one more prayer of thanks: for I'd been given a second chance after all.

54

BY THE TIME GRADUATION ARRIVED,

I HAD DECIDED TO WAIT A YEAR BEFORE COLLEGE,
IN ORDER TO HELP MANUEL RECUPERATE AND TAKE HIM
TO PT AND DOCTOR'S VISITS. I TOLD PA MY DECISION ON
THE WAY TO THE COMMENCEMENT CEREMONY, WHICH
PROBABLY WASN'T THE BEST TIMING.

"I won't allow you to give up your studies," he said angrily. "They're
too important."

"I'm not giving them up," I assured him. "I want to go to college. I'll go next year."

We argued about it all that day and for several afterward. "I promise I'll go," I kept telling him, until he finally believed me—or realized there was nothing he could do about it anyway, other than accept it.

After that I went to work for him part time, landscaping, like I usually did during the summers. I think that turned out to be a good thing, giving us more time together.

On Sundays we started going with Manuel's family to his "welcoming" church, a much smaller congregation on the other side of town. At first I missed all the arm-waving, clapping, and loud passion of Pastor José's services. In comparison Pastor Ruth seemed pretty tame. But her sermons tackled tough subjects, and she didn't give easy answers. Instead she asked challenging questions about God, justice, and our society that made me think a lot.

Maybe most importantly, in Pastor Ruth's congregation I could be myself without people judging me. It was the one public place where Manuel and I could hold hands and not feel the least bit afraid.

One day when I picked Manuel up for PT, he was addressing an envelope. Out of curiosity I asked, "Who are you writing to?"

He licked the seal and said, "Jude."

"*What?*" My entire body tensed. "Are you nuts?"

"Nope. I want to forgive him."

"No way!" I protested. "Why should you want to make him feel better?"

"*Amigo* . . ." Manuel scowled. "I'm not doing it to make him feel better. I just don't want to go through life bitter. That's like drinking poison every day. I'm forgiving him *for me*."

I thought about that, not really understanding it, and mailed the letter for him, figuring Jude would never answer. But six weeks later Manuel showed me the hand-scrawled, horribly spelled reply.

Deer Manuel,

Got your letter. At first thouhgt it was a joke. Didnt believe you'd really wrote it. Then I thoght you sent it to be meen and get back at me cause more I thought about it more it made me feel bad.

One day I showed it to the chaplin here and he said I was lucky. He only heard of one other guy who ever got forgiven by somebody he hurt. So I guess you really did write it? If you did I still dont understand why.

Its bad here in prison. You have to fight everybody to leave you alone . . .

He went on to complain for a page and a half, but Manuel didn't seem to mind. He and Jude started to write back and forth. With each letter Jude revealed more and more things he'd gone through growing up, stuff he said he'd never told anyone, like how he'd been beaten . . . and worse. In one letter he told how his uncle had raped him when he was barely five years old. It turned my stomach to think about that. I wondered, had Jude equated Manuel being gay with his uncle abusing him? Was that what caused him to feel so much rage toward Manuel?

It didn't excuse what Jude did, but it helped me to understand more. Maybe one day I, too, would be able to forgive him.

Although Manuel and I were officially boyfriends now, Angie was still my best friend. In late August I helped her move into her dorm at Texas A&M, where she'd gotten accepted for pre-vet.

That night in her room she made us PBJ sandwiches, which we ate with chocolate milk. And though I tried to fight it, I started crying, knowing how much I'd miss her.

Soon after Angie began school, she met another pre-vet, named Frank. As soon as she got home from their first date, she phoned me, laughing so much I could barely understand what she said:

"You'll never believe what happened. Right away I told him, 'My best friend is a gay guy. Have you got any problem with that?' And do you know what he says? 'Um, nope. Actually, um, my moms are lesbians.'"

God must have an uncanny sense of humor, I thought.

Angie and Frank have been dating ever since. At Thanksgiving she brought him home and introduced us. He's a vegetarian, like her, and equally crazy about critters.

Seeing them together, I felt a little sad, wishing I could've been him. But then I thought back to something Angie had taught me: If you truly love someone, you want them to be happy, no matter who they're with.

More than a year has now passed since the night I went to my childhood church, no longer wanting to exist, and looked in the window at the mural of Jesus. I think I did kind of die that night, to so many things that I had been taught to believe: that the Lord condemns gay people, that homosexuality is a sin, and that being gay is a choice. By buying into that story I had learned—slowly and subtly—to hate who I was.

I had had to let go of those old ideas and admit that I didn't know God's will and could never be completely certain of it. All I could do was surrender, so that Jesus could enter my heart—not on my terms, but on his.

I'm on that new path now, learning to love and accept myself as God created me. After all my prayers for change, uttered and stuffed into my little box, God did change me—just not the way I'd wanted. I still don't understand why I'm gay, but now I accept what I always knew inside my heart: It's just how I am.

I still read my Bible pretty much daily, but differently than before: questioning, challenging, and always—as Abuelita said— keeping love as the standard.

One other big change is that I've started going by Pablo once more, instead of Paul, and I've started speaking Spanish again. Those are small steps in reclaiming my Mexican heritage, but huge pieces in making me whole.

Manuel and I have applied for college together next fall. He wants to study anthropology and tells me I shouldn't give up on my dream of becoming a minister.

"*You're* the one who should be the minister," I tell him.

"Nah." He shakes his head. "I'd piss people off too much."

I laugh, knowing he's probably right. So I'm praying about the minister idea. But my prayers are different now. Like Pa, I'm learning to live my life one day at a time. And I'm trying to trust a God bigger than any box and see where he'll guide me.

Sometimes I grow impatient and ask, "What's your will for me now, Lord?"

If the answer doesn't come, I remind myself of Psalm 46: *Be still and know that I am God.*

And I try to wait patiently, taking hold of Manuel's hand.

GLOSSARY OF SPANISH WORDS AND PHRASES:

ABUELITA/ABUELITO - grandma/grandpa

AMIGO - friend

ARROZ CON POLLO - rice with chicken, a Latin American dish

"AY, QUE GUAPO" - Oh, how handsome

BUENOS DÍAS - Good morning

FELIZ NAVIDAD - Merry Christmas

GRACIAS - thank you or thanks

MARICÓN - derogatory term for a gay person

MI AMOR - my love

MIJO - my son (contraction for *mi hijo*)

SEÑORA - ma'am or lady

TE QUIERO - I love you/I care about you

A NOTE FROM THE AUTHOR

SINCE THE PUBLICATION OF MY FIRST NOVEL, *RAINBOW BOYS*, I'VE RECEIVED THOUSANDS OF E-MAILS FROM TEENS ALL ACROSS AMERICA, TELLING ME THEIR OWN STORIES OF GROWING UP GAY. MANY LETTERS HAVE BEEN LIKE THESE:

Being gay *and Christian* is the hardest thing in the world. One day at church the pastor said the worst things about gay people. It was so hard for me not to cry, and my mom (who I just came out to) stared at me with a sorry feeling. But I still love God, and no matter what anyone says, I am what I am.

My parents are very staunch Christians and when they found out about my homosexuality, they sent me for counseling. It didn't really work. My parents now think that I'm "okay". Only I know that my sexuality hasn't changed at all. I love being a Christian and I know that Christianity is real. But according to church doctrines, it's wrong. Now I don't know where to turn.

Nothing is quite as bad as when you're hanging out with friends, driving down the highway, moshing at a concert, eating tacos at 5 a.m., and you think that there's no place you'd rather be in the world than with these people . . . but you always know in the back of your mind that if you asked them what they thought about homosexuality they would say you're going to hell. No questions asked. Fire and brimstone, forever. I think that's what hurts the most.

Reading such comments made me recall my own faith journey. Growing up, I was blessed to have a mom and dad who accepted me, regardless of my sexuality. But the church presented an image of a God who didn't love me quite so unconditionally.

It took quite a few years for me to get up the courage to revisit the Bible and come to my own conclusions about God. And as I began to hear the struggles of young people, I came to believe that my own experience might help others. The result was *The God Box*.

As I wrote and did research for my novel, the following books were a great help to me: *What the Bible* Really *Says About Homosexuality (Millennium Edition)*, by Daniel A. Helminiak (Alamo Square Press, 2000), *Stranger at the Gate: To be Gay and Christian in America*, by Mel White (Penguin Plume Books, 1995), and John Shelby Spong's books, *Living in Sin?: A Bishop Rethinks Human Sexuality* (HarperCollins Publishers, 1988) and *Rescuing the Bible from Fundamentalism: A Bishop Rethinks the Meaning of Scripture* (HarperCollins Publishers, 1991).

For those who are still struggling to reconcile religion and sexuality, my website, www.AlexSanchez.com, includes a Spirituality page, with links to diverse religious groups that accept gay and lesbian people, including Christian evangelical, Mormon, and Muslim groups.

Know that you're not alone. Have courage. And love, respect, and accept yourself for the beautiful soul you are.

PEACE,

Alex

ALEX SANCHEZ received his master's degree in guidance and counseling from Old Dominion University. For many years he worked as a youth and family counselor. His novels include the Lambda Award–winning *So Hard to Say,* the Rainbow Boys trilogy, and *Getting It.* When not writing, Alex tours the country talking with teens, librarians, and educators about the importance of teaching tolerance and self-acceptance. Originally from Mexico, Alex now lives in Thailand and Hollywood, Florida. You can visit Alex at www.AlexSanchezcom.